The Madness of Despair

Ghalya F T Al Said

The Madness of Despair

A novel

Translated from the Arabic
by Raphael Cohen

Banipal  Books

The Madness of Despair
First published in English translation
by Banipal Books, London, 2021

Arabic copyright © Ghalya F T Al Said, 2021
English translation copyright © Raphael Cohen, 2021
Junoun al-Ya's was first published in Arabic in 2011
Original title: جنون اليأس
Published by Riad El-Rayyes Books S.A.L., Beirut, May 2011

The moral rights of Ghalya F T Al Said to be identified as the
author and Raphael Cohen as the translator of this work have
been asserted in accordance with the UKCopyright, Designs and
Patents Act, 1988.

A CIP record for this book is available in the British Library
Paperback: ISBN 978-1-913043-12-4
Hardback: ISBN: 978-1-913043-21-6
E-book: ISBN: 978-1-913043-13-1

Banipal Books
1 Gough Square, LONDON EC4A 3DE, UK
www.banipal.co.uk/banipalbooks/

Cover painting by Afifa Aleiby

Banipal Books is an imprint of Banipal Publishing
Typeset in Cardo
Printed and bound in Great Britain by Clays Ltd, Elcograf S.p.A.

To dancers on the verge of madness,
before they fall forever into its dark tunnel

1

Dr Nadim Nasra's success in his work and personal life concealed a tale of struggle and perseverance stretching back through long years of hardship that had been a dark night with no promise of dawn. Success had instilled in Dr Nadim a sense of confidence in his abilities and freed him from the feeling of inferiority that had gnawed at him as a result of his limited means and his early halting progress at work.

Here at the beating heart of life, fear and miserable memories were behind him; he was a success and this made for happy memories. It was not strange, then, that he should start enjoying the social life around him, especially the English milieu he worked in and his relationship with his wife Maureen, and his children. He felt that life had smiled on him and offered him a helping hand, and this provided him with a peace of mind he had not known for years. Now, he had space to think about his family who lived in his far-off homeland, the sad country he had not visited since migrating to Britain.

Distance from his family and friends had given him sleepless nights, and he had done his utmost to suppress the longing for home that was always there under the surface. Making himself successful was what really mattered to him, and he had had little spare time for distant memories. But now he had dispelled the uncertainties in his life and set things straight, he began to yearn for his beloved family and their distant land. He had a hankering for anything Arab and oriental: people, food, customs, climate, clothing, even the streets and alleyways. He was drawn to people speaking Arabic, and felt an overwhelming desire to listen to the melody of the language with its different accents, which would combine in his ears while he savoured their impact and resonance. He remembered the chatter of his siblings, his mother, his aunts, and the neighbours, as well as the way with words of his teachers at school and university. In his country, he had spoken Arabic naturally and spontaneously, but in the frosty country of exile all he could do was wait till he was lucky enough to join in with those who spoke his language socially or at parties.

His brilliant success had not stopped him from leading a life of routine; every day followed the same pattern. He might as well have been another Big Ben. He went to work in the morning and came home at the end of the day to spend his evenings in comfort at home in leafy Richmond.

His wife Maureen managed the house, taking care of things for him and his children, while he focused on making money. Everything was going smoothly, not a single dark cloud in a clear blue sky, but then his life was turned upside down. Fate struck out of the blue, and, as they say, the winds don't always blow in the ship's favour.

One day, Nadim left his surgery at lunchtime and headed to a small Arab cafe that sold *fuul* beans, falafel, hummus, and flat bread. A woman out walking some dogs – four, and all of different breeds – went past him, bumping into a man carrying several bags of shopping. The largest dog sniffed at the man's leg, giving him a fright. He fell over, and the contents of the bags – oranges, potatoes, onions, a small bag of sugar, and a carton of milk – spilled everywhere. Nadim helped the man get up and gather the things scattered on the pavement. The woman walking the dogs gave a cold apology for the mishap caused by her dog and headed off, urging her dogs to run behind her, perhaps fearing that the man might get angry and sue her, or the police come and accuse her of being negligent with her dogs. The man pulled himself together and offered his hand to his helper. "I'm Nafie," he said.

The Arabic name grabbed Nadim's attention and he responded delightedly: "Your name is Nafie. You must be Arab, then!"

Nodding his head, Nafie said: "Yes. I'm an Arab. And you are?"

Pointing to a building at the end of the street, Nadim said: "I'm Nadim Nasra. I'm a doctor and my surgery is in that building. Please come with me so I can give you a check-up and treat your grazes. To be honest, I don't think you're in any danger because the dogs here are inoculated against rabies, but heaven knows. Perhaps the dog injured your hand or you were hurt when you fell. It's better to be cautious in such cases even though they appear minor. I'll just disinfect the grazes and perhaps give you a tetanus injection."

Nadim sat with his unfamiliar guest in the patients' waiting room and made polite conversation. After Nafie had had a cup of Arabic coffee and eaten something sweet, he turned to the paintings of oriental scenes on the walls: palm trees, orchards, vineyards, groves of oranges, lemons, and pears. He noticed scenes from the Levant, from Iraq, and from the Nile Valley. The Doctor gave him the necessary treatment and reassured him that there was nothing to worry about and no chance of catching anything from the bite.

The Doctor said to Nafie: "I hope you'll be a regular visitor at the surgery, even if you don't need any medical treatment or advice."

Nafie was pleased by the invitation and thanked him. "My house isn't far from here," he said. "It'll be easy to visit you whenever the chance arises, *inshallah*. A pleasure to meet you, Doctor. A dog bite led me to meet you, and as they say, every cloud has a silver lining. I hope our friendship will grow and last. Both of us left our countries and live in exile. That's why we should help each other. Thank you, and see you again."

From that day Nafie became a regular visitor at the surgery of his new friend the Doctor. These visits delighted the Doctor because he had a yearning for all that was Arab and oriental. He longed to talk about the traditions and customs of the past, and about the Arabic language and stories. Nafie would finish work on the outskirts of the city and take the train to the clinic. The two men would sit together once the patients and nurses had left, drinking Arabic coffee and tea and eating nuts. They would enjoy each other's company until it got late, when they would make their separate ways home.

They reminisced about when they had first arrived in London and the hardships they had both faced in terms of finding work and getting used to the bitterness of life in a strange land. The Doctor had not run after any job that came his way, but insisted on finding work in medicine, which he had studied and for which he had the required experience. But the health authorities made him take extra classes in medicine, which caused him a lot of hardship. The Doctor told his new friend about things that happened to him at that time, some of which had made him happy, while others had made him angry and upset.

He had travelled around on the Underground going from station to station carrying a pile of papers, forms, and job applications. People walked past him as fast as the train itself, confidently heading off with somewhere to go, while he walked aimlessly. His pockets were empty and he wanted someone to help him financially. His heart was empty and he was in dire need of love, affection, and a human touch. He said that he had lived with a woman called Julia who had a house in a posh part of London. Their relationship began when he was looking for somewhere to live and rented a room in her house. The time he spent living there with her helped him to learn English really well and in record time. After he joined a teaching hospital in Birmingham, he split up with her, which made her so sad it nearly killed her. With him not there anymore, she lived all alone in her big house. She felt angry and accused the Doctor of betraying her. She thought he had betrayed her friendship after she had helped him, supported him, and treated him very generously.

One day, Nafie invited his friend Nadim to dinner at his house. The Doctor welcomed the invitation, especially because he rarely had an opportunity to visit Arab people in their homes. He was looking forward to the day when he would enjoy the atmosphere of an Arab home, speak Arabic, and eat food different to what he had at home. His wife Maureen cooked mostly English food without spices and garlic, and he found it bland. The Doctor did not have a particular image of Nafie's house in his head and did not know whether his friend was married.

The Doctor arrived at Nafie's house on the agreed day at the agreed time. He was carrying a bunch of flowers and a box of Arabic pastries. He rang the doorbell. When no one came to the door, he rang again. The front door half opened but nobody was there to greet him. He heard the sound of footsteps, took a peek, and spotted a figure hurrying back inside the flat. He pushed open the door and took a look around. He was hit by the smell of cooking, just like the smell of his family's cooking back home, far away. He remembered his mother's food, the mixture of cumin, lemon, parsley, garlic and spices. He stopped in the doorway waiting for the figure who had opened the door and vanished to reappear. The aroma of cooking made him hungry for Arab food.

The person who had opened the door for the Doctor and vanished like a ghost was none other than Nafie's wife, Maliha. She did not stay and welcome her guest after opening the door because of the saucepans on the stove. The moment she was done in the kitchen, she came back and stood before the guest. The air was filled with the delicious aromas of what was cooking.

Her face was distinguished by shy dark eyes and lit up with an enchanting, playful smile. She was wearing a red velvet kaftan with beautiful abstract patterns embroidered in gold thread across the front. Her appearance created an attraction that did not go unnoticed. The red colour and gleam of the kaftan reflected in the tone of her skin and made her cheeks redder. Her deep black hair flowed like waves in the darkness of night. It was pinned up on top with a coloured clip and locks hung down to the level of her lips, which were painted with a sexy strawberry-coloured lipstick. Nadim's darting eyes met the drowsy eyes of Maliha. He felt miraculously drawn to her, as though there had been ties of affection to this beautiful woman since the creation of the world. Her lovely eyes drew him profoundly in, and he felt he was drowning and melting away to nothingness. His heart was beating, almost audibly he felt, and he was so tongue-tied he could not even say hello. He was intoxicated, her forceful beauty making him awkward. The next thing he knew, he had extended a trembling hand and was shaking hers; a white hand smooth to the touch. Her slender wrist was encircled with gold bracelets that give a ringing sound that spelt seduction. Her fingers were slim like her wrist and bore gold rings set with garnets and emeralds.

After shaking hands and exchanging greetings, Nadim handed Maliha the gifts he had brought. She took them gracefully and thanked him for his generosity. Her wide smile still shone on her face as she looked at him, feeling a longing and a desire she had never known before. He contemplated her face again, examining its features. Her beauty had stunned him, catching him unawares. He noted a precise resemblance between Maliha and someone close to him. Perhaps it was an image long embedded in his unconscious. An image composed of many faces: his mother, his sisters, his aunts, and some women from his old neighbourhood. The image grew and expanded as he inhaled the aroma of the cooking, so like the aroma of his mother's cooking that still lingered in his memory. Maliha's flat was a smaller version of his family's house thousands of miles away. "Is this the vision I have been chasing all these years?" he wondered. "Is she the image that has always appeared to me during my life in this cold country?"

Maliha's beauty evoked the beauty of his distant country. The similarity signifying the long-lost treasure that he had been seeking in his roots. His longing and nostalgia for the warmth of the East grew and this reinforced his sense of the vast difference between the cold English life he led with his wife Maureen and life in his far-off land.

He nearly forgot the custom that called for physical separation between him and Maliha as a woman married to his friend, and almost gave her a gentle and tender embrace. He wanted his body to cleave to hers and longed to say: "At last I've found what I've been looking for in this cold city: you, my sublime Arab beauty. I've found you after all the years you've lain dormant in my subconscious. Where have you been all this time?"

At the last moment, he held back, recognising the seriousness of the mistake he would have made if he had actually done that. Maliha undoubtedly stood for everything he had left behind in his country, and that made him feel homesick. He had finally found those things again in front of him in a flat in London. He wanted to whisk Maliha far away, as if on a flying saucer, and spend the rest of his life with her. He wished he could forget his relationship with Maureen and make Maliha forget her relationship with Nafie.

He recovered from the shock of it all and smiling kindly said: "I'm Doctor Nadim Nasra. I work at a surgery nearby. It looks like I've arrived early. Can I see my friend Nafie?"

The bracelets on her slender wrist shook playfully with a sweet melody as she said: "No, you did not come early. You came on time. Nafie is late back from work. I'm his wife Maliha by the way. Hello, and do come in."

Maliha welcomed the Doctor no less warmly than he had her. She was dazzled by his smart appearance, clean clothes, deep voice, easy smile and kind eyes. She was attracted to him and forgot about the shops and the successful shopkeepers whom she watched out of her living-room window down below on Goldhawk Road, Shepherd's Bush.

She wiped the image of the butcher from her mind. He was short, pale skinned, bald, and stocky, with a large black birthmark in the middle of his cheek that you could not miss. She would see him from her window staggering around his shop wearing a white coat spattered with blood and grease. With his chunky hands in their translucent nylon gloves he would lug kilos and kilos of fresh red meat and put them on the scales, which almost tipped over from the weight, like a donkey stumbling under its burden.

Standing facing Nadim, it became apparent to Maliha that London contained another kind of success she had known nothing about. This was success unmarred by the hardship and suffering of those struggling to make a living. His success differed from that of the shop owners who worked tirelessly all day without getting bored. She watched the commerce in the shops like it was theatre. The main act involved earning money. In London there were different kinds of success: Doctor Nadim had achieved his desires and kept his hands clean and not soiled with blood, unlike her neighbour the butcher, even though both the doctor's and the butcher's trade involved blood.

The clean-cut appearance of the Doctor reminded her of the many times she had wished to make something of her life, enough to change her day-to-day life which was full of hassles. Her life here in London with her husband Nafie was a continuation of the reality she had lived with her family in the past.

Maliha led the Doctor into the living room. She felt that his footsteps were captivating her heart and taking control of her, body and soul. The Doctor sat on the edge of one of the low sofas, an arrangement just as in an Arab house. In front of him was a table whose top was a round copper tray with hand-engraved designs around the edge, like those sold in the shops in Arab markets. The tray was so large that it nearly covered all the floor space in the small room. On the tray was a small decorative coffee set made of copper.

Every object in the small flat reminded the Doctor of the living room of his family house back home, but on a smaller scale. The brightly coloured plastic flowers, the large copper coffee pot, the old floral curtains, the TV, the tinted-glass display cabinet with its perfume bottles and other trinkets all bore the stamp of his old home. "I would never have believed," he said to himself, "that I'd see a house in London with the same character as my family home."

Shortly after the Doctor sat down, Maliha excused herself and hurried back to the kitchen to fetch him a glass of apricot nectar, which she brought in on a small tray in a red glass decorated with gold filigree. The glass might have been spirited away from a folklore museum in some Arab country, and this resemblance increased his desire to drink the apricot juice. He took the glass and thanked Maliha. Then he took a sip. He felt he was getting drunk. He could sense Maliha sitting next to him with no barrier between them. He felt intensely attracted towards her and in a tremulous voice told her how he had met her husband.

Maliha sat up straight; she looked towards the window, and her smile disappeared. She undid the clip holding her hair, which fell down in long black waves of silk, like a velvet night perfumed with jasmine. Sorrow filled her heart as she said: "Doctor, Nafie rarely tells me about his life outside the house. To be honest, I don't know much about what goes on in my husband's head. He doesn't communicate with me and doesn't tell me his feelings or what he's up to. Seeing as you're not a stranger to us, let me tell you that Nafie and I live in different worlds. It's as if we live beyond the world beneath our window. The ebb and flow of events in London is of no concern to us."

Her eyes widened strangely with a mysterious glint, and her features took on a serious aspect as she continued: "You might be surprised by what I'm going to say, and honestly I've never told anyone before. Since coming to this country, Doctor, I've lived a totally isolated and lonely life, skulking behind these walls. I don't know a soul. Again and again, I've resolved to break out of my isolation. I suffer so much. Let's just say that my situation is intolerable, but the real tragedy is that whenever I try to escape my confinement, I ask myself, 'Where am I going to go?' I find myself at a loss, and I make do with opening the window and looking at the outside world, observing life and feeling its pulse, but without any enjoyment. I watch the passengers on the bus and I wish that I was one of them so I could ride to faraway places. I fancy that the bus will take me out of my isolation and let me mix with other people and fulfil some of my hopes and dreams." With that she burst into tears.

The Doctor took a clean white scented handkerchief out of his jacket pocket and offered it to her. He was confused. "But Madame Maliha, as far as I know, Nafie is a really great man, extremely good-natured and generous."

"On the surface, you're right," she said. "But there are things about him you don't know. I'll tell you how it is. Well, Nafie doesn't involve me in anything he does. He doesn't work for a better life. I'd be right if I said Nafie had led us into abject poverty. Nafie is a submissive man, happy to make do with little. He acts as though nothing in life interests him. He's floundering in lethargy. We live a miserable secluded life in a pokey flat. The furniture and stuff we own is no better than what we had at home in the country we left. I've encouraged Nafie to make an effort to improve our standard of living, but it's like talking to a brick wall and he doesn't take me seriously. Aren't we entitled to a part of the luxury we see around us in this rich city?"

The Doctor, aware of her tears, said: "You seem tired, Madame Maliha. Perhaps I've come at an inappropriate time."

She shook her head as if she wanted to encourage him to draw closer, to listen to her words and console her. The only thing the Doctor could do to lessen the sadness that had taken hold of Maliha was draw close and soothe her pain. He hesitated, fearing he might break the social convention that forbade a man from drawing close and touching a woman who was not a relative. But in an effort to convince himself it was okay, he thought he really ought to do something to comfort her.

He stood up and extremely tentatively sat down again next to her and tried to put his hand on her shoulder. Looking at her he said: "It saddens me to see you suffer, Madame Maliha. Just so you know, I'm also a stranger like you and Nafie. I came to this country to work and find a job that would let me fulfil myself financially, emotionally, and professionally. I wanted to build a better future for me and my family, but at the beginning it wasn't easy despite my talents and despite being a qualified doctor. Fulfilling that goal meant putting up with hardships and swallowing a lot of bitter pills. But thanks to God, to perseverance, and continual effort, I managed to reach my goal, gain more experience, and set up a decent practice. That's why I appreciate the situation you complain about, Madame Maliha. Please tell me if there is anything I can do to be of assistance to you both. Why don't you and Nafie come and have dinner at my house one evening? You can meet my wife Maureen and my children."

She did not respond to his suggestion because she was busy drying her eyes. The Doctor was still dumbfounded at what he was hearing from Nafie's wife. A woman he was seeing for the first time in his life was opening up to him about her financial problems and her private relationship with her husband. He had no explanation for what he was hearing and seeing, but he was certain that this woman had bewitched and hypnotized him. He longed to be able to hug her tight to him and console her for her sadness and despair. He wanted to say: "Take refuge in the cool shade of my heart and shelter from the pain and fear of life. For so many years I've yearned for the joy and pleasure of a breathtaking beauty and overwhelming femininity like yours. I'm ready to set sail with you in the ship of eternal happiness and infinite love. Let me visit all the archipelagos in the world's oceans, seas, and gulfs with you. Let us spend a whole week sipping the pleasure of beautiful love, far from customs, airports, and the wicked."

When he became aware that he had been daydreaming, he said: "Just give thanks to God, Madame Maliha. How can you feel depressed and despondent living in London which is so lively and cosmopolitan?"

"What you say is true, Doctor," she said, "but things are the way I have described them. God is my witness that I'm speaking the truth. Apart from my family problems, I can't speak English well enough to help me mix with people and get to know them. Nafie is responsible for getting me out of this dark tunnel. He doesn't listen to my frequent advice to do something to end the problems that dog us at every turn. It's useless. Nafie will never be ambitious and will always be lazy, weak willed, and self-absorbed."

Maliha had barely finished her sentence when Nafie came into the room looking terrible. After a long hard day at work, his face displayed signs of exhaustion and fear. He was afraid of his wife's temper. She would explode in his face for some reason or for no reason and let him have it. He did not want her to attack him in the presence of his friend who was visiting for the first time. Nafie stretched out a trembling hand and, apologizing for being late, greeted the Doctor.

Maliha went off like a time bomb: "Nafie, God help me, what is this? Look at your filthy clothes and hands. Before we sit down to dinner, go and have a wash. We are not on our own today, and being hospitable requires that we present ourselves to our guests looking good and smelling fresh. You look and smell terrible. Please go and have a wash. It won't take you long. Go and get on with it."

Possibly for the first time in his married life, which had involved years of shame and inferiority, fear did not drive him to obey her orders. Instead of going to the bathroom as she had demanded, he sat in excruciating embarrassment on the chair by the sofa.

Maliha left the living room and went into the kitchen to get the food ready. Nafie was very upset by the hurt Maliha had inflicted on him in front of his friend, who was in shock himself because Nafie had just stood there, unable to control his wife. The Doctor looked at Nafie, and they exchanged a few words on random subjects. He avoided looking directly at him until Maliha came back with the plates and they sat down to eat at the round table. The Doctor and Nafie resumed their conversation about London and how expensive everything was, particularly house prices.

As though trying to assuage his wife's anger, Nafie said: "*Inshallah*, in a year's time, we intend to buy a house back home so we can spend the summer with family. Being separated from her family is no easy thing for Maliha. She's desperate to get away from the crowds and problems of London.

"Nafie," Maliha interrupted in a sharp tone, "please stop dreaming. Your income's minimal and won't let you buy a house anywhere, not even a rabbit hutch. Did you hear the rubbish he was talking, Doctor? He says these made-up things knowing full well his income is tiny and not enough to keep us. Actually, his pay runs out a day or two before the end of the week. Tell me Doctor, when we're living this contemptible life, how can this man buy the house he's talking about? Please, ask him?"

Maliha kept insisting with the Doctor: "For God's sake, ask him, Doctor. Perhaps he'll give you an answer. He certainly doesn't answer me when I ask him."

Nafie did not respond to Maliha's words. He shrank into his seat, yet more embarrassed, and began to sweat profusely. But Maliha had not finished and she continued to harangue her husband and belittle his views until he fell silent. Maliha continued her nervous monologue. The Doctor listened to her incessant censure and could see how ashamed her husband was.

"Before buying a house in our country," she said, "wouldn't it be better to move out of this small depressing flat? Doctor, before we moved to this flat, I didn't know it was council property, and that Nafie hadn't bought it with his own money through his own hard work. If I had known, I swear, I would never have agreed to move here. I deserve more than having to languish in shame in a council flat. As you know, Doctor, life in a flat on a council estate like this is really hard. It destroys your nerves and there's no privacy. Outside, we have to deal with all the rubbish piled up around the place, in the entrance and the corridors and the lifts, as well as the incessant noise from neighbours. When you go home in the evening, it's frightening, especially when you bump into a gang of unemployed youths and rowdy kids. They hassle and abuse the passers-by and nobody can do anything about it for fear of getting pelted with stones and bottles or attacked with a knife. Last month, they stabbed one of the neighbours causing him permanent injury, and it was like nothing had happened. As you know, in this country they view self-defence as a serious criminal offence. If you make a complaint, it takes the estate office ages to investigate and resolve the problem. And you can be sure they won't back you, even if you're in the right, especially if you're a foreigner."

Maliha pointed a finger at Nafie and said: "For that and many other reasons, I urge this lazy man to persevere, like other men, until he can buy his own house so that we can get out of this pit where we suffer so badly. I want a house where we can live with our heads held high, in comfort, feeling safe and secure. In our own house, no one would ask what we hang on the walls and what we plant outside. No one would ask us to pay money to maintain the public garden in the street and the block's community garden, neither of which we get any benefit from and which are of no interest to us whatsoever. Actually, I'd like a house with a big garden like our neighbours al-Amini ben Umran, the Somali guy, and his English wife Janet. They were able to buy a house in the suburbs with a big garden and a swimming pool. Now they live in total comfort. But unfortunately Nafie's deaf to what I say. He prefers things as they are and doesn't try to change our situation for the better."

For the tenth time Maliha stabbed her finger towards the

window and said: "My husband isn't motivated like the men I see working hard morning and night. I wish that a little of their effort would rub off on my lazy, good-for-nothing husband. Those men have businesses that make a good profit and plenty of money. They deserve to succeed in their businesses and in their family lives."

Nafie shifted and said in a low voice: "But, Maliha, this is their country and not mine. Isn't that true, Doctor?"

The Doctor looked at the floor and said: "Madame Maliha, what Nafie says is right. Don't you know how hard it is for foreigners in this country to make something of themselves? In the West, making a living isn't easy, particularly in business. The West doesn't shower you with silver and gold like many people think. This is the land of hardships, social fear, and economic pressure. The mansions of the powerful and well-off were built by the weak and powerless, many of whom died without the cruel system taking any notice."

The three of them spent the evening in this strange fashion: the two men mostly silent as Maliha recounted her dissatisfactions with her husband Nafie. The time came for the Doctor to leave, and he said goodbye to the couple and headed to the station to catch a train back home. He did not know then that the visit to Maliha and her husband's flat would be repeated again and again.

The Doctor's mind was full of the image of Maliha and drawn to her beauty despite the sharpness of her tongue and her mockery of her husband. His desire for her grew, and he did not care whether he received many times more the harshness and mockery reserved for Nafie. That night the Doctor went to bed with his heart overflowing with Maliha and her behaviour to such an extent that she kept him awake, tossing and turning, as he tried to think of the right way to get close to her in her small flat on a council estate on Goldhawk Road, Shepherd's Bush. He did not doubt for an instant that he had been smitten. He was ready to shout his love for her from the highest mountain and give her all the good things in life to make her happy.

Without question, Maliha had captured his heart and conquered his mind. He fell asleep and had beautiful dreams of her. He dreamed he had become their private doctor and their lawyer. He also dreamed he had become the person they relied on for everything in their lives. Telephone calls that required a good command of English, the forms that needed filling in for the authorities. He would demand their rights for them when they were mistreated by local officialdom.

He woke up and sat on the edge of the bed going over his dreams. They seemed so real and lucid. Speaking to himself he said: "Yes, I will be Maliha and Nafie's counsel because they are both in dire need of someone to defend them. I will also be their judge because they need someone to listen to their grievances with each other and give a final verdict as to who is in the right and who in the wrong."

2

Nafie and Maliha's wedding had taken place after a series of events that almost wrecked their marriage before it had even begun. The marriage happened after Nafie had decided once and for all to go back to his country and leave behind the many pressures and torments of London. Back home, his gaze fell on Maliha, and besotted, he had to make her his whatever the cost. He did just that and asked for her hand in marriage from his old friend, her brother, Abdel Wahid, who agreed without hesitation. Her whole family also gave their consent.

Maliha, however, refused to accept the idea of Nafie as a husband and swore she would never marry him whatever inducements he offered. But in the end, against her will, she had no choice but to go along with the marriage. However, she decided that her wedding night would be turned into her husband's curse. She executed her fiendish plan the morning after her wedding night. She woke up at dawn and screamed for all to hear in the neighbourhood alleyways that her husband was impotent. To avoid further scandal, and after the advice of Maliha's family, especially Abdel Wahid, Nafie decided to return with his wife to London, despite his fears of the problems he would face there. He knew how hard making a living would be, but he did not tell Maliha that. He did quite the opposite, and made her believe that he lived in the lap of luxury. That very evening Nafie flew to London with Maliha. The taste of his shame lingered bitterly on his tongue and he was still burning with the embarrassment and humiliation she had dealt him with her insult. Strangely, Maliha, after her outburst and upset, became calm and relaxed, as though her limbs were too languid to move and her tongue had lost its power of speech. She never imagined what fate had in store for when she began her new life in Britain.

In contrast, Nafie was flung into an ocean of worry and gloom over the future. How would his wife react to his poverty and the fact that he lived in a cramped room in a filthy hovel of a hotel? Maliha and all their old neighbourhood thought he was a rich man living in an opulent city called London, located on the edge of the beautiful continent of Europe, in a posh neighbourhood, in a big house overlooking the Thames, and possibly in a mansion in one of the areas inhabited by the rich. Nafie wondered what his wife's reaction would be when she saw his home was like a rat hole.

He was certain that his wife would be absolutely livid at what had happened to her. The thing that annoyed her most was that her family had made her marry a man she did not want and she had only agreed to travel with him in the hope he would provide her with some material comfort. Nafie felt he was in for trouble. He looked at Maliha as she slept in her seat on the plane, in a pitiful attempt to derive strength from her and be able to banish the black thoughts gripping him and find some answers to the difficult questions that kept popping into his head. He looked out of the plane window and saw the cities, towns and villages of his country stretching out as far as the eye could see. They were threaded through by rivers and valleys and surrounded by the sea.

He saw mud houses and brick buildings, mosques and churches, fields of figs and olives. He looked hard as though pleading for mercy from the merciful powers of the East to help him through the difficulties ahead.

Since Maliha had no idea about any likely problems, she started to prepare herself mentally for life with her husband in the new marital home. She knew nothing about the life awaiting her, but took consolation from the fact that London was located thousands of miles away from the painful events of the past. She would no longer encounter the faces she had seen on the morning after her accursed wedding night. She imagined that she would live together with Nafie in a spacious and comfortable place, so much better than the miserable house where she had lived with her family. It never occurred to her that she was going to live in a gloomy room in a small hotel full of refugee and immigrant families who had not been lucky enough to find a house fit for living, but found themselves in hotel bedsits with false promises of being moved to suitable accommodation. The image she had was rosy and bright.

Nafie exited the arrivals hall at Heathrow Airport with Maliha. They took the coach to the hotel where he lived in central London. The coach drove along wide streets and drew parallel with double-decker buses and trains. Maliha saw sights she had never dreamed of. She saw the organized way in which people behaved and the fancy shops. They were sights that filled her with happiness and provided proof for the positive thinking that had engaged her on the long journey from the heart of the East to the heart of the West.

When they entered the hotel, Maliha was puzzled. "Where are we?" she said. "I don't think we're in London. This is a hotel, not a house."

Trying to avoid a straight answer to his bride's questions, Nafie said: "Come along, darling. Just come with me. Please, I'll explain it all." Maliha remained uncertain as to whether this was where they would be living in London or whether they were in another city where they would spend their honeymoon.

They kept walking until they were standing in front of the door to Nafie's room. Maliha grew more puzzled at what she was witnessing. Nafie opened the door and they entered the small room. They were met by a bed, so narrow it could only sleep one person. This was more than Maliha could bear and she lost her temper. "What's this?" she yelled. "Where am I going to sleep when there's only one bed?"

Growing yet more embarrassed, Nafie said: "My darling, we'll sort everything out tonight, I promise. Let's spend tonight here. You sleep on the bed and I'll sleep on the floor. *Inshallah*, tomorrow I'll start looking for somewhere else suitable for us to live, by the grace of God, and we'll move to a better place very soon. Just be patient, and trust in God."

Nafie tried to make up an explanation for the awkward situation. "I'm living here temporarily, I forgot to tell you. I had a smart flat but I sold it before I left. I thought I was going home for good and wasn't planning to return to London. But, unfortunately, events were against me. The wedding was very expensive, and I had to borrow a tidy sum from the bank to cover it. I had no choice but to come back here and work to pay off the loan, because if I stayed at home, it would be impossible to make enough money. You know how few job opportunities there are in our country and how badly they pay." Maliha did not reply to what her husband was saying. She lay down on the bed and slept until morning. Nafie slept on a threadbare couch next to his wife's bed.

So, Nafie and Maliha began married life in a cramped hotel room provided courtesy of the benefits system. Nafie started working in a shoe factory, hoping that fortune would smile on him. Life with Maliha was full of pleasure for him; he was madly in love with her despite the scandal she had brought on him. Every morning, he left her and went to work. She remained curled up in the room, like a prisoner, awaiting his return. As the days and weeks passed she grew frustrated and bored.

She started to comprehend the problem she was in. She felt unable to take control of her domestic life and do things like cooking, the laundry, and cleaning the room. Many times, she found herself desperate to cook something she liked to eat, but couldn't because of the difficulty of cooking there. It was hard for residents to cook at the time they wanted to. There was a single kitchen on each floor of the hotel that everyone on that floor shared. In each was a single fridge. Families had to take turns using the utensils, and had to keep their food separate in the fridge so it did not get mixed up with another family's. When a family took someone else's food by mistake, there would be arguments that might last for weeks. There were also quarrels over creating a roster for using the kitchen. From time to time the hotel practically turned into a war zone because of the cramped conditions and the shared use of communal rooms and bathrooms.

The tiny room and the lack of freedom to behave as one wanted and relax when one wanted naturally made Maliha feel stressed out. She would wait, at the end of her tether, for Nafie to come back each evening. The moment he came in, she would knit her eyebrows and lay into him. She had no hesitation in accusing him of failing to find a better place to live and in blaming him for their miserable situation. Showing her annoyance she would complain: "Why did you marry me when you knew you didn't have the money for us to live a happy married life with a decent standard of living? You forced me to get married, knowing that all you had to offer was a tiny room in a crowded hotel. I haven't had a wink of sleep because of the noise that never stops. The walls are thin and awful noises from outside come through. This isn't living, it is just crap followed by more crap."

Maliha went over how things had propelled her into this situation. She asked her husband about the chances of getting out. "It's obvious that this crap is going to continue. I have absolutely no confidence in you being able to change how we're living. What are you going to do about this mess? How are you going to get me away from this? If you want the truth, it's my fault because I agreed to come with you. I should have refused, even if it had cost me my life."

When she didn't feel she was getting any answers, she started threatening him. In tears, she said: "Nafie, I'm giving you one month, no more, to find us somewhere better than this filthy cage. If you don't do that by then, I'll leave you and go back home, where I'll make a scandal for you with my family and the neighbours, just as I did the morning after our wedding night. I'll tell them all about the pitiable state we're living in. You managed to hide the truth by somehow spending lavishly. My family and all the local people were dazzled and thought you must be very rich. They all thought you'd be able to provide your wife with a good life. I'll go home and tell them all the bitter truth and reveal that you're a fraud and a fake."

Then she reminded him of his financial obligations to her family. "Where," she asked him, "are you going to get the monthly allowance you promised them? You can't even provide us with a decent place to live, as opposed to this hole of a so-called hotel room."

In the face of his wife's rage, her violent defiance, and nagging, Nafie did not know how to respond. He was afraid that if he said anything, things would only get worse between them. So he kept quiet, trembling at the lashing from Maliha's sharp tongue. He said to himself: "This country has turned everything upside down between me and my wife. Here, she's in control and I'm expected to follow her orders. Now I'm scared of her, quite the opposite of how it was when she was forced to marry me. Praised be the One who turns things around."

When the nagging got too much for Nafie, he would shut up and make a tactical retreat. He would slip away out of the room very calmly, a weak and nervous man who did not know what to do. In the corridor, the old and threadbare carpet was covered in stains: the urine of drunks, the vomit of children, splashes of wine and other drinks that residents took to their rooms. He reached the reception which was more like a narrow, dark passageway. A slightly built, bent-backed, heavily wrinkled Thai woman, plastered in red, blue, green, and black makeup, sat there round the clock, living and working in the same place. She licked her lips and sucked on her false teeth while out of the corner of her eye she watched a portable TV whose shaky picture always needed adjusting. In front of her were a phone and a computer. She answered the few calls and enquiries from outside the hotel and from the guests themselves. When Nafie walked past her, he would raise a hand and she would respond with a big smile in a desperate attempt to get him to talk to her. She lay in wait for anyone coming and going in the hope of hearing a few words that would help kill the terrible loneliness forced on her by her job. But Nafie did not stop, he was embarrassed and did not want anyone to see his face up close.

He would keep walking on towards the hotel bar, which was located in a desolate corner and filled with drunks and noise. His ears were assailed by annoying music and the voice of an unknown singer striking like a hammer. The smell of stale wine and beer filled his nostrils, along with thick clouds of cigarette smoke. He hunkered down in a dark corner, scared that Maliha might come after him and lay into him in front of the crowd in the bar. He sat at a table, his mind confused and his body in a state of collapse. He tried desperately to rid himself of his worries by smoking. He chain-smoked cigarettes one after another, hoping that their poison would anaesthetize him and allow him to forget his bitter reality, even if only for a few minutes. If the harmful smoke gave him a break from Maliha's violence, he had no problem with that, and was ready to pay the price.

Nafie found many ways to put up with Maliha's insults and nagging. He would lie down on one side of the narrow bed and pretend to be asleep in a deliberate attempt to block out her words. He might cover his face with the heavy bedspread in an attempt to block out the light, which gave him a migraine when it came accompanied by Maliha's voice. For that reason, he was extremely careful to avoid looking directly at rays of light.

On rare occasions he would answer Maliha back, his voice trembling: "My darling Maliha, I'm sorry for what I'm about to say, but I have to say something. Darling, you've got it wrong about me. All I ask for is a bit of time to sort things out. Then you'll see our life change for the better."

Nafie fine-tuned the way he defended himself; he tried to distract his opponent by making sweet and tempting promises. He would say: "All I want from you is a little time, a month or two. I'll try and convince the housing office to move us. Bear with me until I can find a solution, even if it is hard to put up with everything."

But Maliha paid scant attention to his explanations and pleas. Rather, she continued to hurt his feelings, as attacking him was a form of self-defence that would soothe her anger and frustration. She was still raw from her family's betrayal in marrying her to someone against her wishes. She had expected that some of her anger would subside when she reached London but her hopes were dashed by what she found awaiting her. Hopes for a comfortable life evaporated, and she felt she was in a living hell. She said: "This is hopeless, man. And I say man with doubts that you are one since men are usually strong, adventurous, and go-getting but you don't have any of those qualities. I'm suffocating and you're the one choking me. God damn you, you failure."

Then Maliha began to apply a new tactic against her poor husband. A tactic of going to the brink. When the battle became heated, she would run over to the window, throw it wide open, and stick her head out. She would lift her top half up, swing her legs out, and be on the verge of falling. In a loud voice she would shout: "This failure of a man is crushing me. Help me, save me from his evil." Her appearance and hysterical shouting would draw the attention of passers-by below. They would form a crowd, joined by some of the hotel residents. They watched this beautiful woman, her top half leaning dangerously out of the window, fearful that she would fall to the ground in front of them. Sometimes, someone would call the fire brigade, and a fire engine would quickly turn up and extend its long ladder from the street beneath the window, ready to save her if she fell.

Maliha would return to normal and stop shouting, would move away from the window and collapse onto the floor. She was in a pitiful physical and mental state. Nafie knelt down beside her, trying to comfort her, encouraging her to calm down and take care. He stroked her hair and said a few charms he had learnt long before which his mother used to recite to help him recover when he was sick. Once he was sure Maliha was back to her normal state of mind, he would try and make love to her in the hope that she would be happy with him after her body was satisfied. But she always rejected him, pushing him away with her hands and legs. She would run off into the bathroom and lock the door behind her. He used to stand outside the door, pleading with her and begging for forgiveness, saying tearfully: "Come out, my darling. Don't be scared. I promise I won't try again if you don't want to. It was just my mistake, no more. An error I won't make again. I shouldn't have tried to touch you when you are so tired and unwell."

Nafie and Maliha's life became one long series of such outbursts followed by blame and recriminations. Before he married her, he had known little about her. He had no idea that she had such a forceful personality and sharp tongue. He had relied on her brother Abdel Wahid, his lifelong friend, and was taken by her beauty, her attractive figure and pretty face. As a result he had quite a shock and felt very upset and bitterly disappointed.

As things became impossible he was forced to take practical steps to find somewhere better to live than the miserable hotel room. He thought about renting a small flat in the suburbs. It was a good idea but he would not be able to afford the rent as well as the cost of public transport from the suburbs to his work in central London. So there was no alternative but to try to convince social services to provide him with another place to live more appropriate to his and his wife's circumstances. He went to the relevant department that dealt with emergency cases and set out his problem in detail. "My wife suffers from serious psychological problems," he told the housing officer. "Every day she's half hanging out of the window and nearly falling to her death. If you don't believe me, ask the hotel residents and the neighbours. They're all witnesses." As soon as the officials heard what he was saying about his wife, they took it seriously and started the exhausting process of finding him alternative accommodation.

Three weeks later, Nafie and Maliha were allocated a small flat in Shepherd's Bush at the end of the long and famous Goldhawk Road, a street renowned for its many shops and cheap restaurants and its street market, where low-income families could buy clothes, food, fruit and vegetables, furniture, and other things. The new flat was in a ten-storey block; it was a one-bedroom flat, and had a small living room with a window overlooking the street, as well as a kitchen, bathroom, and store cupboard.

With the move to the flat in Shepherd's Bush, Nafie started to look forward to a new period in his life, one marked by calm and stability. Leaving the miserable hotel provided a powerful incentive to try and make himself and his wife happy, emotionally, materially, and psychologically. He actually took plenty of steps towards that family goal, but unfortunately he did not receive the emotional support from Maliha that he anticipated and hoped for. She carried on behaving like a despairing and discontented woman and took a very pessimistic view of everything. What most frustrated and angered her was Nafie himself. Simply seeing him made her scream like someone possessed. For no obvious reason she would threaten him and make impossible demands. Her threats started tearing Nafie up inside, and he became so confused that he thought they were still living in the hotel.

In spite of the language barrier, Maliha started to get to know the new community, the streets, and the different elements of life there. The first thing to catch her attention was how rich the local shopkeepers were, especially when she compared them to her extended family, and to her and her husband. So she thought she was at a turning point where she would be able to find a share of the good life. She would look out of the small living room window that overlooked the street and see displays of wealth in the shops, the goods, the restaurants, the clothes, the cars, even the buses. During the long hours that her husband was out at work, she would scrutinize the life pulsing below. She would look at the goods in the shop windows of Shepherd's Bush with their colourful packaging, smart boxes, and glossy plastic bags.

The jeweller's shop was owned by an Indian man called

Ramesh. In the window she glimpsed gold bracelets and all kinds of necklaces whose gems sparkled like sunlight. The fabric shop belonged to a Sudanese man, Hajj Niamatullah al-Hasil, and was piled high with all different kinds of textiles that he never stopped inspecting. She would watch him moving a bale from one shelf to another. He would measure and cut the cloth and carefully and tenderly feel it with his fingers, as though the piece of cloth was one of his dear daughters. There was a furniture shop crammed with gilt chairs in antique French style, with fine Persian rugs, bright carpets, crystal chandeliers, dinner services, tables, chairs, long and short curtains, bright nylon tablecloths with pretty designs. That shop was owned by Monsieur George Kamoun. Originally from Lebanon, he had lived in London for more than forty years and seen off all competition in the furniture trade. There was a shop for bags and shoes, always full of customers, that was owned by the Moroccan Mloudi Lahbib. There was the butcher's, always busy, whose owner Lewis and his assistants would weigh out cuts of meat – legs, shoulders, rumps, bones, hearts, and shins. One customer would come in as another was leaving, and the numbers would go up in the afternoon a few hours before closing time. That was when people went to buy meat for dinner, the main meal of the day as for many work continued until shortly before six.

Maliha would follow the hustle and bustle of business and wish that Nafie had a shop like those she watched from morning to evening. She asked herself: "Why doesn't Nafie own a shop after all these years he's spent in wealthy London? All he has is his crap job in a shoe factory, whose smells of rotten leather, burnt plastic, and chemical dyes he brings home with him. Even his fingers and nails are dyed." If Nafie had a shop, she would be able to buy everything she desired, and give her family the support they expected every month. If Nafie had a business, she could help him behind the counter, with the books, and with marketing since she had a fantastic background in that field.

In the past she had worked selling all kinds of goods and products as part of her desperate efforts to escape the bitter cycle of poverty. Unfortunately, for many reasons she did not manage to fulfil her dream. Her family stopped her and stifled her; she was hindered by a lack of knowledge after leaving school too young on account of her family's poverty and ignorance; the final straw had been when they forced her to marry, sacrificing knowledge for money, and which time had proved to be a seductive mirage.

After all those years she still remembered the advice of her teachers about the importance of knowledge. The words echoed in her ears as though they had been said yesterday: "Without knowledge, there's no future and no success in anything." She listened to them say: "Maliha, your good looks won't help you if you don't drink from the pure fountains of knowledge. You must take an interest in your classes if you intend you and your family to escape poverty."

It had become clear to her that the teachers had been right. Failure at school meant a continuation of the humiliating and dispiriting cycle of poverty. She was part of a family that depended on the meagre income of her father. His limited pay wasn't even enough to feed them all and so the family was always beset with problems.

Until now she remembered mealtimes. Her mother would come out of the kitchen, her body exhausted, her clothes damp from the oppressive heat after hours spent in a cramped and dark space in front of a temperamental stove preparing meals for her family. She carried what she had cooked on a small tray. On the roof, a thick cloud of flies would land on the plates and start feeding and her mother would wave an arm around to disperse them but without success. Maliha remembered that when she saw the flies swarming over the food, she felt disgusted and nauseous and swore not to go near the dishes however hungry she was. "Better an empty belly," she would say "than eating that." But when her mother put down the tray, Maliha would forget her words and the flies would vanish from her mind. She would smell the food and she and her brothers and sisters would fight over it in heated competition. In the end, they did not eat enough to satisfy themselves and hunger would gnaw at their bellies mercilessly. They tried to fill up on the seeds, nuts, and dried dates and prunes that her mother kept in a tin box, stashed away for visiting neighbours. Hunger drove them to hunt for the box and when they found it they devoured its contents and left it totally empty. This bitter reality gave birth to a strong desire within Maliha to rebel against her family's situation and try to escape deprivation. As a joke she used to call her family house the swamp of hungry flies.

Poverty bared its teeth at school when she noticed the vast difference between her and her classmates in money and clothes. She learnt the reason why: her father did not have enough money to provide his children with what they needed. She suffered from her poverty and that spurred her to look for a way to make a little money to buy the things she needed for school. She longed to get rid of her old school clothes, which her mother was tired of mending and patching, and change her shoes, which were too small and full of holes. Her father had bought them from the wholesale market, they were uncomfortable and their style and colour were hideous.

Her first attempt to rebel began after she saw some neighbourhood women selling junk in the market and making a little money. She saw women roaming the streets and alleys in the area, walking past the school gates carrying their wares on their heads and under their arms – bags of all kinds of stuff: children's toys, snacks and sweets and biscuits, folk remedies and pills for headaches, burn ointments, toothpaste, old electrical goods, makeup, and other light things. They would knock on doors and show their wares to those who wanted and those who did not. Her mother only rarely found any money in her pockets to buy the things she needed for the house, let alone for accessories and makeup. She would eye the attractive stuff, but was unable to get her hands on any of it.

Maliha liked the idea of buying and selling, especially after she saw the roving saleswomen being handed cash by their customers. "You have to give it a try," she said to herself. "Perhaps you'll get lucky and make some money. It doesn't matter what you sell. You have to make the first move, then the money will come." So she started selling to her family; simple, cheap things that when they saw them they wanted them.

Then she progressed to a new stage. She would buy on credit from local shops the things she wanted to sell. Things like nail varnish, lipstick, powder, and perfume. At the same time, she would include anything that came to hand from home, like knitting needles, old clothes, plates, sugar, coffee and tea. She would take the stuff to school and sell it to the pupils, teachers, and other staff whom she trusted not to tell the headmistress. Her scheme was a success and she plied her trade during the lunch break. A crowd would gather round her checking out what she had, and buying this and that. Their justification for buying from her was that they did not have the time to go to the market. Then Maliha started taking special orders from some of her customers. Her fellow pupils were impressed by the beauty products and accessories she offered: nail varnish and lipstick for a few coins.

She would collect up the money she made and use it to settle the debts with the shopkeepers. What remained was her profit. She kept the cycle going, and bought and sold new stock. She was full of hope that her earnings would extricate her from the grip of poverty, but in fact it led her to fail at school and made her teachers angry.

One day the teacher Miss Nabila said to her: "Maliha, despite all my efforts to fill your head with knowledge, it looks like you'll never benefit. Your growing interest in buying and selling and in looking beautiful and attractive takes up the bulk of your concentration. And that's unfortunate. I can't do any more than I have already. I shall leave you to your fate and future life."

When Maliha considered the way in which Miss Nabila went on about learning and failure, she was furious, but she composed herself and began to think logically. "Is that Miss Nabila blind?" she wondered. "Doesn't she see how bad things are for the poor in this country? Or is she just mouthing the nonsense spouted by the rich that the poor are lazy, and out of laziness they go out begging, for an easy living, rather than rolling up their sleeves and going to work to support their families? How come knowledge hasn't helped Miss Nabila understand the lives of poor students? Poor students do badly at school for a host of reasons. First of all, there is nothing that encourages them to learn. They are always struggling with having to make do. Poor families are forced to send their sons and daughters out to work to bring in money, but at the expense of learning."

At the end of the school day, Maliha would stand on the street hawking her wares. In the heat of summer, the cold of winter, and the rain of autumn she was there. She finished late and would arrive home to a good talking to from her mother and a good beating from her brother Abdel Wahid. She put up with it for the material gain that she had convinced herself she so badly needed.

Her school years went by in this fashion until Nafie snapped her up against her will and introduced her to his paradoxical world. Everyone believed he lived a life of luxury that would bring an end to her poverty. The reality, however, was quite the opposite. She never got to taste personally the material success her family talked about. She just witnessed it from the window of her room, at the butcher's, the haberdasher's and the jeweller's shops of Shepherd's Bush.

She kept asking herself: "Wouldn't it be better for Nafie to own a shop like that man who sells fabrics, Hajj Niamatullah al-Hasil, rather than depending on his paltry weekly wages that don't meet our needs for food, clothing, and electricity? The income from a shop would help us change the worn-out, dirty, shapeless and colourless furniture in the flat for new furniture from Monsieur George Kamoun's shop." A big sofa in the middle of the living room that she could show off to her neighbours when they drank cups of clove-infused tea and ate delicious dishes of meat and vegetables and fruit.

Maliha realised that what she aspired to was out of reach since Nafie was incapable of changing the way he lived. He had come to London as a stranger and remained trapped by his foreignness. Upheavals and problems had stripped him of ambition and patience, creating a desire to cling on to the way things were, and weakening his desire to take a risk. He became introverted, seeking peace and quiet, and did not like to mix with people. Maliha told herself: "Perhaps my husband will never recover from the shame of the morning after our ill-fated wedding night."

Nafie would finish work at the factory, go to the shops to buy food and other things they needed, and hurry home. He would sit at their round table and eat dinner with his wife, if she wasn't in one of her all too familiar moods. After his exhausting day at work, she would dish up a sizeable portion of angry reproach, blaming him in the strongest terms for his shortcomings and lack of ambition. "How can you submit to the way things are when you live in London, the city of limitless opportunity? People here have absolute freedom and everything is ready made for them. If you want to work in business, there are no limits to how much you can make. The state only cares about the taxes it takes." Maliha imagined that in such a society there were big chances and opportunities and that it was up to people to grab them and struggle until they succeeded.

Material success was all around her, and from her perspective, the path to making money seemed easy and ready made. You just had to be ambitious, like the neighbourhood businessmen. They made money easily and regularly. They ran their businesses without too much exertion and made a profit out of their clean shops, which were free of dirt and flies, with their floors mopped and polished twice a day. They did not offer credit to customers. The butcher Lewis, for example, stuffed his till with countless notes.

Maliha thought a great deal about what was going on in front of her eyes. She felt she had gained sufficient understanding of the economic and social situation in Britain to become convinced that British society provided shopkeepers with everything they needed to progress and succeed. It encouraged them to make a profit and expand their investments and business. She believed that everything going on in front of her was a success story.

She would see the owner of the draper's shop, Hajj Niamatullah al-Hasil, buried under piles of fabrics; the Indian jeweller Ramesh would handle beautiful jewellery set with brilliant emerald and turquoise stones. Maliha found herself always asking: "How come Nafie has failed to make any of the money that is visible everywhere?" She reached an answer impossible to doubt: "Nafie is lazy. That's why he's failed to succeed."

She devised a foolproof plan to try and get an answer out of the party concerned – Nafie himself. She waited in agitation for him to come back from work. As soon as he entered the house, she began a heated interrogation session. "God preserve you, Nafie.

Now tell me, what have you achieved since the day you arrived in London? Is it credible that you are still living in a flat whose walls are full of cracks due to age and lack of repair? All that's in our bedroom is a narrow bed that we squeeze into every night with difficulty, and a decrepit wardrobe with its doors hanging off. The sofa in the living room is worn out and the edges are ripped. The carpets on the floor are threadbare. The basin in the bathroom is cracked, and the kitchen has a broken light and lacks modern amenities like a dishwasher, a food mixer and a washing machine."

Maliha then made a few adjustments to her plan and adopted a more logical tone. "Let's forget about the sorry state of the kitchen and the flat for a moment. What's strange is that I've discovered you can't speak good enough English. I suggest you work on it. Speaking English clearly and well is the key to making it. If we couldn't make it financially in our own country, that's excusable. Over there only a small class of people do well. They're people in government or businessmen with big enough pockets to pay bribes, or they're backed by the banks with large sums of money. Here, Nafie, things are different. Or have I got it wrong? If you don't believe me, just look out of the window and you'll see success of every kind."

When Nafie failed to obey her words and go and look out of the window, she grabbed him by the collar in an effort to force him to stand up next to her and watch what was going on in the street. She was extremely worked up and angry. Nafie pulled himself free and fled to the bedroom, locking the door behind him and refusing to answer her. He was in no position to answer back to any of her accusations. A single word from him that she didn't like would open the gates of Hell. But she did not leave him to recover in his bedroom sanctum. She kept tapping incessantly on the door, and when he didn't open it or respond, she started pounding on the door with her fist and kicking it as hard as she could. This was followed by fits of sobbing and crying until Nafie opened the door and calmed her down with sweet words and gentle caresses.

3

Quite some time passed after the dinner that brought together Doctor Nadim Nasra, his friend Nafie, and Nafie's wife Maliha. And Dr Nadim was quite sure that his wife Maureen would not relish strangers, especially his new Arab friends, visiting her house.

After her marriage Maureen had changed dramatically from a kind and friendly person into an arrogant and difficult woman who lorded it over those whose culture or opinions were different to hers, with an extra dose of this for foreigners. One way or another, the thoroughly English Maureen wanted nothing to do with foreigners. With her husband already a foreigner, she tried to cut him off from his milieu and monopolize the side of him she wanted, which was that of the successful man with a respectable profession. Maureen had been transformed from an ordinary nurse into the wife of a respected and highly regarded doctor. This change raised her social standing considerably more than she had imagined. Her self-confidence thus boosted she found all the justification she needed to treat others with condescension. She now had a beautiful house with a large garden in an elegant London suburb. Like parvenus in general, Maureen had a superiority complex and disliked people for no good reason.

This was why Dr Nadim was pretty certain that if he asked Maureen to entertain his friends for dinner at home, she would not welcome the idea, and might engage him in a fruitless discussion about opinions he did not share with her, or accept at all. She would likely tell him they were strangers to her and were from a different social environment, from a class who survived on state benefits and lived in a council flat. She would mention how she was supported by her husband's income from his respectable clinic. Now, unlike in the early years of their marriage, Maureen was no longer interested in what her husband wanted, including hosting his friends at home, even though she knew it was something he would like to do.

But it was Maliha who was dominating Nadim's thoughts – she took control of his heart and mind. His infatuation with her grew and he became fixated on her. She was on his mind when awake and visited him in his dreams. Her tall, elegant body, her sweet and winning smile, her languid eyes, her thick black hair down to her waist. He spent hours rhapsodising over her beauty that mixed intense attraction, storminess, elegance and overpowering sex appeal: playful eyes, strong personality, great self-possession and confidence, and a gentle severity. This enchanting mix of smouldering passion and overwhelming seduction made him surrender to the grip of love and desire.

Nadim entered a phase of hopeless romanticism, something he had never been prone to before. This made him forget the unfortunate fact that Maliha was married to his friend Nafie. He convinced himself that it did not matter and there was no need to think about it. No power on Earth could stop the cascade of love in full flow.

He had little desire to reflect on another unfortunate fact: his own marriage. He wished he could end his relationship with Maureen and throw off the shackles of the marriage. His life with her no longer meant anything. Once they had moved into their new house, Maureen lacked for nothing. He had provided her with every form of comfort and luxury, and had nothing left to offer her.

Nadim was convinced that it was now his turn to find personal and emotional happiness and return to his Arab roots, which had long played second fiddle to work and material ambition. Achieving success had not been easy, but he had managed it and given himself, Maureen and their children, a good, comfortable life. Since that aim had been achieved, Maureen had drifted out of his emotional life, and was no longer a substitute for Arab and Middle Eastern things. He did still rely on her to handle his personal and family affairs, but that was as far as it went.

Maliha and her flat became his quest. He became firmly convinced that she, and she alone, would quench his years of emotional thirst and slake his longing for Arab culture that had been stifled by the ups and downs of life. Now he wanted Maliha, and was not bothered by her cultural and social status. He just longed to sit on the low sofa in the living room, he longed for the round copper tray with its Arabic engravings placed before it, he longed for the plain plastic flowers, the smell of the food with its mix of cumin, parsley, sweet pepper, and garlic. Nadim's heart had become beset by an all-encompassing image. His pulse beat faster and he was indeed perplexed by what had happened to him since the moment his eyes had locked with hers, so beautiful and languid. He was sleeping little on account of his constant thoughts about her and how he might see her again, praying that their first dinner would not be their last.

It proved impossible to encounter his new love directly, so he tried to be in touch with her via her husband. Whenever Nafie came to meet him at the clinic, he would scrutinize him, searching in him for Maliha's features, her smile, sweetness and kindness. Nadim tried various ways to get Nafie to talk about her, even if just to mention her name. He spent awkward, nerve-wracking times with his visitor attempting to find a pretext he could use to reunite with the object of his affections, but Nafie was oblivious to the workings of his friend's mind. In any case, he did not care to speak about his wife since being out of the house was his chance to get away from the problems of married life.

Nadim took refuge in the anthems to unrequited love, infatuation and devotion so prevalent in Arabic music in the hope that his heart would be healed and the inferno of love extinguished. In the past he had had little time for such songs, which he thought naïve and adolescent. Love, however, has an iron law and the lyrics turned – praised be the One who turns things around – from being trivial words of adolescent romance, with hackneyed melodies, written by amateur poets with no talent for rhyme into sublime works of art that touched his heart and soul. These songs were a soothing balm for him, precisely capturing the anguish of his smitten heart. Whenever he remembered her, so far from him and so desired, he would listen to Abdel Halim Hafez's "I'm dreaming of you". The cassette with that song on was always with him, like his shadow. He sang along to it in the car, at the clinic, and at home. He would feel the impact of the words and their meaning, as sung by the nightingale Abdel Halim.

Because it had been love at first sight that night of the dinner, Nadim turned from a calm man into a bundle of nerves. His heart had been steady, his soul confident, his mind stable, his work successful, and his family life tranquil, then love for Maliha stormed through his life leaving him vulnerable. Big goals and hard tasks disappeared; he was only hoping to fulfil one goal – to receive another invitation for dinner from Nafie.

He felt hurt by his friend. Nafie would come and visit him at the clinic, but did not invite him home. Nadim said to himself: "That man is living a terrible contradiction, a real puzzle. He allows himself to come and visit me, but he won't invite me to his home. That's strange, only a selfish, mean, devious man would do such a thing. It's my fault, though, for welcoming people warmly and not suggesting they invite me home, which is only my right and I shouldn't give it up." Despite being annoyed about this, Nadim continued playing host to Nafie at the clinic and offering him coffee and Arabic sweets. He received him with kindness and warmth, but when Nafie said goodbye, the link with Maliha was lost and as a forlorn lover Nadim felt terrible.

One morning, after not sleeping all night, he was late leaving home to go to the clinic. When the list of patients for the day suddenly crossed his mind he jumped out of bed like a man possessed. He convinced himself he would have to drive to work rather than take the train as he usually did, as it would be quicker by car. At the end of the day, he left the clinic but was feeling in a shaky state from his emotional turmoil. He did not want to arrive home like that. He was scared he would embarrass himself with Maureen, whose feminine intuition would know what was going on in his head. In fact, the clinic had become his second home. There was a small bed there, a small cooker, and kitchen utensils. He usually made his friends Arab food, such as *fuul* beans and hummus. He could spend more than a week at the clinic, but knew he couldn't stay away from the house for a longer period. He always went home to his wife and children however bad his physical and mental condition. He couldn't be blamed for keeping to the ways he had grown up with as well as fulfilling his marital and parental obligations. A man in love may sometimes suffer near madness, while the object of his desire is sitting relaxed and calm at home.

His legs took him to the car. He started the engine and headed off home to Richmond. On the bridge he felt as though a hand had grabbed his wrists and was taking control of the steering wheel, robbing him of his physical and mental strength. This force steered the car as it pleased, not how he wished, and took him off in another direction. Without realising, his car was then heading in the direction of Maliha's flat. He had wanted to drive around near her house; perhaps see her crossing the road on her way home or see her looking out of the window. With trembling hands and troubled thoughts, he carried on towards Goldhawk Road.

The clock showed 8pm, but he was oblivious to the time for dinner with Maureen. He was oblivious to everything going on around him. His thoughts were channelled onto one task only. He arrived at the street and drove around once, but did not see her. He drove around again checking the faces of the people crossing the road, but her face was not one of them. He drove around and around, checking people's faces from the left. Then he looked upwards to the window of her room, where she might be looking out. Unfortunately, the window was closed. He carried on driving around the block, his mind paralysed; he was unable to decide what to do. The cars behind him were blowing their horns at the man who was driving so erratically, swerving from right to left.

In the midst of all this turmoil, the car stopped abruptly in the middle of the road; he felt as though his heart had stopped, too. He took a deep breath, shook his head in disgust, punched the steering wheel with both hands, and cursed the blasted car for coming to a halt at such an awkward moment. With all the skill he could muster, he tried to restart it but no luck. Shaking at his bad luck, he got out of the car. He tried to push it to the side of the road but, like the lump of metal it was, it would not budge. There was a smell of petrol even though the weather was chilly. He kept on trying to push the car, flustered that it that had let him down at a critical time. The traffic around him was at a standstill, and the road was busy. The other drivers had run out of patience and helped to push the broken-down vehicle out of the middle of the road. When that was done, all the drivers went back to their cars except for one, who checked Nadim's car over, and shaking his head said: "Didn't you notice you were running out of petrol?"

The man's question embarrassed him and he did not answer. "If he knew what I was suffering," he said to himself, "it would have been no surprise that I didn't notice the car was running out of petrol." He got into the car, feeling lousy, mentally confused and slightly feverish. He sat before the steering wheel and shut his eyes. "There's been a massive change to my personality," he said to himself. And he was right. He was no longer the sensible Doctor Nadim in control of all aspects of his life. He shook his head in an expression of regret. Despair was eating at him and driving him crazy. He sat up and looked at his watch. It was almost midnight. He was shocked at how late it had become. "What am I going to tell Maureen?" he said, fearfully. He had no idea what to do and put his head in his hands.

Dragging himself out of the car, he headed off down the road, he knew not where, after realising he had to get some petrol. He came to a small garage where a young guy was behind the till. Looking at the empty container, he said to Nadim: "Sir, you know that the law does not allow me to sell petrol in that way. We have to pump the petrol directly into a vehicle. I'm very sorry."

Pleading with him, Nadim said: "Please, I have to get home to Richmond. I have to be at work early tomorrow morning and it's well past midnight now."

The guy at the till saw a tired man in front of him and said: "OK then, take the petrol you need, but leave your name and address. The supervisor might ask me why I broke the garage rules."

"I promise you I won't use it to start a fire or make Molotov cocktails." Nadim walked back to his car and poured the petrol into the tank, and set off back home.

When he arrived, he found Maureen waiting for him, irate and annoyed. "Where have you been so late?" she demanded. He explained what had happened, but of course saying no more than he had run out of petrol. He hurried up to his room, undressed and lay down in his cold bed. He could not sleep, but tossed and turned. Anxiety kept him awake and his eyelids were smarting. In this bitter struggle between wakefulness and sleep, he asked himself what had happened to him to make him lose his peace of mind and sense of composure. Everything in his life had been turned upside down, to such an extent he no longer knew himself. In the middle of his musings, his eyelids grew heavy and he fell fast asleep.

In the morning, he was late going to work, and treated his patients in a terrible state of exhaustion. At midday, behind the screen that separated him from the waiting room, he could just make out a woman coming in accompanied by a man, who then left. She sat among the patients with her back towards him. He shook his head in surprise. Who was this strange woman who had entered the waiting room like a ghost? He was even more taken aback as he failed to recognize her. He consulted the list of that day's appointments in the hope he might discover her identity. In the list prepared by his secretary Cynthia, he found the name of a woman, but it was too early for her appointment. He said to himself: "If this strange woman isn't one of my patients, what does she mean by coming to my surgery?" He answered his own question: "Perhaps she is the ghost of Maliha, come to relieve me of the torment, which has turned morning into night, and to restore my mental and emotional balance." He wanted to consolidate his relationship with Maliha, but that could never happen because of her relationship with Nafie. This was the secret behind his anguish, sickness, and despair. Since meeting her, he had had no rest, not even for a moment, because he had been unable to see her again. Could he stop himself from thinking about her and start a relationship with another woman? He shook his head in sorrow and said to himself: "I don't think so, but there's no harm in trying. The next few minutes will reveal what fate has in store."

He stole a glance at the strange woman and mumbled: "She looks fit and healthy. I wonder what illness she's suffering from." The strange woman remained sitting in enviable composure. He wanted her to be the last person to come into the examination room, so he could spend sufficient time with her to learn why she had come to see him. He finished a hurried examination of the next patient. Then he washed his hands and face, and sprayed cologne on his face and neck. Why all these preparations? Had the woman made a date with him? He made sure his white coat was buttoned correctly and went into the waiting room. He found her sitting in the same spot, dressed in modern clothes: flared jeans and a flowery blouse with rolled-up sleeves and a red leather handbag beside her.

When the woman heard his footsteps in the room, she turned round to face him and to his great surprise it was none other than Maliha. His heart jumped and he was so startled he nearly raced over to her and buried his head in her chest in tears, begging her to free his heart from all its agonies. He wanted to end the torment he had been through the past few weeks. At the last moment, however, he stopped himself, and rather than doing so he looked away from her to hide the hot tears rolling down his cheeks. He did not want the tears to give away his wayward desire. He took a deep breath and felt as if he had been freed of a great anxiety. His balance returned and he felt better physically. He was now standing before the person he had been seeking for what seemed like an era of geological time, not a few days and weeks. This was the first time his eyes had set sight on her since the dinner that night. Here was Maliha in the flesh, here for a private meeting.

He felt wonderfully lightheaded and said to himself: "My Lord, you have saved me from certain disaster and from the madness consuming me. I almost lost my mind. You have restored the blood to my veins and brought me back to life from nothing, Lord. My body is full of life. I can hardly believe that the person I was seeking with all my might has come to visit me unannounced, come to visit me without her husband. Praise God, there must be a powerful motive that made her come to the clinic. Perhaps she sensed my torment or was even suffering herself. Reaching the very bottom means you have to start rising again. The migration of birds and their long absence means their return once again. However long the drought, rain will come again and the springs and rivers flow."

He looked at her again and was stunned by her beauty: the radiant face, the beautiful eyes, the soft cheeks, the arched eyebrows, the rose lips. Very politely, he took her soft hand with its elegant fingers and, giving it a gentle squeeze, raised it to his lips and kissed it. His eyes registered nothing around him except her attractive face. The surgery with its desks and chairs vanished. Maliha instinctively understood the effect she was having on him and she smiled warmly. She listened intently to his few sweet words: "Welcome to my clinic, Madame Maliha, your presence is an honour."

"I came unannounced," she responded, "and quite frankly that is wrong. If it seems I lack manners, please forgive me. For your information, it was Nafie who made me do it because of his work. It's his day off today, and he was supposed to spend it at home. But he got a call from the factory asking him to come in, some kind of emergency. He suggested that I wait at your clinic until the evening when he will pick me up."

His heart danced with delight because he knew she would be with him until the evening. "Welcome," he said. "I'm honoured that you've come." He noticed that his receptionist Cynthia was still there. Her hours were not over, and there were still patients to see in the afternoon, but Nadim had to remove every obstacle in his path to the precious quarry. "Please excuse me, Madame Maliha," he said, "I have to tell the receptionist about a medicine we need for a patient this evening." He hurried out without glancing at her face since he was afraid she might tell he was lying. He told his receptionist: "A representative from an Arab embassy has arrived for a meeting with some businessmen who will consult with me on a project to set up a clinic to treat chest conditions. It's probably best to cancel this afternoon's appointments, and so there's no need for you to stay. Please, take the rest of the day off." In spite of her incredulity, she immediately began to finish up and leave.

Once he had given his instructions, he relaxed and hurried back to where Maliha was sitting. "Forgive me," he said, "for being gone so long. Let me get you something to eat or drink. The kitchen is rather basic, I'm afraid, but we'll make do." She smiled and nodded her assent. He went to the small kitchen, picked up a packet of cakes, and offered them to his guest. "These are very plain cakes," he said to her. "My receptionist stops me buying chocolate. She says sweets are bad for your health, and their only benefit is the pleasure of a sugar rush. And sugar causes tooth decay, obesity, and heart disease." Maliha reached for a cake and he spotted that there were no rings on her fingers, not even a wedding ring. He remembered the night of the dinner when she had worn her red velvet kaftan. Today she looked very modern, young and elegant. She smiled delightedly and thanked him for being such a good host. She was very surprised by the appearance of the clinic, whose contents and style made it seem like an old Arab house on a side street in some oriental city and not a Western medical clinic.

The clinic was small, cramped, and dimly lit. On the walls of the waiting room hung strings of prayer beads of different colours and sizes made of glass and wood. They were all covered in a thick layer of dust and cobwebs. The place was like a long-lost cave. There were also many oriental souvenirs: carvings, pictures, and figurines that he had acquired over the years or had been given by friends and patients of his who had travelled to Arab and oriental lands. Beneath every set of prayer beads, there was a note about its material and where it came from – Iraq, Egypt, Lebanon, Gulf countries. There were pieces of oriental carpet woven from wool and silk, old-style earthenware bowls, hand-engraved copper pots, and old books of poetry, literature, and dictionaries. Some curios were piled up on small tables or wooden shelves that bulged under the weight. Nadim looked at Maliha and sensed she found the place strange. He asked her: "Do you like the prayer beads? They're presents from friends and patients. I've been collecting them for years."

He moved on to another subject unrelated to the souvenirs: "Madame Maliha, it's important for me to talk about things with my friends. Subjects like poetry, language, politics, and economics. You might find us browsing the papers and discussing the day's news, especially anything to do with the Middle East. Madame Maliha, even though I am far from my country, I am a very keen observer of its politics and love to be engaged with what's happening there. I still support Arab causes, first and fore-most because I'm an Arab though also because I'm an educated man concerned about poor countries and humanitarian affairs east and west, north and south."

"But you're a doctor not a professor so how do you explain your interest in such complicated matters?" asked Maliha.

"It's an indication of my great interest in the Arab world. I follow events there with fear and dread in my heart. I'm particularly interested in the Israeli-Palestinian conflict, and also follow news of political and economic corruption, suppression of individual liberties, and the lack of democracy. Those things are an expression of the political clampdown going on, especially in the Arab world.

"The loss of Arab identity because societies are bowing to outside influences makes me weep. I'm not calling for Arab isolationism, quite the opposite; there must be collaboration and cooperation between societies throughout the world. But one has to be aware of threats and not accept any form of subservience. The advanced nations use their media power to exert control. Their TV channels broadcast programmes and films around the clock, presenting their lifestyles in a way that attracts poor viewers from developing countries. They're enticed to imitate those lifestyles, but it doesn't make sense.

"I hope, Madame Maliha, that if I had been able to enter politics, I would have made some difference."

Nodding in agreement, Maliha said: "I don't know much about politics, but I do know that poverty is the greatest obstacle humanity faces. I'll be honest with you: I've tasted the bitterness of poverty and have never forgotten its hardships, like ill-health and psychological stress. Nafie, like me, suffered from poverty and could not complete his education. In our societies, there's no lack of educational opportunities for children from well-off families, while the poor have no hope of finding a better future and a decent life. The children of the rich learn but they don't need their education as a weapon against poverty, unemployment, and disease. Their families already have the means to meet all their physical and psychological needs."

Nadim looked glum as he said: "Poor students can use their education to help them acquire skills so they don't have to rely on others or the resources and capacity of the state. But, unfortunately, states in the developing world do not devote the attention they should to schools."

"Poor students like us," responded Maliha, "are not given the chance to learn. From birth, we are at a big disadvantage, particularly because of having to work from an early age. My family are a living example of how hard it is to balance having enough to eat and getting an education. Our father's incompetence made us ashamed to go to school because we couldn't afford the things we needed."

"The reasons always go back to people exploiting other people," added the Doctor. "Resources are abundant, they're just not distributed fairly so that people, communities, and countries can have a decent life. People who become desperate rebel against the situation oppressing them. They don't hesitate as they have nothing to lose. Unfortunately, it's politicians who are deaf to what we are saying, and who refuse even to recognise problems until they get so bad that they explode, shaking the Earth, storming the sea, uprooting trees, and killing people."

Doctor Nadim smiled and went on: "Madam Maliha, let's return to our lives here and stay away from the world's problems. I was telling you about having my friends round to the clinic. I invite them every now and then when work permits. My friends prefer to visit me at the clinic because my house is in the suburbs and most of them live in the centre. Really, I couldn't live without them. They mean a great deal to me. You don't like the cakes? Let me make you a cup of Arabic coffee, then. I make very good coffee myself, and tend to avoid the bad coffee served here in London."

With a hint of happiness in her voice, Maliha said: "Doctor, is this a waiting room of a London clinic or a reception room in an Arab house?"

He shook his head and with a touch of sadness said: "I wish it were an Arab reception room like the old sitting rooms in our country. I can still remember what they were like so clearly. They had high windows with old wooden latticework, beautifully carved. The windows were tall and wide, making the rooms cool in summer and warm in winter, and kept out the wind and rain. This room looks like an Arab room, but it's not on the same level. I've made an effort to make it an Arab sitting room, because I love Arab traditions, and I don't have anywhere else I can arrange in a way that suits me. My house is basically my wife's private domain, and she chooses English-style furniture that lacks any Arab character."

A cloud of pain and sadness covered his face as he spoke: "Before we got married, Maureen claimed to love Arab culture. She even started learning Arabic. But as soon as we got married everything was different. She became intent on starting a family, and no longer wanted to live in our central London flat. We moved to the suburbs and bought a big house with a big garden. Maureen said that such a large house would give the children room to play, unlike the flat that would have stifled them. Over time, she shunted me off into a small room on the first floor. That's where my books are, and my bed, and my Middle Eastern things. On the walls I hung coloured prayer beads and pictures of sights back home."

With a lump in his throat her went on: "Maliha, the only things with Arab features left in my life are two small rooms, one at home and the one you're sitting in right now. The problem is I love my country. Thank God, I've kept my Arabic and see it as my identity and strongest tie to the past. It would have been easy to lose it given the years I've spent in England and my marriage to an English woman as well as the fact I treat patients who don't speak Arabic. But I promised myself I'd protect my language whatever challenges came my way."

He started to digress: "Let's forget about unhappiness now, Maliha. I have much to be sad about, and nostalgia for my withered roots is the reason for the anguish in my wounded heart. In the future, you'll learn more about my sufferings and torment, and realise that you aren't the only one to suffer the misery of exile and the failure to fulfil your dreams and achieve your goals. I'll tell you about how I left my country and other reasons behind my pain. I long for my mother's delicious bread, for our beautiful neighbourhood, for our nice house, and for my kind and generous family. My heart is full of bitterness at having left them. The only consolation I have is tears. Being estranged is the reason for my misery, which will only leave me if I go back to my Arab roots."

Hot tears flowed down his cheeks as he said: "I wish my wounded Arab star would meet another Arab star in the heavens' wide expanse." Maliha was upset by his remarks and spontaneously stood up, embraced him, and held him tenderly to her bosom. He inhaled her scent and remembered the aroma he had encountered at their first meeting in the Shepherd's Bush flat. He felt comfortable with such an aroma, which went back to his childhood and the time of innocent crushes and sweet passion. That aroma had stolen into the corners of his soul and the depths of his pain. Maliha was reminding him of the scent of his distant home that he had long been deprived of.

He held on to her, wrapping his arms around her as though secretly imploring her to help save him from his inferno of desire for her. He was terrified she would slip out of his arms and vanish like dust in the wind. They became enveloped in a passionate embrace, seduced by a wave of pleasure that melted them in a frenzy of attraction. The planets stopped in their orbits, humanity froze, wind, rain, and clouds stopped. The whole world was condensed into this small room crammed with oriental furniture, pictures and souvenirs. After their long and impassioned embrace, which had seen them peeling off their clothes till they were both naked, he led her by the hand to the room next door. There they joined in stolen and forbidden pleasure until late afternoon. They did not cease from the thrill of unending indulgence until Nafie's fingers pressed on the doorbell. They quickly disentangled themselves, unwrapping their limbs and reassembling themselves emotionally and physically. They re-emerged from their quest for overwhelming feelings, warm affection, and rootedness, and in a crazed fear that Nafie might see them naked and in a state of arousal, they ran to the waiting room in search of their clothes that were scattered everywhere.

With that encounter, the story of Doctor Nadim Nasra and Maliha, the wife of his friend Nafie, began its course along desolate and difficult paths. Together they set off, dancing in tandem until the end of their long journey.

4

Nafie had come to Doctor Nadim's clinic to take his wife home. He was in a deplorable state: pale-faced, downhearted, and physically exhausted. The Doctor asked him what was wrong but he did not respond. "What's happened to you?" asked Nadim. "You look very anxious. Calm down a bit."

Nafie sat down, his face puffy and his eyes red, took a deep breath and haltingly, and stammering, told them what had happened to him at work that day. "Listen, you two, there's been a real disaster. They've sacked me and I have to join the dole queue. This morning, when I got to the factory, I saw many of my workmates gathered at the main gate and they were really angry. They had placards condemning the management, and were shouting things against the managing director and the board. The managing director's secretary came out and told all the workers and the staff that the bosses were being forced to close the factory because it wasn't making enough to remain profitable. The number of outlets and shops that bought the factory's products had gone down a lot this year and that had had a major effect on the budget, she said. It didn't make sense to spend any more money and throw resources at a factory with no foreseeable future."

He was crying and sobbing as he continued: "Management decided to fire us and give us three months' redundancy, plus some of the staff keep their pensions. I'm crying for myself and my future and the future living standard of my wife." Doctor Nadim was visibly upset, too, once he understood the dreadful situation facing his friend Nafie, husband of the woman his heart had settled on. In consolation, he said to him: "Listen to me, Nafie. You know that no one in this country dies of starvation. If you don't have any money, the benefits system provides help you can rely on. It's very likely you'll be able to find another job, and keep your benefits and pension, too, if you don't tell government agencies about it. It's better to get some work on the side so you get two livelihoods, then you and Maliha can have a suitable standard of living."

Nadim knew that his suggestion was against the law and dishonest, but he was undoubtedly driven by his feelings towards his friend and his wife. He had taken into account that his friend and his wife were Arabs like him, suffering in exile, and it was his patriotic duty to help and advise them in any way possible, even if that meant breaking the law of the land and behaving improperly.

Nafie relaxed a little after listening to Doctor Nadim, and his suggestions in particular. He would do that and make some money to replace his lost income from work, he thought. That would help him meet their needs, and persuade Maliha to treat him less harshly for having lost his job.

After the torrid session in the clinic, Nadim was invited by Nafie, and Maliha, to go home with them for dinner in gratitude and respect for his concern and support. On the way, conflicting thoughts flashed through the heads of all three.

They reached the flat and went in, along the narrow hallway to the living room. Nadim inhaled the air and felt happy: after his long period of suffering he had been able to return to this beloved place. He sensed that his travails, waiting for a chance to see Maliha were over, and no longer left a mark on him.

He looked around the flat, checking every corner, contemplating every inch and every piece of furniture. He saw the many pictures hanging on the walls, the shoes by the door leading into the living room, and many other things, such as old clothes that the lady of the house seemed intent on getting rid of. It was a surprise to him that during his first visit he had not noticed the pictures on the hallway walls. Now he noticed a photograph of Maliha's parents, a photo of her brother Abdel Wahid in his work uniform, which made it seem he might be a policeman, photos of women and children, and one of the whole family with Maliha in the middle.

Nadim's desire to study the flat and enjoy its aroma grew. He hoped the taste of anxiety, anguish, and loss he had gone through over the past few weeks would be wiped away. Today was a joyous day because he had seen Maliha, made love with her at the clinic, and then come back with her to a nest of love and affection.

He went back into the living room thinking: "I want to take all the things in this flat and hang them on the wall of my heart to make it strong enough to bear my longing. I don't want my link with it severed. I want a relationship that does not end overnight. I want to set down roots in Maliha's flat so that things are under my eyes and ears. My attachment to this place has become an indisputable fact, not up for negotiation. Tomorrow during my afternoon break, I'll go and see my solicitor and ask him to write irrevocably into my will that when I die I must be buried inside Maliha's house."

Nadim had no doubt that he would ask his lawyer to have him buried in Maliha's flat because he could no longer bear the idea of being far from her even when dead. But seeing as he was still alive, he wanted to be someone who belonged to that place, to smell the old Arab fragrance in it and touch its pure Arab soul. Having become part of an English family and being away from his country for all these years had increased his desire to belong to an Arab family, like the small family that Nafie had created with his wife Maliha. It did not matter that theirs was a simple family of humble social background. What he wanted to be part of was something simple, beautiful, and easy to deal with.

He remembered that on the night of the first dinner he had promised to join Nafie and Maliha in all they did, and dedicated himself help them as someone entrusted with responsibilities and obligations. He wanted to know more about their lives. So much more that he could write a fly-on-the-wall novel or conduct research into the life of a small Arab family in an alien environment. He wanted to be an effective and useful member of the family, as an honest expression of his serious connection with Maliha and of the material, spiritual, and emotional conditions she was enduring.

Maliha excused herself to go to the kitchen and prepare a meal in celebration of Nadim's visit and in gratitude at his generosity and help to Nafie in finding a job. She stood in the pocket-size kitchen at the small cooker and started cooking with the old pots and pans that were dented and worn inside and out. She peeled tomatoes, onions, potatoes, and garlic and then chopped them and minced the garlic and some parsley. She took the bottle of olive oil and poured some into a pan. Fumes rose from the pan into the flat. Along with the fumes, her imagination took flight as she fantasized about Doctor Nadim's arrival at her flat for the second time. Her mind went back to what had happened between them that afternoon. She had never imagined that life in London would fling her into the arms of a man other than her husband, a man who told her of his burning love and great passion for her. This man had reached a mysterious place in her heart, making it pulse with a hot passion she had never experienced before. This man had made his infatuation for her clear and shown her the place she occupied in a world of beauty, even though she was the wife of his friend. She reached an important conclusion: Dr Nadim's feelings for her were so strong and solid that he would do the impossible for her.

"My heart pulses with love and desire," she thought. "You are my angel, the apple of my eye. I have travelled thousands of miles from the east to the west, to sip from your pure and clear fountain and listen to your sweet words and see strength, valour and manliness embodied in a man. You combine the science of the west, its skill and precision, with Arab pride, generosity of spirit, and bravery. Tell me when I will meet you and where we will be joined. Tell me that land, sea, and space have heard of our love."

Now they had reached this stage, there was no doubt that Nadim would ask to see her again. How, where, when would these meetings occur? It occurred to her that the Doctor had promised to help Nafie find work, which would make it easier to meet in a way that did not invite suspicion. She would be able to visit Nadim at his clinic without compromising herself. His assistance was acceptable, and Nafie would probably be overly generous-hearted with Nadim and continue to invite him to the flat. In the midst of these flights of fancy, she was taken back once again to what had happened at the clinic that afternoon. She said to herself: "Things are happening really quickly and getting complicated. If I hadn't married Nafie, who knows what my life would have been like and where it would have led me."

She would have been stuck at home, having to put up with the cruelty of her brother Abdel Wahid. But who knows? Perhaps she would have been able to find work as a seamstress in one of the many clothing factories. But work in one of those factories would have been hard, because the bosses gave the good jobs to their friends and relatives, and she did not have any acquaintances to help her, or any money to pay a bribe. The only thing she might have succeeded at was buying and selling; she had the experience, skill, and vision to have done so.

She remembered how she had shouted at the top of her voice when she sold her wares and how little money she had made. She kept the money in a small box, which she tried as hard as she could to hide from the hands of her family. The lack of privacy at home made that difficult. The only place to hide her possessions was behind a crack in the bathroom wall, and so she would secrete the box holding her profits there. When her brother Abdel Wahid found the box one day, he opened it, took the money, and threw it in her face empty. Naturally, she was unable to stand up to him. She was weak and helpless while he made a show of his strength and viciousness. She burst out crying and pleaded with him but he just laughed and kicked her as he made his way out of the house to spend her hard-earned money. He often threatened to hit her if she didn't stop lying about him. When she did manage to hide the box again, she would sit alone in a room out of sight and count what she had. She would divide the money into small piles and say: "This is to buy food, this is to buy cosmetics, and this is to pay the debt to the shopkeeper. If I can make more money, I can buy the things I want for myself."

In those days, she dreamt that when she succeeded in making a good profit from her business, she would buy a large shop in the heart of the city market to sell trinkets, domestic goods, and cosmetics. She wished she could be a proper businesswoman who went abroad to import the best and highest quality goods. Her greatest dream was to buy a house of her own and escape the overcrowded family home. In her own home, she would have space to keep all her own things, her cosmetics and clothes.

She recalled what her teachers had said to her about her dreams never coming true if she didn't take advantage of her intelligence and do well at school. The teachers would say to her over and over again: "Maliha, you're clever but you don't concentrate on your studies." She tried hard but despaired: making progress at school needed more than intelligence. There were textbooks, paper, pens, and enough time for homework. But she had to help her mother with many domestic chores: in the kitchen, washing and mending clothes, sweeping and mopping. Apart from the lack of time, there was nowhere comfortable for her to do her homework undisturbed. The house was crowded and the rooms were dark. There was a lack of fresh air because of the clouds of thick smoke coming from the nearby gas plant. The rooms were crowded with family members, visitors, relatives, and neighbours, and it was hard to find a spare inch to sit down and go over her studies. This meant she had to use the bathroom, to which she would flee, locking the door so as to finish her maths homework, but soon enough someone would come knocking on the door.

She rued her luck at not having the things needed to do well: "It's not fair that poor students face problems and at the same time are responsible for their own failure. Teachers, family, and neighbours blame them. Kids from well-off families have it easy: they do their homework in peace and quiet. Their homes are spacious, they have their own rooms and armies of private tutors, who are schoolteachers themselves, to give them extra lessons, so it's no surprise they're fully informed of the syllabus and the exam questions."

She looked into the saucepan in front of her on the cooker and give it a stir. She took a deep breath and carried on her internal monologue. "Praise God! The poverty I endured in my country has followed me to London." All her family and neighbours thought that leaving would free Maliha from want and that she would live the good life of European capital cities where people could receive money from the state to meet their needs. Social security, designed to guarantee a decent standard of living without the pressures and humiliation of poverty, would protect her. But there was a difference between the laws as they were written and their application in reality, which made receiving benefits difficult and at times impossible.

When the voyage through her memories came to an end, Maliha turned off the ring under the saucepan and put the food on the tray. She carried it to the living room and laid out the meal on the round engraved copper table. The two men were sitting down with a beautiful woman between them having dinner. Harmony and happiness prevailed and they almost believed that peace reigned, love triumphed, and conflict had ended. The evening came to a close. Doctor Nadim said goodbye warmly to his friend Nafie while he gave Maliha a look full of love. He took the train home, feeling completely certain that the spiritual and physical relationship with Maliha had become so strong that no one could separate them. The period of fear and being torn had ended and the period of confidence and stability had begun.

5

In the afterglow of their passionate encounter at the clinic, Maliha and Dr Nadim's relationship went along perfectly, even though at Nafie's expense. The way was open for Maliha to get together with the new man in her life, and she became even more indifferent towards her husband. As far as she was concerned he could eat, drink, and wear what he wanted; she left him to wallow in glorious isolation once she had given up encouraging him to pull himself together, fulfil his responsibilities, and shake off his laziness and lethargy. What more could she have done to persuade Nafie to persevere and become ambitious? "Life's attractions," she thought, "are of no concern to Nafie, so I'll let him get on with his life in whatever corner of the sitting room he pleases."

Most of the time, she found him sitting on the floor – he had given up sprawling on the sofa by the round copper table. When Maliha asked him to help around the house, he would comply before quickly withdrawing back to the safety of his distant spot. As much as he could, he avoided her gaze in fear of her hurtful words and blazing looks.

Nafie started keeping his things in his corner, his shaving gear and a little food. He packed a large wooden trunk, which bore his name and address in black capitals, and which he would lock, keeping the key in his pocket at all times. In the trunk were dried foods, edible seeds, pistachios and peanuts, dried figs, and a range of sweets. The trunk also contained a large photo album of pictures of his friends and family, some old clothes and shoes, illustrated magazines, old newspapers, the complete poems of Antara, and a small cassette player and tapes of old songs. When ensconced in his favourite corner, he would listen to the songs over and over, especially to the booming voice of Fahd Ballan whose words he would repeat after him: "I can't do it, I swear, girls of my country."

Maliha's voice would impinge: "Don't you ever get tired of listening to those songs. I can't take any more of your crooning along to Fahd Ballan. It's so dreary." Nafie would fall silent and start eating watermelon seeds, peanuts, and pistachios. Very often he would turn to the poetry of Antara ibn Shaddad. He would look at the first few pages of the book and read the following description: "The collected poems of Antara al-Abassi, pre-eminent in the arts of the Bedouin Arabs and the settled Arabs. Although one may not be certain that he was the greatest horseman, there is no doubt that he was the greatest poet."

It was Nafie's habit to open the works of Antara and leaf through the pages from cover to cover. His eyes would scan the verses, his head would bob, and his lips hang loose. Sometimes he would seem amazed and delighted. He would do all of that, but in reality he was a poor reader with insufficient intelligence to grasp pre-Islamic poetry. He was of limited abilities, but for some indiscernible reason, he could be found pouring over the poems. He would turn the pages and when he reached the end of the book he would start reading again from the beginning. Over time the cover of the book and its pages became torn and ripped.

Nafie and Maliha were living in two different worlds, a situation only exacerbated by Maliha and Nadim's burgeoning relationship. They rarely talked about their life together as might be expected of man and wife. And on the few occasions they did converse, she made her contempt for her husband plain with her cold offhandedness and lack of kindness.

In fact, Maliha seldom heard Nafie's voice or saw him wandering round the flat. He became taciturn, scarcely opening his mouth as though he was a dumb mute. When the Doctor paid a visit, Nafie would say a few words so as not to offend him. During their evenings together, Doctor Nadim felt pity for Nafie when he saw the looks of fear on his face, and tried to draw him into the conversation with Maliha.

The couple continued to share a bedroom and a bed, but whenever Nafie tried to touch Maliha, she drew her body away in obvious distaste sending a definite no. If he tried again, her distaste and rejection magnified. All his efforts to break the barrier between them were unsuccessful. They were two bodies lying side by side separated by a vast chasm.

Maliha adopted a new excuse for putting her husband off whenever he tried to have sex with her. The moment he touched her, she would pretend she was having her period so that he would leave her alone and not persist. Although Nafie had doubts about her claim, he was unable to put up a fight and expose her lie. She refined the way she deceived him in order to force him to give in. For example, she used sanitary towels as a weapon, buying them in vast quantities and leaving them on every surface of the bathroom. She placed them in prominent places so that he would easily catch sight of them and doubt his belief that she was making her excuse up.

Sometimes Nafie would get angry and dismiss Maliha's excuses and evasion. He knew she was lying so it was no surprise when his patience wore thin and he confronted her. In a fit of rage, he would try and force her to have sex. But she would push him off the bed, screaming hysterically. On one occasion she said: "The only thing to do with you, Nafie, is to contact the religious authorities and bring a case against you for your constant attempts to have sex with me when you know I'm impure. If you don't believe me, come and see for yourself. Anyone with doubts would be satisfied, then. Come along, don't be shy. You're always giving me suspicious looks as though I was lying."

Nafie did not move, frozen like the Sphinx. Maliha carried on screaming at him as she drew closer in an attempt to pull his hand down to her crotch. He resisted and pulled back. This only infuriated Maliha and made her scream louder. "Why won't you come near and find out the truth," she shouted. "I think you want me to strip in front of you so you can see the blood for yourself just to upset me."

Then Maliha changed her tactics. She no longer threatened to get the religious authorities involved, but women's rights' groups instead. She said to her wounded husband: "In our situation I think it best if I contact organizations that look after women and let them know what you're doing to me. I'll tell them that you won't leave me alone even though you know I'm not well and not up to anything. My advice is that you protect yourself and stop acting like a stupid guy. Men always treat women badly in this way. They imagine we are just bodies to excite them, and ignore our feelings and our health.

"You should know the kind of woman you're dealing with and trying to dominate, her and her body. I am Maliha, with an unbreakable will. I'm different to most women in the strength of my personality, my experience, and my talents. I'm not scared of you anymore and will not be offering myself to you whenever you desire. You think I'm a sex slave under your control, a defeated woman.

"I am so over the shock of our dreadful wedding night when you forced my body to submit to your brutal attack. You took me by force, you animal. I can honestly say you raped me and used my brother to defend yourself. You took advantage of the law to magnify your hidden desire to control me. Here, we're far away from our families and yet you still shamelessly try to keep on assaulting me physically and stripping me of my dignity to satisfy your lust. But I swear that whatever you do, you'll never get your wicked way. If you were a real man, you would be ashamed of yourself, you coward.

"You forced me to marry you even though you knew I didn't want to. I was too weak to say no and had to obey my family's wishes. If I had kept refusing I would have lost my family and maybe even my life. If only I had died, and so avoided a marriage I didn't want. You're not a real man because you resorted to violence. Nafie, you have to listen to what I'm saying and take it seriously. My body isn't there to be mounted whenever you want. I'm not a plaything for your crazy enjoyment. My body is mine and no one else's. It's me who's in charge of it. I know perfectly well you believe that because you're my husband, you have a right to my body whenever and however you want, but those are sick ideas. Wrong and wrongheaded. I'll never accept that logic and those justifications. You can be sure I won't allow you to hurt me with your rough handling and dirty fingernails."

When Nafie heard Maliha's threat, he felt scared because he knew the problems he would face if she turned to women's rights' organizations: an investigation into her complaints and legal hearings that could end in her favour and with him being punished. So he tried to calm her down and not hassle her.

On one occasion he took her hand and said: "Please forgive me, my darling Maliha. Forgive the things I've done. It was a misunderstanding that made me behave badly. Forgive me. It was my great desire for you that made me try it on with you in that violent brutish way. But, my love, months have passed and I haven't come near you in bed and haven't even touched your fingertips. Maliha, you're my first and last love. Why do you react to my affections with disdain and rejection? You're the woman I love and desire and whose body I want to hold and whose fragrance I want to inhale. I want you more than you can imagine. You're my wife, there is no one else. Try to understand me."

Maliha responded harshly. "Damn you, man," she shouted. "Isn't it wrong to ask me to have sex when I'm not physically up to it? Give me your hand so you can see the truth for yourself. Come and feel so you can know I'm not lying. If I've deprived you of what you want, well, your faith doesn't prevent you from marrying someone else. You've every right to marry another woman. Why upset yourself over me? Why not make us both happy? I'm no good for you anymore. I can't give you what you want because my body's messed up. Can't you understand and believe what I'm saying?"

In a faint voice Nafie answered: "God preserve me from what you're saying, Maliha. Seek God's help against the Devil in your heart whispering against me. The Devil is behind what you're saying. What you're saying, my darling, is shocking and wrong and I never want to hear it from you. How could I marry another woman when I love you and will love you as long as I live. You'll be my wife until the end of the world. I swear I'm not the kind of man who tries to be in control and give free rein to his lusts. I want our sex life to be based on love and respect. Let's enjoy the freedom in this country to make something of ourselves and help our families without being enemies and making threats."

He made a move towards her and tried to embrace her, but she pushed him away coldly and cruelly. He went into the living room where his favourite corner was. "My darling," he said, "why don't you go to hospital and get seen by a doctor about feeling unwell? The doctors here are excellent and will diagnose and treat diseases. They can help you. I'm sure of it. Don't let illness and pain destroy you. I beg you, my darling, take my advice and get seen at the nearest hospital or surgery."

Maliha usually kept well away from Nafie and neither listened to what he said nor answered him. He would go to his corner of the room, with his head bowed, his body trembling and his shoulders crumpled. He would sit beside the trunk, the cassette player, and his collection of old songs. He always left the bedroom feeling sad, hurt, and down. The constant clashes meant distance between them. Nafie abandoned the marital bed and most of the rest of the flat to his wife to strut around as she pleased. She had plenty of freedom to sit on the bed or go to the living room window and look out at the shops with their shopkeepers and customers. If Nafie was there, she would recount to him all the buying and selling that she saw below, the merchandise, and the piles of cash going into the tills.

On one such occasion she said to her husband: "If only you could see the lengths of black Italian silk and lace being handled by the Sudanese draper Hajj Niamatullah. He's measuring it out right now to sell to the Italian woman who owns Mama Nicola's restaurant. She's a widow, by the way. That's why she wears black clothes, which are made of lace and silk. A young dark-skinned guy with big muscles from Ecuador helps out at the restaurant. He's called Manuel. The restaurant is well known for its delicious Italian food. The floor of the shop is piled with beautiful, beaded cloth. He's taking loads of money off the customers. Now I can see our friend Lewis, the butcher, standing outside his shop ready to receive tons of fresh and frozen meat and poultry. Where's our share in it all, me and you? Where's our share of the profits made by these shopkeepers? If someone had told me how much businesses made in Shepherd's Bush before I'd seen it for myself, I wouldn't have believed them. But I've seen it for myself. I've seen how much Monsieur George Kamoun makes selling furniture, and I compare that with our financial situation. We're sick and tired of how little we have. Actually, it's me who's sick and tired. You are not fed up with having no money and don't care that people around you are rich."

She carried on with her description and musings: "We're living in a bounteous country, but we have hardly any of the things we want and dream of. We see the things in the shop windows, but cannot have them. I thought we'd overcome the ordeals of poverty and leave them behind. Unfortunately, I'm now convinced that poverty has wings powerful enough to fly a long way and hound the likes of us wherever we go."

Nafie replied in a faint voice: "But wealth comes from God, Maliha. God has given all those people the living you see. One day He'll grant us the same as them, or more. I beg you, my darling, don't despair of His mercy. Thank God that we're healthy and don't go to bed starving. We shouldn't be envious but content with what God has given us."

The same scene played out between Maliha and Nafie day after day. But there was never a resolution to close the chasm between them.

6

The emotional and physical relationship between Maliha and Doctor Nadim went from strength to strength. Their meetings were frequent and passionate. They would always sit alone together in the room at the surgery, which came to be their love nest. For Nadim their encounters made him feel truly alive and he became wildly infatuated with her. He no longer cared that she was a strong-willed woman with a sharp tongue. She represented the emotional happiness and physical pleasure that fulfilled his longing for the Orient.

Simply recalling her name made Nadim tremble. He lived in hope that he would always be with her. He admitted to himself that he was love-struck and would never be cured, even if he wanted to be. Loving Maliha had shaken him to the core and made him forget sleep. It was no surprise then that he should turn to writing poetry. He was always muttering one of his many long poems on the sufferings of the wounded heart. If it had been possible, he would have published his poems in enough volumes to fill a library.

There was just one obstacle, albeit a complicated one, standing between him and her. Nadim was married to Maureen and

Maliha was married to Nafie. For the thousandth time he wished he could end his marriage with Maureen, especially as he no longer got on with her or felt any affection for her. The atmosphere at home was as gloomy as a dark cave. Quite the opposite of what he felt with Maliha and Nafie, despite their simple flat.

Every evening after work, Nadim would go and eat dinner with the couple and watch TV and play cards. Of course, those were the evenings when Maliha was in a good mood with her husband. When it was tense, there was a cloud over everything because of the shouting and the accusations directed at Nafie. On those evenings the Doctor would glance furtively at his watch and wait for the chance to leave the conflict zone. In a trembling voice he would say: "Sorry everyone, it's time for me to go home. I don't want to miss the train and it's a long way." Maliha said nothing, while Nafie looked pleadingly at him not to leave him alone to face the storm. "Don't leave yet, Doctor," he would say hoarsely.

This time Doctor Nadim insisted it was time to leave. He reached for his bag with a trembling hand scared that the fight between the two would lead to his papers and prescription pads being torn up. He sidled out of the living room and opened the front door. He made his way towards the lift along a long dark corridor that smelt foul and whose dampness made him gag for air. He reached the courtyard of the building feeling highly per-turbed.

The neighbours' eyes followed him from the windows of their flats, from the courtyard, and from the surrounding streets. They knew the link between him and Nafie's wife and found it a strange story with no good justification. The man was an Arab like them, so why didn't he respect the rules of family and friend-ship? How could he simply ignore all those things for the sake of a passing fancy? Whenever he passed by they would whisper to each other, and the youngsters would raise their voices so he could hear them.

"Why are you in such a hurry to get home this evening, Doctor?" said one.

"Dinner wasn't rich enough for him tonight," came the answer. "The meat was all lean with no fat and there wasn't enough salt or appetizing spice."

"The woman of the house is angry tonight," said a third. "The evening wasn't relaxing enough for our Doc and he left early. That's one of the secrets of flat 70, the flat of the friends of our dear Doctor."

In the face of these sarcastic taunts, the Doctor continued walking in a desperate effort to keep control of himself, and be brave. The kids continued their attack. They clapped and whistled, cracked jokes and made hurtful remarks about his shirt and wide tie. They asked embarrassing questions that made him upset and annoyed.

When the road curved around towards the station he was at last out of their sight. He took the train home and went straight upstairs to the first floor and his bedroom. He moved like a cat, calculating every footstep so as not to disturb any member of his family. The excessive caution was because they no longer cared about his comings and goings after he stopped keeping to his old routine. Love had destroyed his old pattern of life and made his sensible mind go soft.

He went into his bedroom and looked around at its contents, focusing on the dictionaries and poetry collections, the old and new books, the files, newspaper cuttings, and the many posters from the Arab world and the Middle East on the walls. He lay down on his bed in a state of turmoil.

One night, he was tossing and turning anxiously staring at the ceiling. He had a strange thought that he could not get out of his head. He decided that to solve his problems he had to buy a bed. "Why suffer?" he thought. "Why do I leave their flat late every night whatever the weather? I'll buy a single bed and put it in a corner of the sitting room. The nights when I don't feel like going home, I can sleep there. Then I won't have to put up with the taunts of all those envious people in the neighbourhood."

What the Doctor actually had in mind by buying the bed was spending more time in the flat, much much more than was currently possible. It had nothing to do with the difficulty of getting home in the winter cold, or because of train cancellations. Those were just flimsy excuses to hide the real reason. He imagined being with Maliha permanently. Buying a bed would help him do that. Love was an ocean without shores, a path without end. "Let me spend nights with my love Maliha," he said to himself. "I can't bear to be apart from her."

As usual with the Doctor, the idea of buying the bed brewed in his mind and dominated his thoughts. Like every crazy idea that took hold of him, he could find no way to avoid carrying it out. The next day he waited impatiently for lunchtime when there would be no patients at the surgery. As soon as the clock struck one he left the surgery and went straight to the nearest Argos store. He looked through the catalogue, his head filled with clashing voices debating the purchase of the bed.

The voice urging him to buy finally won him over. He looked harder and saw many pictures of beds, expensive and cheap. He chose a single bed and thanked God. Then he realised that the bed would need sheets, pillows, and blankets. He picked out Egyptian cotton sheets and pillowcases and a heavy woollen blanket and asked for the things to be delivered to Maliha's address. Having carried out his plan, he hurried out of the store as if afraid he would change his mind and cancel the order.

His head was abuzz with confusing, clashing images of the future fate of the bed. He imagined himself lying on the new bed on a winter's night after Maliha had put it in a corner of the living room: he woke up early and had breakfast with them – toast, cream cheese, thyme, olives, hummus, feta cheese, and sweet coffee; lying on the bed, he thought how different his breakfast was from what he was used to having at home – an English breakfast of eggs, toast, jam and honey prepared by Maureen.

Argos confirmed they would deliver the bed to the address the Doctor had specified, and the bed indeed arrived at the flat when Maliha and Nafie were at home. The delivery man knocked at the door and handed the receipt to Maliha for her to sign. She took the papers in total surprise and asked: "What's this? We haven't bought anything from you. This isn't for us."

Handing her the delivery order, the man said to her: "Here, take a look for yourself. Isn't that your name and address?"

She nodded yes and said: "Perhaps someone meant to have it sent to their house, and wrote down our address by mistake. It is my name and address, though." Maliha signed the delivery note, and the man hurried back to his van and, with his colleague, brought her the boxes. "We'll wait for the Doctor," Maliha said to Nafie, "and ask him about this strange thing."

When the Doctor came later, it was as though he had forgotten all about his trip to Argos. He looked at the boxes in the hallway and asked: "What's all this, Madame Maliha? Couldn't you resist the price cuts when you went to the shops? What are all these boxes?"

"They arrived an hour ago," said Maliha. "They said it was a bed, and that you were the person who'd bought it and asked for it to be delivered here."

Only at this point did Nadim remember having bought the bed. "I almost forgot about this bed," he said. "Madame Maliha, this afternoon I was at Argos and they had big discounts on furniture – beds, wardrobes, bedroom suites. I couldn't resist the temptation and thought I'd buy this bed for you. You might need it in the future."

The couple had no doubts that what Nadim was saying was true and so it was no surprise when Maliha said: "If you'd told me about the sale I would've gone myself and picked up a few things that we really need. Thanks for being so kind and generous. We'll put it in the corner where Nafie sits until it's time to make use of it."

Doctor Nadim had a pang of conscience and reflected on the muddle he had got himself into and how irrationally he was behaving. "You must be hallucinating and going crazy," he thought to himself. "How else could you have bought a bed and had it delivered to Maliha's house? You're acting foolishly with a married woman, and you're also married to Maureen. How and when are you going to use the bed? It's inconceivable that you could spend the whole night away from your wife and children, having already been absent for the whole evening."

Until that point Maureen had not asked him about his absences after work. But things would become complicated and risky if Nadim decided to sleep away from home. Maureen would definitely complain and try to interfere in his private life. She would impose her conditions – given that he was her lawful husband. She could pay him back for his neglect by stressing his marital obligations.

That evening at the flat Nadim was preoccupied and caught up in these thoughts. His head was in the clouds, and that must be making him behave irresponsibly, he thought. He had bought a bed without knowing how the household would react. He was convinced that evening that what he had done would cause him serious problems. This meant he could not eat the food offered by his beloved Maliha. It was obvious to Nafie and Maliha that Doctor Nadim was going through an anxious phase, but neither of them broached the matter with their guest, so that the evening could pass without incident until Nadim said goodbye and left. On his way to the station he felt terribly confused in his head, terribly weak in his body, and terribly disturbed in his soul.

7

Because he was madly in love with Maliha, Nadim started spending a lot on her and lavishing her with gifts of every kind. He gave her whatever she asked for, and what she did not ask for, with or without an occasion. The doctor thought that this generosity would calm and mellow his beloved. He hoped she might get over her bouts of temper and replace them with bouts of love and affection.

Maliha never went home empty-handed now, but would be weighed down with bags of new clothes, perfume, jewellery, shoes, handbags, as well as kitchen equipment such as food processors and coffee and tea sets. The living room, kitchen, and bedroom were crammed with luxury and electrical goods until the flat looked like part of a major department store. With stuff piling up Maliha started selling some things to her neighbours. This delighted her as it gave her the chance to practise her old job and test her bargaining and marketing skills as she chased after any customer who was slow to pay what was owed.

The love that Nadim displayed for Maliha made her far more concerned about her appearance, her clothes, and her makeup than before. That proved to be no problem, thanks to the money she had access to from her generous lover. She started going to beauty salons once a week, and having her hair done in the latest style trending in the world of fashion. She went to the finest stores in central London to buy clothes that matched the new fashions among the young, hip, and middle class. She said goodbye to the traditional, loose-fitting clothes she used to wear. Modest Arab dress went out the window to be replaced by tight-fitting Western clothes that showed off her curves.

Doctor Nadim, however, was not happy about the major changes Maliha had made to the way she dressed, though what she had done was no more than conform to current fashion. He wanted his lover to be Arab to the core and preferred her to wear loose-fitting Middle Eastern garments such as long brightly coloured kaftans and the traditional patterned dresses worn by Arab women in villages.

Whenever he saw Maliha in modern clothes he said: "But, darling, I love to see you in your beautiful Arab clothes. Why do you want to wear these tight-fitting monstrosities? Trust me, jeans are a Western design the Americans have foisted on the people of the world, and it's very sad that people have accepted them without any thought. To be honest, those monstrosities were designed for Western women. The flashy outfits aimed at women today were made for one reason: to make women sex objects. People who sell women's clothes don't care that women will lose their dignity as human beings, whose values are deliberately buried beneath clothes and makeup. Darling, it isn't wearing clothes like these that attracts men. No, it's modest femininity, a beautiful soul, refined culture, and deep thoughts that are attractive. These clothes are appropriate for the bodies of Western women because they are free to think what they want, and don't need to worry about presenting a modest appearance. In Western society, everything is a commodity that's up for being bought and sold. Women here are just commodities that flaunt themselves erotically."

Maliha shook her head: "How do you mean?"

"What I'm saying is the result of my long and intimate experience of Western societies and their culture and mentality. Western women are expected to attract men and excite them sexually because they are viewed on the basis of their desirability in a materialistic world that lacks spirituality. As for you, my dear darling, you're more suited to demure Middle Eastern dress, not tight nonsense. These kinds of clothes don't go with our Arab customs and traditions that are based on covering up. I love you as an Arab woman, not anything else. Look how vivid and beautiful Middle Eastern clothes are and how funny modern Western blouses and dresses look. Just seeing you in them gives me a terrible headache, especially when you wear those damned blue jeans. Blue jinns more like!"

Maliha listened to Nadim going on about fashion and clothes, ignoring most of what he said and shrugging her shoulders indifferently. Rather than accept his opinions, she asked him to buy her the latest Levi's. Without any hesitation she continued to wear tight jeans and visit the surgery, parading herself before him and strutting around in a manner to attract and arouse.

"I'm smitten with your beauty," commented Nadim, "not the tight-fitting whatever it is hugging you. Please, take it off and put on a lovely kaftan. You've got lots of beautifully embroidered and tailored ones. Let me enjoy seeing your beautiful Arab character." Maliha said nothing, but threw herself into his arms and flung her arms around his neck. He responded with hugs and kisses of his own and forgot his opposition to tight jeans. Trembling with excitement, he led her to the reception room where they could enjoy the hot ecstasy of passion and quench their burning desire.

Maliha started to feel quite optimistic about her relationship with Doctor Nadim. She envisaged that her life would go from strength to strength thanks to the dear cultured man who was encouraging her to move forward. Her first step in that direction was to take driving lessons. She bought magazines with adverts for new and used cars, hoping that Nadim would buy her a car of her own. But she failed the driving test and didn't get her licence. Then she took English classes, but soon found that hard going and went back to being bored despite remonstrations from the doctor.

Nafie felt unable to ask Maliha where all the presents and purchases she brought home were coming from. He felt unable to confront her about other things he was unhappy about. She went out whenever she felt like it, for no obvious reason, and without telling her husband where she was going. Nafie was convinced that the presents and purchases his wife brought home were not coming out of his miserable wages. The money he made as a cleaner in a restaurant and his benefits were barely enough for essentials.

Maliha had everything she asked for, and dreamed of, from Nadim in exchange for a few quick moments alone with him at his surgery. Meeting Maliha had assuaged the loneliness Nadim felt as a result of the decline in his relationship with his wife. Maureen had started to dislike him because he no longer seemed to care about her, or about being at home for his children. She had no qualms about disconnecting him from her life and that of her children. To begin with she wanted to kick him out altogether, but when she found no way to do that, she agreed he could stay in the house on condition he kept well away from family life.

Nadim started living in an outhouse at one side of the garden. It was like being an animal in a barn, eating, drinking, and sleeping unnoticed. He went home one day to find Maureen and the children had taken his things from his room on the first floor and dumped some in the outhouse and were scattering the rest around the garden. He shouted at them: "What are you doing with my stuff?" Maureen did not respond and, together with the children, continued throwing his things around with no concern, no respect for her husband, the father of her children, who was shouting and wailing in front of them.

A fierce argument erupted after Nadim refused to give up his room in the house, where he had been ensconced with all his things for a long time. "Maureen," he protested, "you should remember that it was me who bought this house where we're living with the children as a family, and all its members have the right to enjoy it fully. You've spent a great deal of my money doing up the house, yet you act as though it is your own property and you also want to keep me away from my children, without any pity or compassion."

"Oh, shut up, you loser," Maureen retorted. "You're talking like someone who doesn't know the law. What do you mean when you say you paid for the house? It looks like you've forgotten I supported you when you were getting qualified. I also played a big part in helping you succeed in your work and make the income to buy the house. Remember, I looked after the house and made it nice. While you were out at work every hour of the day and night, I was never remiss, not even for a moment, in taking care of the children, bringing them up, feeding them, and playing with them. The balance is in my favour because of the big part I played in creating a safe and stable family environment."

At the end of the argument, the children intervened and persuaded their mother to take pity on their father, let him live with them at home and stop harassing him and threatening to throw him out. They said: "Whatever you think of him, he's our Dad and we can't give up on him so easily." The mother agreed to her children's request, but only on condition that their father lived in isolation in his own room upstairs and therefore minimized any chance of their spending time together. From then on he was like a prisoner, staring at the walls full of books – science books, literature, dictionaries, poetry, historical and geographical studies – and listening to his collection of old songs by Abdel Wahhab, Umm Kalthoum, Sayyid Darweesh, and others, and watching videos of old Arab films and series by renowned scriptwriter Duraid Lahham.

The family started functioning without him and without taking his views into account; it was as though he was not there at all. They would eat without him, leaving him to eat on his own like someone with a contagious disease. They went on holiday without him, and without even telling him where they were going. They travelled to Italy, Brittany, the Far East, and other tourist destinations that he was unaware of until he saw the souvenirs they brought back with them or holiday snaps left lying around.

In contrast, his relationship with Maliha and Nafie grew ever stronger until he felt he was part of their family. Nadim's shaky relationship with his own family encouraged him to become closer to Maliha and her husband. He visited them in their small flat evening after evening. He brought them many things: Arab foods and sweets, coffee, fruit and vegetables, some of which were essentials and others simply out of habit.

When Maliha was in a good mood, they would all enjoy a convivial evening, eating and drinking, watching TV, and chatting. Maliha would cook and they would sit together harmoniously, playing cards, watching TV shows, the news, football matches, and the racing. Nadim would comment on the programmes, making points he thought important for understanding what was going on in the world.

But if Maliha felt stressed, she deliberately did not come home early so as to avoid Nadim and having to cook dinner and join in the conversation. She would arrive home, her head spinning with strange thoughts about what she had seen in the street. She would talk about what she called the good life, the big money to be made, and the vast wealth. The city was in motion like a beehive with all the activity in the shops. As soon as she entered the living room, she flung down her coat and handbag and took off her shoes. She would take a deep breath as though there was a heavy weight on her chest and mind, and sit on the edge of the sofa, looking glumly into the room or at the window onto the street. Then, in a state of severe depression and despair, she would turn her gaze on the two men. The roar in her head jarred with the apparent calm of both her husband and her lover, who seemed oblivious to the storm in her head and her disturbed features.

She burst out agitatedly: "I'm fed up with the lack of any change in our lives, for all three of us. I've reached the point that it's making me ill and desperate. I'm sick and tired of your passivity, Nafie, and I'm angry at you, Nadim, because you love the miserable life we're living in this tiny flat. This isn't a new life, it's a constant repetition of events to a point beyond boredom. Despite this, I find my dear husband resigned to it and relaxed, and Nadim saying he loves our life because it's Arab and nothing like the modern, fake, life."

In truth, this was a subject Nadim and Maliha disagreed on. Dr Nadim certainly loved Arab things, which he saw as a sign of authenticity. As a result, whenever he entered Maliha's flat he felt both nostalgia and contentment. He often told Maliha, when they met at the surgery: "If I had a super life with palaces and wealth, I would never alter my love for the atmosphere of your flat. It represents the life as it's lived by my family, my kin." Maliha, in contrast, would complain bitterly, whenever she met her lover, about the lack of money, the monotony of life, and about Nafie's passivity, weakness, and lethargy when it came to the challenge for him of earning a living. "He sits in his corner like a hen sitting on her eggs. He does nothing except listen to macho music at full blast while looking at one photo after another of the past, then placing them with supreme care into his big wooden trunk. It's driving me mad."

Nadim was quite indifferent to what she said and took no practical steps to resolve the psychological crises of the poor woman. He thought her words were a kind of grumbling stubbornness. He often said to her: "My darling Maliha, I don't know exactly what you mean by the monotony of life and your harping on about change. Aren't we, thank God, enjoying good health and a good lifestyle? Or do you want to swan around on yachts and go to expensive restaurants? Those are things for foreigners and I have no wish to join in, and I can't sweet-talk you. My age won't allow it. I can't stand travelling any more after so much moving around from one city to another when I was a student and later for work. I don't like cruises where you spend weeks at sea, going out for visits at every port. I don't like going to fancy restaurants. I think eating out is a waste of the money we work so hard to earn. There's no reason to go out when we have the chance to sit together every evening, relaxed and in harmony around a healthy and hearty meal."

Maliha felt a surge of anger, but she kept quiet and let him keep talking. She realised she would fail to change him just as she had failed to change Nafie. When she had first met Dr Nadim she had thought he would rescue her from the boring life she was leading and introduce her to a life of comfort and joy, like that of people she saw in restaurants eating, smoking, laughing, and enjoying music. But she discovered that the Doctor would be deepening her despondency with yet more indifference to her plight. Unfortunately, he liked to see her in a cramped flat made up of a small bedroom, living room, tiny kitchen and bathroom, and lacking any style – even its plastic flowers were faded whereas elsewhere there were beautiful real flowers.

She loved real flowers but couldn't afford them given her limited means. She saw them in front of her, full of vitality, beauty, and freshness, leaning out of tall vases in shop windows and under the awning of the florist next to the station. She often told Nadim how much she wanted some real flowers: "Darling Nadim, I love real flowers. I go especially to look at their beauty and radiance. They take me back to the gardens in my country with their flowers and plants. Green things were right under my nose there, but I paid no attention to their real beauty until it was too late. I'd love to buy some real, fresh flowers and put them in the flat to add a touch of elegance."

"Sadly," replied the Doctor, "real flowers have a very short life, just a day or two. And for that, the consumer has to pay quite a lot. But, my darling, if you like real flowers, I'll get you some so you don't have to do without. Tomorrow, I'll go to the shop near the surgery and buy you enough to decorate the flat."

The fact was that Dr Nadim had a complex about buying flowers. He thought they cost a lot and did not last long, and so not worth the expense. But since Maliha loved fresh flowers so much, he decided to make the woman he loved happy. He went to the florist's and asked how much the flowers cost; the prices made him wince. He asked the florist: "Why are they so expensive? Who's going to pay so much?"

"Sir," replied the florist, "the prices are high because the flowers are real, not artificial. There's nothing more beautiful to look at than fresh flowers and nothing more fragrant. Customers think we charge too much and are only in it for the money. But we work really hard to preserve and look after the flowers so that they stay fresh and in good condition. Flowers are delicate and we handle them like fine art. That way we meet our customers' desire for pleasure and beauty.

"You want flowers at a reasonable price – a request we agree with. Let me tell you a secret that will meet your wishes. Come here this evening an hour before we close. You'll find us getting rid of left-over stock at knock-down prices since some of the flowers won't last until the next day. We sell them off to make room for new stock."

Nadim followed the advice of the florist. The next day he went back shortly before closing time and bought a bunch of carnations for a modest amount. He took them to his beloved Maliha's house, and when she opened the door, he offered them to her with great delight.

"Dr Nadim," she said angrily, "who are these wilted flowers for?" Who tricked you and sold you something only fit for the bin? Don't tell me you paid for them."

Nadim defended himself: "But Madame Maliha, we're talking about flowers, not fruit or vegetables. It's not essential to buy fresh roses because, to be honest, we're only going to look at them, not eat them. Decoration, in the end, is something that people disagree about and for which there are no hard and fast rules. I picked out these beautiful red flowers with great care, after consulting an expert in the field of keeping and tending flowers. And, by the way, I paid a tidy sum for them."

She picked up the bouquet and threw it in the bin. She was certain that expensive, fine-stemmed, brightly coloured roses were not something that Nadim, despite his means, was going to buy her. She remembered what he had said to her on the subject: "Darling, what's the use in buying expensive flowers, seeing as they wilt and fade. To be honest, I think buying expensive roses is a gross waste of money, and I don't like wasting money."

Alongside flowers, there were many other issues that Nadim

and Maliha argued and quarrelled over: whether to buy fresh meat or frozen and their being unable to go out in public for fun or to the cinema, a museum, or the park.

Confronted with Maliha's psychological state, the evening get-togethers were often pervaded by a heavy gloom that the two men could neither dispel nor contain. Maliha would erupt like a volcano, venting her toxic anger at times towards Nafie and at times towards Nadim. She would condemn the passivity of the two men and their aversion to adventure. The sessions would turn into waves of anger, rage, and quarrelling. Sometimes things would become too much for her to bear. She would then start pulling out her hair clip and throwing it at whichever man was in front of her. Then she would tear open her blouse, exposing her heaving white bosom to the eyes of her husband and her lover. Once she became aware of the state she was in, she would hurriedly gather up the edges of her torn blouse which was slid-ing down her back in spite of her husband's efforts to cover her up. She would launch into curses and reproaches, take off her shoes and hurl one at her husband and the other at her lover.

Once, she stood at the window shouting: "Nafie, come and have a look. Nadim, come and have a look: people, living in lux-ury and happiness, not like us this stupid evening. People, living life as it should be, enjoying full nights and busy days."

In tears, she continued: "Lord, why are You testing me? Two useless men and a dull life, even though I'm living in the most el-egant capital city in the world. Blasted poverty is my constant companion and I can't get rid of him. What have I got compared to the rich?"

Nadim went over to her in an effort to soothe her and calm her down. It was his custom to address her in a brotherly tone of ven-eration when speaking to her in the company of her husband. So it wasn't strange that he should start with expressions like lady, madam, and sister. He said to her: "It seems my presence every evening is annoying you and making you upset and angry. If that's the way things are, I'll stop this repulsive habit, and not come and visit you again. I just wanted a chat. My bed is cold, and a hard day's work lies ahead in the morning. It's as if I'm a robot, programmed and unable to change whether I'm on or off."

As if his tongue had suddenly become untied, Nafie intervened: "Not at all. We're not tired of you, Doctor. Why would you say such a thing and think like that? You're our friend. As long as we live, we will remember your kindness and help towards us. Let me tell you, Maliha isn't angry about you coming round. She's angry because of the endless demands of her family. They make a lot of demands, as if my poor wife was sitting on piles of gold or the streets were paved with it. They hassle her with demands beyond her means. I was practically killing myself at work to fulfil them. Then came that terrible day when I got the sack. If it hadn't been for you, that would have been a disaster for us. But God helped us and sent you to save us. In my wife's family people are asking for help to buy a car, to build a house, to get an entry visa to the UK, and to pay for their weddings. They're all asking at once, as though we were Lloyds, or Barclays Bank."

This was not the first time Dr Nadim had heard the likes of what Nafie was saying. He had heard it before from Maliha. He had gone quite a few times with her to Western Union to send money to her family. Even so, he reacted to what Nafie had said: "Madame Maliha, tomorrow morning I'll write you a cheque for you to send to your family to help them pay for what they need. I beg you, don't let your family's demands get you down. We all know our countries are suffering from falling living standards and low incomes, while governments stand by with their hands tied as though they had nothing to do with it. Those who have been able to get out have a moral, patriotic, and humanitarian duty to help their relatives. We mustn't abandon our poor families and allow them to fall prey to hunger and disease. At the same time, all of us, and you especially, Madame Maliha, must not allow stress to ruin our mental and physical health."

Pointing at Nafie, Maliha said: "My family think I married a millionaire with wealth and status. Nafie seduced them by splashing out money and giving expensive gifts. It didn't occur to anyone that he was actually terribly poor." Her tears came flooding out.

Nafie stood beside her to comfort and calm her. Nadim asked her to be patient and spare her health. Then Nadim looked at his watch and said: "Sorry, everyone, the time has flown by and I have to go now so I don't miss the train." Nadim went, leaving Maliha and Nafie drowning in a whirlpool of confusion and despair. And all the way home, he thought longingly about seeing his lover soon, either at her flat or the surgery.

8

Doctor Nadim Nasra no long felt the slightest embarrassment about making himself quite at home in Nafie and Maliha's flat and sharing the most intimate details of their married life. He came to see his participation in everything they did as something natural, as though he was one of the family. The reality, however, was not quite as he imagined. The neighbours were concerned about his puzzling relationship with Nafie's family. They did not approve of the constant presence of a strange man in the midst of a supposedly decent, respectable family. The residents of the block and their visitors would not have liked to find the Doctor ensconced on the sofa in front of the engraved round table.

Without much ado the neighbours concluded that there was something just not right about the relationship between Maliha and the Doctor, particularly when they noticed that the latter's evening visits included Nafie himself. Many of the block's residents were Arab and Muslim, economic migrants or asylum seekers from conservative traditional societies. As a result, they were outspoken in condemning what was going on at the flat. It might have been acceptable in an open-minded society like Britain, but for the community in the building in Shepherd's

Bush, it was unacceptable and contrary to traditional values and morality. The women were more critical than the men; the young had more misgivings than the old. The customs they had grown up with and which they insisted on keeping did not allow it. They were shocked by what was happening, and felt threatened. They condemned the presence of a man who turned up every evening wearing a suit and tie and carrying bags of shopping, fruit, and vegetables. Sitting between the husband and wife, he would have dinner with them. He ran the household as though he were the breadwinner, and it was his rightful responsibility. This feeling was exacerbated when they learnt that he had taken the outrageous step of buying a bed and putting it in the living room.

He always seemed the centre of attention, sitting up on the sofa in the middle of the flat, giving orders or issuing prohibitions just as he wished, without anyone to tell him right from wrong. He was completely free to watch TV and used the phone to make calls to the council to deal with the couple's disputes with the housing department over rent, and to the electricity and water companies. Sometimes he read their post, and replied as he thought appropriate, without consulting them. The Doctor was fully in control of the family's affairs and managed the flat and its contents.

Men were naturally afraid that their wives and daughters would get used to this unacceptable situation and it would become acceptable. How could a strange man leave late at night for a place they knew little about? It was rumoured that he returned to his house in the suburbs, but there was nothing known for certain about where he lived or worked or his social standing. The scant information about the Doctor drove the rumour mill.

The residents of the building, driven by an instinctive fear of the unknown, made strenuous efforts to discover his identity and solve the riddle of his relationship with Nafie and his wife. That the Doctor did not want to give anything away or talk about his private life only made things worse. He was determinedly evasive when they asked about his origins and where he was born and raised before coming to the UK. The people longed to uncover the secret of this man who had appeared out of nowhere. Some residents even referred to him as the ghost of Flat 70.

A few residents asked the Doctor "What nationality are you?" His face showed his anger and he said, as though talking to himself: "Strewth! God give me strength! When will annoying nosy people learn that my nationality is my business? No one has the right to know or ask about it. I speak Arabic very well, without an accent or mistakes. I have a strong Arab heart between my ribs, and my habits, character, and actions show it. If that's what I'm like, what does it matter what Arab country I'm from?"

The Doctor thought his background was a private matter, and people had no business asking. That was simply rude. In his view, that kind of question divided Arabs when what they most needed was unity, not being split into nationalities, countries and regions. If someone asked where he was from, he would reply with passion: "I am a proud Arab patriot. That is enough to define me. I need say no more." People stopped asking to avoid his anger and contempt, and took to guessing.

A number of contradictory theories were advanced. The Doctor wasn't Arab at all, despite his eloquent Arabic, thought some. He was a migrant from Eastern Europe, who had been a prison governor. The regime in his country jailed its opponents and its irritants, and he would torture them mercilessly. Eventually the opposition, with hefty bribes, got him to stop his cruelty and help the prisoners escape. Once he had saved a big enough amount, he tricked the security service and fled to safety in the UK.

No, he was an Iranian from Ahvaz province near the Arabian Gulf. For some reason or another he slipped away across the border.

No, he was a Russian agent who had betrayed the state to an enemy country and then escaped disguised as a woman. After enormous efforts he had sailed on a merchant ship to the UK where the authorities had helped him to stay in exchange for information.

No, he was a Chechen, born and raised in an Arab country so that when he left he spoke perfect Arabic.

In the fervid speculation over the Doctor's background, one resident swore that he was a drug dealer who had crossed a gang leader and was going to be eliminated. Once he learnt what was in store, he had fled and sought asylum by claiming to be a dissident back home. The authorities gave him a false identity to save him. Another demonstration of the humanity of the British state for persons displaced by war or whose lives are threatened in their home countries.

To others the Doctor was an unknown fighter who had lost an arm, a leg, and an eye in a distant war-zone. Initially, he walked with a crutch and had a black patch over his missing eye. Then, taking advantage of the NHS, he swapped his crutch for an artificial limb. His eye had to be glass, claimed the neighbours, because it sparkled so brightly but never moved; his false arm was very realistic, they affirmed, but his fingers seemed rigid when shaking hands. The neighbours insisted on shaking his hand, and would feel his fingertips and jiggle his arm in search of the truth. His limp was obvious, apparently, but he still made an effort to walk normally. The inhabitants of the building, young and old, had all heard talk of his disabilities. Children would seize any opportunity to follow him when he was there, and look into his eyes, trying to differentiate the glass one from the real one, and in amazed excitement, they would try and touch his leg and arms.

The neighbours finally concluded that the Doctor had risked death to come to Britain aboard a boat full of refugees. He was not originally Arab, but was smitten by the beauty of Arabic and its rich, bewitching literature and had learned Arabic perfectly. His relationship with Maliha and Nafie had only one objective: to converse in Arabic with Arabs about their culture. The Doctor avoided revealing that he wasn't Arab to prevent any barriers growing up between him and the Arab community.

The Doctor maintained silence about his identity, and the situation began to resemble a detective mystery. The neighbours couldn't tell the couple how unhappy they were about the strange Doctor being in the block and intruding blatantly into their lives. Once, an old woman who lived in the building dared to ask Maliha and her husband about their relationship with the Doctor. Nafie responded angrily: "The Doctor is one of my best friends. Anyone who isn't happy about him coming round to my flat, mine and my wife's, can go to hell. Let us live how we please. Besides, you should know that Doctor Nadim will carry on visiting us until he gets the signal from me, but *inshallah* that won't happen. He'll keep coming round despite you lot, whatever you think. Our door is always open for our friend, always." After that, the neighbours shut up. The Doctor's presence left a bad taste, but they could do nothing about it.

One evening, a strange incident happened in the street nearby. The Doctor had left the building to catch the train. The street was totally silent. It was raining hard and the light was dim. He opened his large umbrella and made his way to the corner. Suddenly, someone leapt out in front of him and pushed him hard in the chest. He almost fell to the ground as the attacker shouted something incomprehensible in his face.

From behind the assailant, a group of youths and men emerged, their faces masked with printed pieces of cloth. One of them sprayed him with sticky red dye. Another threatened him in Arabic: "The resident of Flat 70 doesn't know how to deal with you. He's failed to stop your invasion and violation of his home. So we've decided to do the job ourselves and are taking the matter into our own hands. We know how to handle you. You're a coward who disrespects our customs and traditions. You going round there every night is a slap in the face. We'll defend ourselves whatever the cost." The Doctor's attacker jabbed his finger at him and continued: "Today we'll make do with a warning, but if you don't listen, we'll really shake you up. Be quite sure that we can do a lot worse than this. And when we do, you'll know who you're dealing with, you coward."

Before he could take in what was happening, the group had vanished. He was left trembling in fear, covered from head to foot in sticky red goo. He had no idea who had jumped him. He certainly couldn't go home and face his wife in such a state: how would he explain the red gunk on his face and clothes? In the end, he decided to spend the night at the surgery. The red dye had dried and he spent hours scrubbing it off, using every last bar of soap and drop of detergent in the place.

He slept on the sofa and dreamt the strangest and most disturbing dream he had had since coming to Britain a quarter of a century before. He was in the middle of a vast barren desert, criss-crossed by tracks that twisted together like serpents. There were no plants or animals, as though life had yet to begin. The wind blew and the tracks writhed and hissed. He saw a group of people dressed like his family and tribe. They were riding horses, camels, and donkeys. He asked them about his mother and father. No answer came. He asked for a drink of water and a piece of bread. Their leader looked at him angrily and indicated to one of the riders to give him water and food. He raised the water container to his mouth but was unable to drink. The riders departed, leaving him in fear and terror. He saw a train and thought: "I'll get on board and should quickly get to safety." The inspector and soldiers said: "You don't have a ticket so it's not allowed." He began to run incredibly fast. The horses, camels, and donkeys disappeared. He saw lights shining from a city suspended midway between heaven and earth. He did not know which direction to go, but kept running. His legs sunk into the sand. A snake bit him. He screamed at the top of his voice, woke up, and thanked God.

9

Dr Nadim had a practical idea and without hesitation he started to put it into practice. He would bring everything needed at Maliha's flat – tea, flour, oil, spices, fruit and vegetables, washing powder and cleaning products – at the beginning of the month. There was no way his lover should have to traipse from shop to shop and carry her purchases home. Her having to ride the bus in the cold made him feel sorry for her.

At the beginning of every month he turned into an old-style Middle Eastern patriarch, a familiar figure in his country in the days when women were women and men were men, before everything had been turned upside down and women had taken control while men trailed behind following their orders. The Doctor, sweating and his body aching, would go up and down to Maliha's door with different sized bags and boxes. His exertions carrying them would surely make Maliha happy, he thought. For him, buying material things was the highway to her heart, given how much she loved possessions. Her dreams were coming true, she would certainly think, thanks to the generous, gallant Doctor.

Maliha, however, did not fall into his carefully laid trap of seduction by way of the market. She opened the door and there he was, surrounded by bags full of shopping, with an exhausted smile on his face. Rather than smiling and welcoming him in, however, she frowned and acted with indifference. He felt awkward at her cool reaction and tried to disguise it behind a sardonic smile. "Madame Maliha," he said, "please take these things inside. I have to go back down to the car for the rest. Then I'll go and find a parking space. I left the car by the front entrance and I'm scared I'll get a parking ticket."

She didn't respond directly to his ramblings, but in a cold, dismissive tone said: "Wouldn't it be better to finish the things we have first, and then get us more shopping? Can't you see the kitchen is full of food? Rather than buying us things it would be better to move us out of this cramped flat that's barely big enough for us. Please leave the things here. They won't have gone anywhere before you fetch the rest."

Maliha's words hurt the Doctor and dispelled his feeling of happiness. The disgust written on her face was enough to put off any reasonable person, but the Doctor's response was not reasonable. He didn't stop making a show of getting the shopping, instead started buying even more. He thought he had not provided enough, and that Maliha was actually encouraging him to bring more. He had to change his tactics, then, change how and what he bought.

Until then he had bought meat retail, but he resolved to buy it wholesale. A whole carcass might change things and win him the approval of the only person in the whole world whose approval mattered to him. He would buy a whole lamb of the sort Maliha talked about whenever she saw the carcasses going in and out of Lewis's, the local butcher's. He would not buy it from Lewis, because he did not sell halal meat, but from an Arab grocer where the meat was slaughtered in accordance with Islam. The idea of buying a whole animal dominated his thoughts, and he could not shake it off however hard he tried.

He went to Arab shops on Edgware Road, the central London street renowned for Arab and oriental goods. In the past he had paid it little attention, even though he had heard a lot about it and its Arab foodstuffs. It was famous for its many Arab customers who drank Arabic coffee in the cafés. Arabs came in groups or individually in the summer for tourism and medical treatment. Some owned houses or rented flats on the street itself or nearby. The Doctor wandered around Edgware Road looking closely into the shop windows at the meat and Arab foods that delighted the eye and heart as he searched for the right shop to buy the lamb from. He was not prepared to accept cuts of meat, however good they were. He was after a whole carcass, lacking nothing. He went into a few shops, but Edgware Road, despite its history, was just not good enough.

He headed for Queensway, and then into the back streets off Moscow Road, which were packed with Arab cafés and shops. He stopped in front of a small Arab shop called Zein Market, which was owned and run by three brothers from Lebanon, Ramez, Michael, and Marwan. Marwan was standing behind the refrigerated counter housing the cuts of meat.

"I hope your prices are good," said the Doctor. "I'm looking to buy a whole slaughtered carcass, a lamb in particular."

"Sir," replied Ramez, "our prices are good, and we have the best quality meat from England, and elsewhere. Sir wishes to buy a lamb? We have lamb that comes from Wales where the animals graze only on fresh green grass, not on any harmful chemical feeds."

The Doctor nodded in relief as soon as he heard Ramez's explanation. "I want to buy a whole animal," he said, "including the innards like the liver, intestines, and heart. Please prepare me the best animal you have. I'll come tomorrow afternoon to pick it up."

Ramez was very surprised at his customer's request. Only rarely did someone ask for the innards – even the Gulf Arabs, or Arab ambassadors who bought whole animals to roast at their celebrations of national days or the birthdays of kings, princes, sheikhs, and presidents, asked for the innards to be removed to avoid the nasty smells associated with animals' insides.

Ramez could tell he was dealing with a very determined customer who was expecting a yes to his strange request. "Don't worry, Sir. I'll sort out the animal for you tomorrow. It'll be ready around one. I'll let you know then how much it will cost. As you're know, meat is sold by the gross weight, and I won't know how much it weighs until it arrives and I put it on the scales."

The Doctor assented: "Just please don't forget, I want a whole carcass. There's no need to cut it up or clean it."

Ramiz nodded his head nonplussed. "Can you let me have your name and phone number, please."

"My name is Doctor Nadim Nasra," he said, as though to himself, and gave Ramiz his phone number. He left the butcher's shop, leaving Ramez puzzled at his strange request.

In the street, the Doctor imagined something very strange: Maliha standing in front of the carcass, taking great pleasure in seeing how big it was. She turned it round to the left and right, her eyes widening in delight. Maliha could do what she liked with the lamb. The enormous quantity of meat would make her happy and convince her that she was on the verge of becoming rich. Large amounts of meat would distinguish Maliha from her less-fortunate neighbours, and transport her into clouds of happiness. In his vision she was sitting on tonnes of fresh meat while the local women scrabbled in bins for scraps of old and rotten meat. He saw himself presenting Maliha with different kinds of meat, and she cooked up a feast, while those exhausted women fought over bits of meat with cats and dogs running after them.

Once the Doctor had gone, Ramez shook his head in disbelief: "How can this guy want to buy a whole uncleaned carcass, even a small one? How will he handle it, and how will he be able to cut it up on his own? It's not easy cutting up a carcass, especially if you don't have the right knives and some experience in slaughtering and butchery."

The Doctor himself spent the whole day in a hazy reverie. As usual, when he wanted to put into effect something his imagination had conjured up, he spent a sleepless night waiting in fervid anticipation of the action next morning. He was preoccupied by the carcass and kept thinking about its size and weight, the quality of the meat, its external appearance, and its innards. Talking to himself, he said: "It's best not to go to the clinic when I get into London; I'll go straight to Zein Market to make sure the Lebanese guy has done everything I asked."

At this point, an image of shoppers camped out in front of the shops for the sales popped into his head. The doors opened in the morning and they dashed madly inside to get their hands on the best bargains. It would be best for him to spend the night in front of the doorway of Zein Market. When Ramez came to open the door, he could quickly take the carcass. That would be better than spending the night thinking. He did not want to toss and turn in bed with his mind churning. He would wait until first light and leave for London.

Then he remembered that the animal would not be ready until early afternoon. He shook his head in sorrow and sat down on the edge of the bed. He rubbed his eyes and placed his trembling palms over them in an effort to snap out of it. "I take refuge in God from accursed Satan," he told himself, and went back to bed and slept till the morning.

He left the surgery at lunchtime and headed to Zein Market. He entered the shop, very eager to see his order. Only Ramez was there, who greeted him with his customary smile. The Doctor looked at the cuts of meat carefully piled up in the cold units. "I've come to get the whole carcass that I asked for yesterday. I hope you haven't cut it up. I want it whole as requested."

Ramez was amazed that the Doctor had come back even more insistent than the day before. He had thought the Doctor would forget the intact carcass, that his request was perhaps a joke. But he had come back and asked again. "As you requested, Doctor," he said, "I've prepared a whole animal for you that you will really like. It's not been touched by a knife or cut into joints. Unfortunately, I don't have paper big enough to wrap a whole carcass. It's not very often a customer asks for one. So I've left it in the cloth it came in. If it's hard for you to carry, I can chop it into large pieces and then wrap it in paper." Ramez said this in the hope that the Doctor would change his mind. But the Doctor gave him a hard stare and almost shouted at him in anger. The veins on his forehead stood out like pipes of blood fit to burst, but he realised the young, polite Ramez was only trying to serve him and fulfil his wishes.

Shaking his head sorrowfully, he said calmly: "It seems that these days, customers have little choice. Don't try to fob me off with cuts of meat after I made it perfectly clear to you yesterday that I wanted to buy a whole carcass."

"Calm down Doctor. Think of your heart. What you want is my top priority. You will get what you asked for. But in my capacity as manager of the shop, I have to give you some guidance for your benefit. You will certainly have difficulties handling it, because it's not been cleaned inside. Unfortunately, we don't have big enough paper to wrap up a whole carcass. So I will have to leave it wrapped in the cloth it came in. It'll look worse than a shrouded corpse. Doctor, the way it looks will frighten you and others. But you're the customer. As manager, I am serving you and doing what you've asked, as best I can. My aim and that of Zein Market is to make you happy. We would like to keep you as a regular customer who buys all their food from us. If it's no problem for you to carry the carcass in the state I've described, I pray to God that no one notices you going from here to your car."

The Doctor calmed down a little. He was impressed by Ramez's manners and the way he talked and dealt with him. "I took the train today and left the car at home," he said shaking his head.

"Doctor, if you don't have your car with you, things will be extremely difficult. But in the end, you know best what you can do. It's in your hands."

"Don't worry, brother, I'll manage. Anyway, ask yourself how we lived in days of old. How we managed our daily lives before cars and all the other silly modern forms of transportation.

"Our ancestors were used to life without cars and other kinds of rapid transport. And they didn't have any problems to speak of. They carried their things on their backs. The women fetched water from distant wells in jars on their heads, walking for miles to get home. They also carried firewood for cooking and heating. Brother, modern transportation has ruined people's bodies and made them slow and sluggish and prone to illness. As a result of their reliance on modern transportation, the environment and the air in cities and towns have been polluted. Today, I intend to carry the carcass over my shoulder until I get home, however tiring and awkward it is. We'll see how it goes."

Ramez shook his head incredulously. "As you wish, Doctor. You can have what you want, I am at your service. I will try to wrap the carcass so the blood does not drip out and make people stare. Blood from a slaughtered animal does not dry quickly."

The Doctor shook his head defiantly. "Blood does not bother me. I'm not squeamish, I deal with it on a daily basis. I'm a doctor. Blood is my specialty, even if people don't like the sight of it." Ramez realised there was no point in trying to dissuade him from his crazy plan. He hurried inside and fetched the sheep, which was wrapped in a white cloth, and put it on the counter. The three brothers helped the Doctor sling the carcass over his shoulder and said goodbye to him.

The Doctor left Zein Market with what looked like a shrouded corpse slung over his shoulder. The slaughtered sheep was slipping around inside the cloth, and blood was clearly and unmistakeably seeping out. The Doctor paid no attention; his focus was on getting to the tube station as fast as possible. It was not far, and no one paid any attention as he headed to Bayswater tube station at the end of the street. When he arrived, he took out his ticket and put it in the slot in the barrier. The narrow gate opened and he hurried on to the platform.

Passengers waiting on the platform suddenly became aware of him. Suspicious and fearful, they started staring. They whispered to each other, exchanged glances, and covered their noses with their hands. Panic rose inside them and they moved as far away as they could, all gathering at the end of the platform. When the train arrived they all got on quickly hoping to escape the Doctor and his bloodstained shroud.

He looked for a carriage that wasn't crowded to share with his little lamb. After some effort, he found one with ten or so passengers with their bags, umbrellas, and newspapers. He sat down in a seat at the end of the carriage, put the little lamb on his knees, and gave a sigh of relief. He thought his problem with the nosy passengers was over.

His hopes were soon dashed. Initially, the passengers had not noticed anything, because they were all sitting calmly reading their newspapers. Little by little they began to smell a funny smell. They lowered their papers and saw droplets of blood oozing out, and they reacted like the passengers on the platform. Their sense of panic increased when blood dripped onto the floor of the carriage. Some thought, and some were certain, that their fellow passenger was carrying a dead body.

The Doctor sensed the unease of the passengers and gave them a mental ticking-off: "I swear, the people in this country think and behave irrationally. I don't know them as well as I should, despite having lived with them for years. What are they frightened of? Is this the first time they've seen a passenger with a little lamb? What's so frightening about seeing a slaughtered animal being carried on a train? Haven't they seen meat on display in butchers' shop windows?"

He became aware of the lamb resting between his thighs and noticed the blood spotting his trousers. He kept a firm hold of the carcass to stop it slewing around as the train took a sharp bend. The train sped along, its wheels screaming on the rails, and he began to feel indescribably embarrassed.

Suddenly an alarm went off. The train stopped inside the tunnel between stations. The passengers were asked to wait calmly. The train started moving again and pulled into Earl's Court. The station workers evacuated the frightened passengers from the train. A group of station guards and armed police burst into the Doctor's carriage. They surrounded him and told the other passengers to get off. He felt he must have done something terrible in their eyes.

He asked himself: "How could you travel with a whole carcass on a train full of children and old people? How could you do it in a country where people like to follow public health rules? How could you travel with a sheep carcass, stripped of its hide, and dripping red blood? Didn't you realise that the sight would provoke people and bring the police?"

The police began to ask questions. They were worried there might be a murder involved. There was little he could do to defend himself, and he admitted the shocking thing he had done that was now staring him in the face. One policeman came and stared intently at the strange bundle on his lap. "Can you tell us what's inside that cloth? Can you explain the blood all over the place? The Doctor was trembling with shame and fear. "I bought this sheep to feed my family for a month. It's much cheaper to buy a whole animal than buy one already cut into joints."

The policeman took a knife out of his trouser pocket and pierced the cloth. The lamb's head came into view with its bulging eyes, crooked jaw, slab teeth, and thick tongue. Everyone gasped in shock: "What is it?"

"Are you satisfied now?" asked the Doctor. "Or do you want a sample for lab tests?"

The policeman in charge ordered the sheep to be wrapped up again. He handed the Doctor back his business card. The police reached the conclusion that they were dealing with a mentally deranged individual. Sarcastically, the officer asked: "Is it for your family or did you plan on carrying out some experiments in your medical lab?"

As the policemen led the Doctor away they asked him for his address. He gave them Maliha and Nafie's address, and they took him there in a police car. They were content with telling him not to do it again: "Look, you've lived years in this country and know the law here. Causing alarm to people is a crime." The Doctor nodded his head and did not utter a word. He realised just how disturbed he had become. He thanked God that the police had not arrested him or charged him for violating public health provisions.

He arrived at Maliha's flat carrying the carcass over his shoulder.

His whole body was shaking, his thoughts were confused, and his nerves shredded. As soon as he got through the front door, he flung the slaughtered sheep off his shoulder and onto the floor. When Maliha saw it, she screamed in fear: "What's that, Doctor?"

He replied calmly: "It's a slaughtered sheep. I decide to get us fresh meat for dinner. We can say goodbye to cheap cuts that have no flavour or nutritional value. I'm bored of eating frozen meat. This is a slaughtered lamb, from Wales. They eat grass without the chemicals that are in animal feed. After cutting it up, you can keep it all in the freezer.

"Next time, I promise, I'll ask Ramez, who owns Zein Market, to cut it up and clean it. I've had a hard day because of British stupidity. I nearly got caught up in a legal disaster. The idiots thought I was carrying a human corpse. When they learned the truth, they shut up in embarrassment. According to them I'd broken the law and distressed passengers on public transport."

Indifferent to his trying experience, Maliha answered: "I can't deal with a whole sheep in this tiny kitchen. And the freezer compartment in the fridge in also tiny. It's only big enough for two tubs of ice cream."

Nafie appeared from behind Maliha. He looked at the sheep and was delighted: "Is all that for us, Doctor? Listen to me, Maliha. Leave the carcass to me and the Doctor. We'll manage it like real men. I want you to know something important, Doctor. Something I haven't told you before. Back home, at Eid, I would slaughter all different kinds of animals. Those were good times, and I hope they come back again. Seeing this animal, I'm reminded of the good old days. It's only a small carcass, it should be no problem. It won't be hard for us to cut it up in record time. Maliha, you're the witness. Keep calm, just for the time it'll take us to chop up this little lamb. You can leave the kitchen, too, as there's nothing for you to do here."

Weakly, the Doctor said: "You're right Nafie. People always long for times passed. Back home we lived happy, simple lives. I ask myself, 'Where is the simplicity of our lives these days? Our fathers and grandfathers lived very relaxed lives, while we live fast and furiously."

Maliha left the kitchen and made for safety. She was certain of a very annoying fact: however hard she tried, she would never work things out with Nafie or with Doctor Nadim Nasra. She flung herself down on the couch, and after a short rest, got up and went over to the window.

Back in the kitchen, Nafie told the Doctor: "I wish I'd slaughtered this little lamb."

"Today," said the Doctor, "I proved my bravery to those who wanted to test it. I bought the sheep and carried it over my shoulder through the streets of London and on the train. I proved that I can be free of the groundless fears that people have of the law and its enforcers. People are as scared of the law and the police here as they are in developing countries of the state and state security."

Nafie and the Doctor tried to cut the carcass up into small pieces. They found this difficult because they lacked experience and did not have the right knives for the job of cutting through flesh and bone. As time raced by they wrestled with the little lamb. The kitchen floor and the narrow hallway in the flat were awash with the blood draining out of the animal. The place became a red lake, and there was a risk of it leaking down into the flat beneath. That would give a fright to the elderly couple, Mary and Ned, who lived there. Nafie started mopping up the red blood with kitchen paper towels and cloths. Then they were all used up. The Doctor took his jacket, which was hanging up, and threw it on the ground in a desperate effort to soak it up.

Aside from the blood, a foul stench was coming from the

carcass and spreading through the flat. Nafie opened the window, and came back to continue cutting up the lamb. He cut his finger deeply and started wailing in pain. The Doctor tried to find a clean piece of cloth to wrap around the cut finger, but all he could find was his tie.

As soon as he was done treating Nafie, the Doctor noticed it was past midnight. He was scared that it was then too late for him to get home. He looked for his jacket, which he found on the floor among the pile of sodden paper towels, cloths, and clothes. It was covered in blood. He gave it a farewell look and left the flat. He stopped at the door to the building for a moment and managed to hail a taxi to the station. He looked back of the car window and imagined he could see Nafie standing in the midst of a pile of chunks of red meat, holding his injured finger in pain.

10

Maliha no longer cared about the kitchen, about preparing food or other household chores. That did not impress the Doctor. He wanted her to be an Eastern woman through and through: one who cooked and cleaned and devoted most of her time to her home and family. Maliha's heart was set on a different course, one that she thought more interesting and enjoyable. After all, since childhood she had longed for the good things in life.

She felt miserable, but others envied her. She had become a focus of envy and jealousy of her neighbours. Their husbands worked long hours and brought in little money. Why weren't they like their lucky neighbour? Fresh meat and vast quantities of fruit and vegetables and other good things arrived right at her door every month. The Doctor spent lavishly on her from his high salary, while her neighbours lived in permanent shortage. Where was the fairness in that?

Maliha's neighbours in the building were furious and bitter. One of them told another how she felt about Maliha: how she took great pleasure in good food and drink; how she cooked copious quantities of meat for dinner and never worried about it running out, because she knew that as soon as it was finished, the

Doctor would buy more. On religious holidays, Maliha outdid all her neighbours. The Doctor would buy a larger sheep than usual, a weighty, fatty animal, and he would distribute part of the meat to the neighbours as a pious act of charity.

The women would try to look through the windows into Maliha's flat. The scene of roasting meat and the preparation of food and drinks inspired envy, as did the sight of the three of them sitting around the copper table eating pieces of grilled meat and lamb's liver, or sumptuous festive dishes. Some of the neighbours got used to the things which went on in the flat. That meant they handled the Doctor's relationship with the couple tactfully. They submitted to reality and hid behind a veil of liberation, openness, and individual freedom. When they sat with the three friends, they thanked God that they lived in a free and open society, and enjoyed the value of freedom granted by Western society, unlike their old closed societies.

They were, however, expressing the opposite of what they really felt. In the flat, they talked about personal freedom and the need to take the initiative. But once outside they made jokes about the miserable relationship between the merry trio, as they called them. They indulged in gossip about Maliha, Nafie, and the Doctor, and swore it was a shameful way to live.

Life continued for Maliha, Nafie, and for Doctor Nadim, who was up to his eyeballs in love, in a way far removed from custom and convention. He formulated justifications for his presence with the married couple: he was an Arab living in an alien land who missed the taste of Arab life; his wife Maureen did not understand his feelings and she could not create an Arab atmosphere at home.

The level of cohesion between the Doctor, Maliha, and Nafie grew. The floods of presents, clothes, and luxuries continued. He bought her what she asked for and what she didn't. He spoiled her with perfumes and beauty products, yet Maliha began to grow more stubborn and contrary. She didn't care for her husband or her lover. Her movements became more awkward than before, and her gaze took on a strange character, not fixing on anything.

Her eyes would wander to left and right, as though searching for a lost treasure. Nafie and the Doctor could not fathom the secret of her quest and were unable to help her in her desperate search. She started walking quickly, panting when she breathed. Sometimes she would take a deep breath down into her lungs and let it out with a loud sigh, as though she held a heavy burden in her chest. When she felt trapped, she would undo the buttons of her blouse and run over to the living room window. She would lean as far out of the window as she could and watch the people walking below. She would spend a long time there, without moving. It would get cold, and her husband would ask her to come in and shut the window. So she would go and lie down on the sofa, stretching out rigid as a corpse awaiting burial.

Over time, Maliha began to treat the Doctor more harshly. She knew how to take advantage of his intense hunger for her tenderness. She withheld it from him, and he became like an anxious child. She waited for him to beg her to set a date at the surgery, and he would confess his intense raging desire. On the day of a date he would be ecstatic and arrive early in the morning to prepare everything. On the way he would buy a bunch of fresh flowers; he would clean the surgery, concentrating on the small reception room, the location of the eagerly anticipated date. He sprayed air-freshener and straightened out the couch; he chose the music and food. All his actions were lively and animated, as though he was at a wedding. He counted down the hours until he finished examining his last patient and went to wash his hands. Then he would go into the small reception room and cast a final eye over it before Maliha arrived. Songs of joy coursed through his mind as he awaited his beloved's footsteps.

He waited for Maliha, counting down the hours. Many passed and still she did not appear. The more he waited the more anxious he became. He could not cope; the situation was driving him mad. He called her up to ask why she was late. The ringing of the phone seemed like a crow cawing right into his ear and made his eardrum throb and hurt. He couldn't bear to listen anymore. Maliha did not answer. Annoyance and despair overwhelmed him, and he threw the phone down in anger, as if he wanted to smash it. He collapsed onto the sofa, his heart constricted in pain. Disappointment had ruined his peace of mind and physical strength. He could sense emptiness and darkness bearing down and suffocating him and he wished the sofa would swallow him up. He could not shake off the bitter taste of humiliation His awareness of his lover's betrayal grew and his tears fell silently as he wept at the rejection and treachery.

He realised the time for their date had passed, but he could not leave. A faint hope rippled in his heart. He carried on waiting an hour or more. At any sign of movement outside his heart leapt with joy: it had to be Maliha's footsteps. He went over to the doorway and peered at the steps leading to the outside door. The movement was just a gust of wind. Feeling weak, and with hands trembling, he went back and continued waiting. He was scared that if he left, Maliha might turn up and not find him.

The Doctor tried to kill time by looking through his collection of books and poetry. He read without focus. He changed the music. He grew bored and tired of sitting on the sofa. He opened the window and felt a breeze, which relaxed him a little. He watched the traffic. His attention was drawn to couples walking together. Men and women of various ages holding hands. "They look so happy," he thought. "No problems are holding them back.

I wish things with Maliha were like that. I envy those couples. I envy their emotional stability."

He thought about older couples. Love struck at all ages, it had nothing to do with being young. He thought about couples who were addicted to drugs and drinking. Love came in spite of illness and addiction. "What's the secret of your relationships, dear lovers?" he mused.

He closed the window and threw his trembling body down on the sofa. He was sure Maliha wasn't coming. He got up feeling listless, his joints loose and his body barely able to support him. He dragged his heavy feet and prepared to leave. He blew out the candles and turned the music off. He put the plates of food back in the fridge. Suddenly he felt a surge of rage. He picked up the plate of hummus and threw it against the wall. It smashed into pieces. Then he left the clinic and headed off to the flat for dinner – as usual. He decided to confront Maliha in the way she needed to be confronted: in a man's way. He dreamed up dozens of questions to put to her. Nafie being there made it difficult, but he would still be able to question her when Nafie went to the toilet. Nafie would go at least once over the course of the evening. That would be his chance. This time he would be firm with her. He would frown at her, shake her by the shoulders, pin her against the wall. He would ask her questions that made him nervous. This evening, he would threaten her like he had never done before. He would abandon her if she did not stop playing with his feelings. He was tired of the ups and downs of their relationship and could no longer bear her mockery and sarcasm.

His boldness increased as he approached the flat. Nafie opened the door to him. Immediately his eyes searched for Maliha. He went to the living room, but she was not there. "Maliha hasn't come back yet; she went to visit a neighbour who's just given birth," said Nafie. Hearing this only made the Doctor angrier.

Maliha was playing cat and mouse with him. She was out on purpose, he thought. If he could see her, his storm of anger would subside and Maliha had denied him this chance of a little peace of mind. He would therefore spend the evening waiting for her, whatever the price. She knew he normally left at ten o'clock.

Nafie continued his vacuous chatter. He asked the Doctor to explain a few verses from Antara's poetry. The Doctor responded out of his love of poetry. Ten o'clock passed and then eleven, and there was no sign of Maliha. He knew he could not stay longer or he would miss the midnight train. He left, broken in body and mind after the painful events of the day.

11

Maliha's attitude and behaviour towards the Doctor really baffled him. He was good to her and spoke kindly to her, but she treated him badly and spoke hurtfully. He often asked himself question after question, trying to find answers: Why doesn't she care about the way I feel? Why does she treat me cruelly and indifferently? Why does she scorn my concern for her and my tenderness? Doesn't she know she means the world to me?

No answer was forthcoming to the incessant questions that kept him awake. He did not know how to resolve this eternal dilemma of love and hate, and was in sore need of a way to deal with his cruel lover. How to deal with her caustic nature and get her to be tender with him? Buying fresh meat for her had not lessened her cruelty or motivated her to treat him well. He remembered her screaming in his face during a special date. When he wanted to become physically intimate with her, she pushed him away violently, like a cat defending its kittens. She shunned his feelings, and his touch. She resorted to her old avoidance techniques: when the Doctor suggested they go to bed, she said: "Doctor, I'm having women's troubles and am impure."

Then she screamed hurtful words at him: "You claim to be

highly educated and cultured, yet the way you look at me is just like my husband, who lacks learning and knowledge. You act like someone who knows nothing about married life. You've got excellent medical qualifications and long experience diagnosing and treating diseases. You're an avid reader of different sources of knowledge, and a keen observer of the media. But you're like all men! You only want one thing from women. It's the same thing from the intellectual and the educated as it is from the boorish and ignorant. Are you Nafie or Nadim?

"You claim you're a big intellectual, an aesthete who loves poetry. I'll say the same thing to you as I said to my husband: I won't give up my body for you and him to ride and play with. You want my body under your control, to enjoy its youth and ripeness as you please. And when the youth fades and the ripeness passes, you'll look for new prey.

"I'm not a woman whose body is in servitude to the lusts of men. Sweet nothings in my ear from a man are at the very bottom of my list of priorities. You're ignorant of the real power of a woman's body, but you race to satisfy your animal carnality. I can say the word no. Just listen to me, dear Mr Doctor. I've decided to withdraw the weapon you use. I've decided to stop your damaging work against my body. Let the evenings in the Shepherd's Bush flat go to Hell. Let the plates of meat and veg sod off."

Once or twice Maliha did turn up at the appointed time. She arrived angry, her face bare of makeup, wearing baggy clothing, which made her look flabby and graceless. Her hair looked untidy under a loosely tied paisley headscarf and smelt of cheap jasmine scent. She found the Doctor waiting for her like the proverbial cat on a hot tin roof. The room was always festooned with roses in copper vases that had Arabesque engravings. The couch was carefully arranged and there was a blanket in case they needed to cover themselves on account of the cold. The corners of the room were lit with red candles fixed in empty glass bottles.

The Doctor bent over backwards to turn dates with his lover into Arab get-togethers. He had in mind the old Arab gatherings as described in famous tales like the *Thousand and One Nights*. He recalled the works of orientalist painters who were inspired by life at night in the orient. The Doctor was infatuated with that mysterious, exciting life and the place for his encounters with Maliha had to reflect that infatuation. The Arab décor and inscriptions were essential. He bought them from both Arab and Indian shops so the scene was not entirely Arab. He was reliving the acts of the great lovers of old from Arab legend. He was Jameel and Maliha was Botheina.

He played Arabic music like the song "The Ruins" by Umm Kalthoum as he was transported by its lyrics and music. When Maliha arrived he replaced Umm Kalthoum with a song by Abdel Halim Hafez, which went: "I'm dreaming of you". A young person's song in accordance with Maliha's taste. He brought light Arab food he had prepared himself and set it out in small pottery dishes. He sat down on the sofa and invited her to sit beside him. He stretched his arm behind her and she leaned against him. He rested his head on her shoulder and inhaled the scent of her neck. His spirit relaxed from the torments of unfulfilled desire. Without her knowing, he asked God that his happiness at being with the one he loved could last for ever. He began to make gentle and romantic gestures, touching the tips of her fingers, raising them to his lips, and kissing them. For a short while Maliha submitted to his groans of yearning as he whispered words of love into her ear.

"I've missed you more than I can say, Maliha." She looked at him and he continued: "As God is my witness, it's true, my darling." She surprised him by withdrawing her fingers from his grasp and turning her face away from him. She stood up, ramrod straight and with an annoyed flourish yanked off the paisley head-scarf, an action that made her seem like a Spanish gypsy getting ready to dance a heated flamenco. She tossed the scarf into his lap in a theatrical flourish full of flirtation and sexiness. He looked at her long wild hair in amazement. Curls rained down like lava onto her lower back. The scent of the cheap jasmine filled the space and he breathed it in. The scent of oriental perfumes took him back to his mother, his neighbours, and the village girls.

Maliha started to undress seductively, taking off one item of clothing at a time. She flung one here and another there. More and more of her curves came into view. He looked at her and his body caught fire, but he was unable to go near her, either to touch her or to stop her undressing. She climbed onto the wooden table and sat down cross-legged, stark naked. The light from an old lamp hanging from the ceiling fell across her body. The Doctor was spinning in a haze of amazement as she uttered words he had never heard the like of before.

"I give you fresh dates and honey. My master, come and take from this eternal bounty. I will give you what you want. Take what you are used to taking from me whenever you invite me to come and meet you in this dark and dusty room. Hold my hand and let me take yours. Stand up."

The Doctor looked dumbstruck, frozen to his seat, and did not respond. She continued: "Stand up. I beg you, come close. Why won't you come near me? Take me, I'm ready for whatever you desire. I shouldn't have to ask you. Just do what you want with me." Maliha's anger and storminess increased. "Come on. Why are you still on the sofa staring like an idiot? Is my body a frightening ghost? Didn't you ask me to come for just this purpose?" Her tears came, hot and profuse.

The Doctor shook his head in sorrow, and in a weak, submissive voice thick with passion, said: "My darling Maliha, what are you saying? Why are you always so stressed out when we meet? Why do you think that our love is based on short-term pleasure? Why do you imagine that my invitation to you is for one purpose only? My relationship with you is not for my own pleasure. You know I am tied to your soul, not just your body. Do you know what you mean to me?"

He was standing like a child, beside the table, and continued: "My darling, you mean the whole world to me. I have no pleasure in the world unless I can look into your beautiful eyes. I've written so many poems to your love." He stroked her hair and caressed her shoulder. "Don't worry about having sex with me. Put your clothes back on. There's no need for us to do anything if you don't want us to." He started to collect up her items of clothing scattered over the floor and hand them to her.

"Calm down, darling. Get dressed. Come and sit beside me. I'll make you a cup of coffee. Don't you feel like tasting the food I made you? After that I'll read you some poems. You can look at the drafts. Here they are." He pointed to a small table next to the sofa. "Please, Maliha, my love, don't be angry with me. I'm the one infatuated." She calmed down a little. In great trepidation he edged closer to her. She let him embrace her and he put his head on her shoulder and started to cry. He was quick to cry and his eyes quick to fill with tears.

"Maliha, you don't know how much I desire you and long for you. I've missed you so much. It's been weeks since our last time together. Please, my darling, don't be chary about meeting me. Be kind. It's torturing me how seldom we meet. Yes, we meet in your flat every evening, but you know that there I can't get as close to you as I'd like. I can't take you in my arms as I want. I long to whisper sweet paeans about your beauty and my passion in your ear, but it's impossible to do that in your house. It's impossible to repeat lines of poetry for you alone to hear when

Nafie's there. You're the only thing left in the world that matters to me. Please, grant me the wish for us to meet. Darling, let our time together be wonderful and calm. Let us enjoy these moments of sharing each other in eternal love."

Maliha was suddenly overwhelmed by anxiety. In disgust she repeated what she had said to him time and time again, probably more than a thousand times: "God, you've got no idea what I suffer. Maybe you do know, but you pretend you're stupid and don't know. I am oppressed. I have to watch that wretched man Nafie wasting his life in front of me day after day. He's a pile of flesh and bone stuck next to an old suitcase. His possessions are worthless: a cassette player and cassettes of old songs. That poetry collection he borrowed from you and hasn't returned yet – the diwan of Antara – he pretends to understand it. He must have read the same page a thousand times a month. He sits scratching his head all day long and munches on watermelon seeds, peanuts, and pistachios. Life passes by before him and he pays no attention, he makes no effort at all. He takes me in bed without thinking, as though I am not fit for any other purpose. Of all the things the world gives, all he has is his body. He's totally in love with himself and his masculine prowess. He ignores the things that make me happy and fill my heart with delight. He lacks the ability to capture my heart. His interest is limited to getting on top of me in bed with his flabby, tired-out body.

"Listen to me, Nadim. You say I mean everything in life to you. So why don't you save me? Get me out of my crushing life with Nafie. He's absolutely useless. He sits in a corner at home and accepts the little that life sends his way. You say you love me, so why don't you help me get out of my cramped council flat? Save me from the man stuck there. I want to enjoy life with you, like lovers do. Your relationship with your wife isn't up to much. What are you waiting for?"

The Doctor's heart shrank at Maliha's words. She wasn't like she was before. When he first knew her, she was happy with the things he gave her. Now, she was no longer a compliant woman. She was paying no attention to his many purchases from London's cheaper shops; she did not want things imported from China, Thailand, and Korea; she did not even want things from Argos. What he had bought her was no longer of any interest to her.

The Doctor longed to be in touch with his Arab roots, and Maliha helped him, but her caustic character made this hard, if not impossible, to achieve. She had big ambitions for their relationship. She wanted him for herself alone without any rival. He realized that he had to deal with these ambitions with great caution. If he failed, the balance of his family and his whole life would be upset. That was the risk. He was unable and unwilling to wreck the stability of his family. All these issues were racing around his head as he listened to her heated remonstrations. He shook his head in fear and confusion and gave her a fearful, broken look.

"You're my beloved. What do we lack? We see each other whenever we want. I spend a lot of time with you. I don't go home after work, but come to see you and sit with you. I've given you everything you could have wished for. And I won't leave you in need of anything. Are you short of meat? This month I'll buy two sheep, not just one.

"You can change your hairstyle at any time. I'll open an account for you with the famous hairdresser Trevor Sorbie. He's expensive. Or with Stephanie Pollard, the well-known stylist. If you want to wear jeans, no problem. For your comfort, what's hard is easy. I'll buy you luxury brand jeans, like Calvin Klein, Versace, or Dolce and Gabbana. Soon, I'll give you some money to buy a house back in your country. Take care of it, don't waste it on frivolous purchases. And I'll give you cash so that you can get out and about. Go to restaurants with your friends. Travel to Paris or Madrid.

"You're so difficult, Maliha but I care for you more and more every day. What do you lack? Haven't I given you everything you asked for? Why put me in an awkward position? You're asking the impossible. You know better than most that I cannot break up my family. Divorcing my wife would cost me a lot. It would push me to the edge of poverty and I could not cope with that at my age. Do you want that for me? If I became poor, I wouldn't be able to help you. Go on, tell me what you think about divorce. Be realistic, be fair."

Maliha responded: "How can I keep quiet about this unbearable situation? Can't you sense my fear? It's all because of the tension in our relationship. Our love has no aim. Look at my tears and my sorrow. Listen to my cries, my anguish. Empathy with my pain will help me feel better, so come on, Nadim. I can't and won't keep quiet anymore. Do you hear? I won't keep quiet about where our relationship has got to. All your attempts to shut me up will fail, for certain. I'll resist to the last, and in the end victory will be mine."

The Doctor and Maliha's rendezvous was over before it began. A rendezvous as arid as a desert. Maliha left the clinic and slammed the door behind her. She left the Doctor alone, swallowing a bitter draught. Heavy silence and darkness surrounded him. His heart was filled with pain and his feelings bruised. He thought about doing something to counteract the torment and pain. He put on Arabic music, and as he listened the tears rolled down his cheeks.

12

The relationship between Dr Nadim and Maliha continued in the same vein, and Maliha grew more frustrated. She hated both her life with Nafie, and her relationship with the Doctor, with his repeated evening visits for dinner and company. Her despair mounted day by day. Their private meetings at the surgery upset her, and she only went when he begged and pleaded.

Her whole life was just one long routine. There was nothing challenging; it was just as it had been with her family. Her dreams had evaporated. Once, she had dreamed of changing her life for the better, but having lived a long time in London, she was certain she couldn't do anything because she and her husband had become dependent on the Doctor's helping hand. He supported them in everything big and small: food and drink, legal matters, and official procedures. Their reliance on him had become an unbreakable chain. How to break free? How to change her life radically?

The Doctor was assiduous in buying Maliha her monthly carcass and supplies for the house, even though she paid little heed to his efforts. He started to feel annoyed that some of the monthly provisions were used up very quickly – by the second or third week of the month – and he would have to plug the gap from local shops. The waste and lack of management made him angry, and he gave vent to this when Maliha told him one day that some essential household product had run out. It was a dangerous turn in the relationship: before this point, he had never been critical or hurtful speaking to her. She was the one who criticized and hurt. Now it was her turn to listen to him.

"Darling, please excuse me. I'm sorry for what I'm going to say, but I have to say it: you're extravagant and don't know how to run your household. The money that goes into your bank account, and all the groceries that I buy, should be enough for at least two families to live on."

Maliha listened, fuming. She cried a great deal and for the most trivial reasons. She became agitated. Her voice cracked and she complained bitterly about her husband's weakness and her failing relationship with the Doctor. The relationship was not bearing any of the fruits she had expected, and her situation had not improved. It was just evening visits, meetings on their own, and slaughtered animals.

"You're being harsh, Nadim, and your accusations just aren't fair. It's easy for you, you're well paid and so it's fine to talk about economizing. The life you lead is completely different to ours. You might always be coming around to our house and seeing up close our lives and standard of living, but you only see the surface. You've failed to see into the heart of things. You're like someone who goes to the theatre, has a good time, and at the end of the play goes home. Our drama embodies our misery. My husband and I are real people with bodies and feelings, not actors. Every evening you watch the show and when the curtain falls you leave. You forget our troubles and unhappiness and go back to the comfort of your nice home in a nice quiet suburb. You're not worried about anything. You're not in need, like us. You don't have a problem paying the bills. And you come back the next day to the same theatre and watch new acts of the marvellous play.

"Whenever the postman pushes a bundle of brown envelopes through the letterbox, my stomach contracts. It means bills to pay. We pay for water, electricity, and the phone. Just the phone bill is a disaster. Sometimes the phone gets cut off. Then there's the incessant and growing demands of my family and my husband's family. We're trapped by them. They want huge amounts of money, even though we have so little. I just wish I could make the suffering and pain go away. You and Nafie are a big disaster. Your face is as cunning as a fox's, and his as blank as a chicken's."

The Doctor listened to her, and felt sorry. The relationship had reached an unimaginable low. His feelings were hurt; his efforts not appreciated. He sought attention from her however he could. Without it what meaning or flavour did life have? Maliha's face flashed with anger, and he felt frightened. The truth was painful and hurtful: his lover's estimation of him was getting lower and lower. The relationship was heading over a cliff. He was terrified that Maliha would soon abandon him. Being dumped meant misery and a return to a life without Arabs. The Arabic language was his third lung. Talking in his beloved language and mixing with people like himself was vital to him. "I'll be so lonely and desperate," he thought, "if she dumps me."

His marriage had become as cold as ice, ruled by betrayal and separation. Maureen was always travelling. She would go away and come back for a short period, only in preparation for another trip. Her bags were always packed. He didn't even know when she left and when she came back. Once he found a female contraceptive device in her bag. It hurt that their relationship had sunk so low, and he was convinced he could not stop his marriage falling apart completely. Now he had conclusive proof of his wife's infidelity but he could not bring himself to look inside the packet that contained the contraceptive device. He tried to disregard the evidence of her sexual activity – it was a provocation hard for any man to bear.

He hurried to his room. Repressing his anger was painful. He locked the door and flopped onto the bed, his whole body feeling tormented. He became silent and despondent. He wept and suffered in pain and spent days on his own. No one in the family asked after him and he, in turn, had no idea what was going on with his children. He did not even know where they worked. He had had many problems with them. He had exhausted himself trying to teach them Arabic, and had failed miserably. He wanted his children to understand Arabic culture and had given them dictionaries, books of poetry, literature, and travel. He told them about the brilliance of Arabic music and played them old songs. He dreamed that one of his children would become an Arabic-English translator.

All those dreams evaporated, like a gulp of water in an arid desert. Whenever he tried to draw close to his children, they had avoided him. Their father's origins and his place of birth were of no interest to them. He was just their father. Roots and language did not matter to them. They had no desire to know any of the things he talked about with such pride and passion.

His wife was worse than his children. She adopted a policy of poisoning the wells and destroying the crops. When their first daughter Samar and their youngest son Ayman were born, she insisted on giving them her surname. He accepted this though it was hateful to him. His wife said arrogantly: "Things are different these days. Fathers don't have an absolute right to pass on their name to their children. Mothers also have that right. They have families just like fathers. Samar and Ayman will take my family name, Duckworth."

She had quarrelled with him about the children's upbringing.

Stressed and angry she had shouted out: "Please! Don't you exhaust my children with your old-fashioned ideas. They're free either to know about your origins or to ignore them. They might learn your language, or they might not. No one is going to force them to do anything. You have to obey the law of the land and the system here. So, don't you dare pressurize my children with all your old-fashioned demands. Don't push them more than need be. Better, leave my children alone, otherwise you'll only have yourself to blame."

It was quite possible for her to kick him out of the house – the law was on her side, he thought. If she did, it would be a disaster for him. His children were British, and she warned him about manipulating them. For sure, the state would defend them from his interference in their private lives.

The Doctor remembered his wife's words when he was with Maliha. He shook with fear because he was trapped by fire on both sides. Maliha complained to him about bills that had come in the post and he responded fearfully: "Just tell me what needs paying. Come along, give me the bills you're talking about. I'll pay them all. I do it out of kindness. Please, my darling. Your tears are too precious to waste on these worthless things. Let's be happy with our love. What you say is right, absolutely right. Time is racing by and our days are numbered. We have to love, enjoy, and laugh. There's no point in being sad and down."

Maliha listened to the Doctor for the thousandth time as she had done before. She did not reply, but remained silent, frowning. She shook her head in disbelief at the contradiction between his words and his actions. He lived in a world removed from reality. He imagined he was living the life he had left behind, a traditional Oriental lifestyle. He enjoyed the fantasy of her flat in Shepherd's Bush but was ignorant of her feelings and did not ask himself whether this was what she wanted. He wasn't interested in dreams other than his own. He imposed his fantasy on her life. He wanted her to fulfil his desires, emulate his vision of life, and conform to his traditional Arab ideas. She had to be an obedient mistress, who visited him in his reception room that was filled with the ghosts of old books and was where he rested his head on her shoulder and inhaled the scent he had been deprived of for years.

Maliha had turned into a symbol of the distant Orient of his past. She had to put up with his crazy ideas and fancies, and translate his desires and demands in the space of her tiny flat. In exchange for her tenderness, he paid a high price. The monthly shopping and the help to meet the needs of both Maliha and Nafie were very expensive. Why did she treat him so cruelly, then?

The situation remained on hold. They were neither in heaven nor in hell, but walking a dark, treacherous path. There was no goal. Days flashed past. He was verging on despair, and Maliha had fallen into the same slough of despair. They were spinning out of control.

Her despair grew worse once she realised the Doctor would not lead her to a new life, and that fact made her indifferent to their relationship. In parallel, the Doctor was feeling more messed up in his head. The ground, no longer solid, was slipping from under his feet. During the early part of his infatuation his steps had been firm. Now he had a permanent tremble in his hands and a weight on his chest. Would he end up ripping his clothes like Maliha?

Fear engulfed him. He was terrified of being cast aside by Maliha and having to leave the Arab microcosm of the flat on Goldhawk Road. It was a place that embodied magic, enchantment, and mystery. Having to leave it would expel him from paradise and wreck his life. That small flat in Shepherd's Bush was like the very air he breathed. If he lost it, his soul would suffocate and his body wither.

Maliha entered a phase of despondency and deathly despair. She was all anxiety and frowns, and her smile faded. The glow of optimism always reflected in her pretty face had vanished like a snuffed candle. A pale face and sunken eyes reflected the new situation. She stopped putting on black mascara and eye shadow in various shades of green, blue, and brown. That was all gone – for good. Her lips had been as succulent as grapes, but had become dried and split. She no longer had any desire to show off or flaunt her beauty.

She neglected her appearance, which had once been her weapon to brandish against men. Her new weapon against the Doctor meant hiding her beauty, an appropriate way, she thought, to express her unhappiness and indifference. Neglecting her appearance became a symbol of her resistance to his ideas and behaviour. He wanted her to fit the image he had, to be the elegant Arab woman who wore embroidered kaftans and full makeup, an oriental candle to illuminate their evening sessions and the darkness of his surgery. She would deprive him of the pleasure of seeing her in all her Arab beauty and captivating femininity.

Maliha became oblivious to the Doctor's shopping and gifts. His offerings paled and lost their sparkle. Now she received purchases from Argos and other cheap London shops. She had a video recorder, a washing machine, plastic flowers, pictures with oriental scenes, and electronic goods. The Doctor intended to make his beloved happy, but Maliha did not open the door to take delivery and the goods would be returned. Sometimes she accepted them, but left them for days in their packaging in the hallway. Food would go off and smell bad. When the Doctor asked her gently why she did not do anything with the purchases, she would shrug her shoulders and give no answer.

Maliha had reached a bitter conclusion about the shopping and gifts. No good would come of them. The problem was more serious than that. She was living a double life, split in body and mind between Nafie and the Doctor. What mattered to her had no connection with the Doctor's purchases. She wanted things that would make her comfortable, but, unfortunately, he was determined not to do that. The top priority for her became salvation from the clutches of Nafie and his filthy, miserable flat.

She resisted the evening sessions at the flat and gave the two men scant attention. She did not speak all evening and would not be drawn into the conversation. She turned her back on them and carried on watching TV as if she was sitting alone. She remained absolutely silent. Withdrawing to the window, she watched the activity in the street below and did not turn round, even when the Doctor made to leave.

The Doctor suffered from Maliha's coldness and abandonment. She was indifferent to the love that should bind them. He imagined that the moment when her heart would reject him completely was close, and then she would not allow him into the flat. The final rupture was at hand and Maliha was strong and tough. He swallowed the bitter pain of abandonment. He begged to see her, and she set a date to meet him. On that day, he waited for her to come but she didn't show up, and didn't answer his calls.

The Doctor tried hard to treat the sickness he thought was afflicting his relationship with Maliha. He wanted to make the relationship warm again and see it flow on course. He wanted to keep it going and try to remove the obstacles. He would fight with all his material and emotional resources. He felt his relationship with her was a foregone conclusion that no one could take away. He would never leave her; she was the centre of his existence. To himself, the Doctor repeated words of determination:

"I will fight with every weapon I have to make my place in Maliha's life solid, whatever the hardship."

Maliha, however, kept up her attempts to get out of her relationship with Dr Nadim. She made her rejection of him plain, expressing her true feelings towards him in body language. She ignored him and frequently didn't turn up to their dates. Their usual evening sessions, she skipped, only going home after the Doctor had left to avoid seeing him. All the signs that their love was over were on display.

There were many reasons behind her attitude. The Doctor himself knew that his lover was unhappy with her situation. He understood things, and ignored her requests on the basis that they were a passing fancy. He thought she was going through a petulant phase, one familiar to most men. The relationship was going through a bad patch but things would soon return to normal. Love, like the year, had seasons, a cold winter and stormy spring.

If he gave more, she would go back to the way she had been. He was even more generous, but the love object continued to spurn him. Maliha was going too far in ending things, but the Doctor was forced to admit the bitter reality. Her abandonment weighed heavy on his heart. He realised the time had come to give the matter the attention it deserved. What was he going to do to get Maliha back to her old ways with him? He had not fulfilled her most important wish, which was to leave her husband Nafie. With a little thought it might be possible to solve the problem of the tiny flat she hated living in. If he got her out, where would he take her? The idea of changing her flat flew around his mind. If it happened, it would help keep him in her life.

Ideas and questions swirled inside his head. Answers or solutions, he failed to find. And so, acting as a proxy for Maliha and Nafie he decided to contact the housing department responsible for low-income families. "I'll persuade them that they have to move them to a new flat, something bigger in a better neighbourhood. I'll be devious and use all the tricks, a trivial thing for my darling's sake. I'll tell them that the flat is full of mice and insects. I'll explain the risk the damp poses to the poor family's health. The council will believe me. I am a doctor, after all."

The Doctor wrote a letter outlining their fictitious circumstances. The couple's health was at risk if they remained in the flat. To his great surprise the housing department offered Maliha another flat. He went to inspect it, and found it even smaller than their present place, and stuck in a poor suburb, miles from the centre of town. In the role of the couple's proxy, he said that they no longer wanted to move. Maliha was furious, but things were not over; battle involved retreat as well as advance.

13

Maliha continued to spurn Nafie and avoided him in bed. From time to time he would make advances, using kind words and affectionate behaviour in the hope she would take pity on him. He wanted to touch her and have his way, which he considered his marital right.

Before the sun was up one day, he touched her, softly and hesitantly. Her body was always wrapped in loose clothing, and this time she was wearing a long nightdress and thick trousers. She had a scarf over her silky hair, which was always pinned up, plastered in henna, or sticky with conditioner or oil. She claimed these products encouraged hair growth, and slept with such concoctions on her head, while on her face, she daubed unpleasant smelling skin creams. Her real motivation was not hair or skin care, but keeping Nafie from trying to have sex with her by making herself unattractive.

He pressed his body against hers and embraced her from behind. As usual, she gave a sigh and elbowed him in the chest. Then she got up and turned on the light. This hurt Nafie's eyes and he rubbed them so hard they nearly burst. She adjusted her clothing, pulled her thick trousers up, and pulled her headscarf down round her forehead.

"Nafie, why do you assault me? It's like you were taking on an enemy in battle. You woke me up, d'you know? Sleeping in this blasted bed isn't at all restful. What do you want from me? Tell me. Haven't I told you a hundred times I'm not well enough to have sex with you? My period is still all over the place, like it has been for years. Why don't you believe me? D'you think I'm lying to you and buying tampons to turn you on? Come and feel, and then you'll believe me. Come here. It's better I show you the doctors' reports. Wait till I fetch them all. I'll keep shoving them in your face until you accept my health is getting worse."

She walked over to the bedroom door and tried to leave, but Nafie tugged at the end of her long nightdress. She fell back onto the edge of the bed and gave him an angry look, a look he feared and tried to hold off. "Tell me what you want from me, Nafie. If you want me to agree to you taking another wife, I already gave you my consent ages ago. How many times have I told you that I agree to you marrying again whenever you want? Put your trust in God and get married. I stand by what I say. You have the right to marry someone else, or more than one. Why deny yourself what is permitted you? Why not do it and enjoy what the Law-giver allows?"

Nafie scrutinized her irate face. He did not lower or avert his gaze, but stared into her face as though he were trying to penetrate the hidden depths of her being. In a serious and measured tone he said: "Maliha, why do you keep your distance? Isn't it about time we had sex? I want you to have a baby. I want to see the fruit of my loins. I want children to make me happy. Why don't we start trying today?"

What Nafie said that morning came as a surprise to Maliha. He was saying something new and it gave her a powerful shock. She had never expected this, and was thrown into confusion. She didn't let him finish what he wanted to say. She shouted incomprehensibly at him and flung herself onto the bed, lifting up her nightdress and exposing her belly and breasts.

"Come on. Take me now before the sun comes up so we can have a baby like you said. You want me to bring children into God's wide world. You want them to live in this wonderful flat, eat off social security, drink from your miserable job in a scuzzy restaurant, and be educated at the Doctor's expense? You're going to be disappointed, Nafie. I'm infertile. I've known that bitter truth for a long time. I can't have children. Didn't you already know? Perhaps you didn't. I wanted to keep it to myself. It's nobody else's business. Only my business."

Nafie looked sheepishly at Maliha. He hadn't expected that response from her. He mouthed the usual things he would exclaim when he was sceptical about what she had said: "God is my refuge from the accursed Satan. What are you saying? Who said you can't have children? Thankfully, my darling, you are in perfect health. Look at your glowing cheeks and complexion. You're in the prime of youth. You say you can't have children. Why didn't you tell me before? We could have got treatment. Lots of women despair that they can't have children, but medical treatment makes it possible."

Maliha ignored what she was hearing. She got off the bed and stood in the middle of the room. In an agitated fashion she grabbed her handbag. She stretched out her hand around the door and snatched her coat off its peg, almost tearing it in the process, and it took both her trembling hands to free it. She ran out of the room towards the front door. Nafie's bunch of keys was dangling in the lock. She turned the key and pulled out the bunch. "Enough," she mumbled, "I've had enough." She stormed out of the flat, still in her nightdress. She slammed the door behind her and locked it from the outside. It would not be possible for Nafie to leave and catch up with her. She ran down the long winding stairway to the courtyard. The area was dark and still. She kept on going to the street.

She began talking to herself: "I'm tired of living with that man. I'm tired of this life. It's just one annoyance after another." Without thinking, she headed off to the Doctor's surgery, and decided to wait for him at the front door to tell him about Nafie's new demand. She would try to convince him that he had to help her. Something had to be done to avoid her husband's crazy demand becoming a reality.

Nafie heard the door slam behind Maliha, but he did not move. He stayed on the edge of the bed, his new idea whizzing around his head. Because it had come at such an early hour of the morning and so unexpectedly, he wondered whether he had done something wrong. He had never imagined she would be so angry. He should never have opened the subject. He always tried to avoid provoking her anger, and did not know what had driven him to talk about having a baby. He could have waited till the following evening; such talk would have been more appropriate once the Doctor had left.

Talk about having children was the last thing she had expected from him. There was something strange about it. Nafie had never said he wanted children. In the early days of their marriage, yes, he would stroke her stomach and tease her, saying: "I hope God blesses us with a baby. That would be fantastic." Maliha thought he was teasing her to bring a smile to her stern face and calm her chronic nerves. But what had happened today for him to suggest her getting pregnant? Had his family put him up to it? Had his mother's words influenced him? But Nafie always spoke to his family in front of her. Behind the crazy request someone was plotting. Maliha could find no satisfactory answer, and thought it was a new ploy to get her to sleep with Nafie.

The truth was different. The secret lay with Maliha herself. Behind her husband's back, she had started taking the pill as soon as she arrived in London. She had decided not to get pregnant with Nafie. She thought children would complicate the change she longed for. On her way to the Doctor's surgery she came up with a plan. It would be an important meeting with the Doctor. Matters had come to a head. He would have to make a decision about their relationship. How many times had she tried to make him stand by her so she could leave her husband? Would he now submit to her demand?

She reached the surgery. Anger was making her tremble. Her eyes were full of tears. She stopped at the entrance, the greyness of night still colouring the world. She waited for him in the doorway, shunning suspicious looks of passers-by. Whenever someone cast her a glance, she took refuge further along the passage leading to the building. She was consumed by fear and tried to hide like a mouse.

She heard the Doctor's footsteps approaching. He reached the door of the clinic and started fumbling in his pocket for his keys. He heard her voice behind him: "Doctor, it's Maliha." He turned and asked, in a voice full of surprise and curiosity: "What are you doing here so early in the morning?"

"Quick," she said, "I'm dying of cold. I've been standing here for more than half an hour waiting for you to arrive." He opened the door and they hurried inside. He turned on the light and they headed straight into the reception room. There the Doctor opened his arms to embrace Maliha. He put his head on her shoulder and inhaled the scent of her neck. It had been months since their last date. After that short moment, Maliha freed herself from his arms and pushed him away. She sat down on the couch and started to cry.

He felt scared: "What's happened? Why all the tears? Did you quarrel with your husband?"

"Me and Nafie don't fight any more. We're past that stage. I came to tell you something serious. I've come to ask for just one thing."

"What is it, my darling? Tell me straight out."

Trembling, she said: "Let me be a servant in your house. I mean what I say. I'll cook and clean and do the washing. I'll look after the big garden. Just get me out of the hell I'm living. I'll lose my mind or I'll murder him, and spend the rest of my life in a mental institution or in a prison. I can't face living with him anymore. Today he was suggesting something really crazy."

The Doctor looked at Maliha suspiciously. Something serious had happened. He had tried to put it off for a long time, but had she come to lower the curtain on their relationship or to ask for help about something? "Why do you want work?" he asked her.

"Ask me those questions later. You say you love me, so please do this simple thing. Do what I ask before it's too late. Save me from the mess and confusion of my life."

Feeling puzzled, he said: "What's wrong with your life? Nafie loves you and does many things to make you happy and provide for you. He hasn't made you go out to work to help him. I know you need a bigger income, and so I do my part for you in terms of money very well. Don't you think so? What are you missing, Maliha, my darling?"

"My life with him is hell, as you know. I've had my fair share of bad luck in life. I've tried to escape my life and release Nafie from life with me. Our life together isn't bearable any longer. There isn't any more to say than what I've already told you. I've explained my suffering with him until it's made me ill. Who could put up with the life I have? Nafie, sitting in the corner of the room, with his big trunk and a pile of old songs grinding on. He lives a shadow life, and I've given up trying to change him.

"I'm asking you for one thing, and I won't ask again. If you love me, save me from this hell. Save me from this schizophrenic life. Hear my plea and my groans. Save me before it's too late. I want to be a servant at your house."

Her body convulsed with crying. The Doctor got up and put a hand on her shoulder. The telephone rang, but he ignored it. He felt confused and shocked. "Why are you saying these things? Is working as a cleaner for me a realistic option? Suppose it happens. Would you accept serving my wife? Would you accept my wife bossing you around and giving you orders? What you're saying isn't sensible. You should know something really important. My life is restricted, just like yours. Do you know how I live at home? My family are strangers to me and I'm a stranger to them. They don't speak my language. They don't even eat with me. How could I take you home with me? Should I tell my wife I've brought an Arab woman to live with us?"

"Nothing I've said is a lie," she retorted. "I've been abundantly clear about what I want. It's time for things to change. I can't stay in that flat any longer. We gather round the table. We put food on it. I have no desire to eat or cook. If you think that's one of the rituals that keeps our love alive, you're deluding yourself.

"I've got a shocking piece of news. It's what made me rush to see you so early and wait in the dark and cold for you. This morning, Nafie surprised me with a crazy request I could never have imagined. And I don't imagine I can do it." The Doctor continued staring at her in surprise, waiting to hear the news. She went on: "How can I do what he wants when he's never done anything I've asked? Since coming to Britain with him, he's stayed the same. Despite my constantly urging him to change his way of life, he hasn't paid any attention."

Somewhat more calmly, she continued speaking as she got off the sofa and took his hand. "I'm begging you. Save me from depression and being trapped. My life with Nafie is like the madness of despair. Take me home with you. I won't ask for payment for my work. I see you're going to insist you can't do what I ask. I'm suggesting a sensible solution. Marry me and save me from being torn apart."

"Marry you, Maliha? How can I do that, darling?"

"I don't want to live the rest of my life with Nafie. I've had enough. Things can't carry on like this. I've burst in on you so early today, Nadim, to ask you to marry me. I agree to be your second wife and will accept any situation you think suitable."

"What about your family?"

"I've broken away from my family. It no longer matters what they say. Anyway, they know about my relationship with you. Someone told them you were my lover."

The Doctor was stunned at what he heard. He asked her anxiously: "Are you telling the truth, Maliha?" Nadim recalled the people who had jumped him by the block in Shepherd's Bush, covering his clothes and face in dye, but he stopped himself telling Maliha.

"One time," she said, "my mother called and said my father and brother Abdel Wahid wanted to know the truth about rumours of my relationship with you. I denied it, of course. I said you'd helped Nafie find work. I threatened my mother and told her not to interfere in my life. 'Stop torturing me like this,' I told her. 'Before, you married me off to Nafie against my will. I'm far away here and I'll drop you all for good. I'll stop sending money every month. And you can't do without this help.' Nafie stood by me at the time. He told them you were his friend and that they shouldn't believe rumours and gossip."

The Doctor listened intently to Maliha's account and then asked her an important question: "What about Nafie? He'll stop you leaving him as soon as you try. Aren't you afraid of that? He brought you to this country, and he's a close friend of your brother. It's likely he'll block any attempt by you to leave him."

"Yes, you're right about that. I'm scared of Nafie and his friendship with my brother. Still, I'm looking for another man. I hope you will be the one who saves me. But it seems you prefer family life over our relationship."

She continued talking about why she was still with Nafie. "His friendship with my brother interfered with my happiness and freedom. It stopped me leaving him. If I left Nafie, the family would go mad, and I'd never be able to go back to my country. My family wouldn't accept it. They'd think it was a scandal. Despite all the hassles, I can't break off my ties to him. If I left him, my brother might kill me. Being far away wouldn't stop him. I know what I'm talking about. Abdel Wahid could kill me even though I'm here.

"The bottom line is this. Nafie is oblivious to what's going on around him. My presence in his life is important and it doesn't matter if that comes at the expense of my happiness and his. Nafie worships my brother and worries that they might lose contact. He clings to that tie any way he can. Unfortunately, I'm the tie.

"There's something even more important. As I've told you time and again, Nafie's on another planet. He can barely tell night from day."

The Doctor interrupted Maliha's account. In a trembling voice he said: "My darling Maliha, I really love you, but I have to live in the real world. I'm married to a woman from this country. We have children together and share a house and possessions. I have commitments and face consequences. Believe me, if I could get out of my marriage with Maureen, I would. I would have said goodbye to her the day I first saw you. But I can't because of my commitments. I can't just drop them. If I divorced Maureen and left my home and children, I'd lose a great deal."

"So what's the solution, then?" she said. "Has Nafie been incited by someone to suggest I get pregnant? His suggestion came out of the blue. We've lived together for a long time in the same way and we've never spoken about having children, even in passing. Where and how am I going to give him a child? How can I keep making excuses? His new idea will be another restriction to add to the many I have to put up with. This new restriction will be more stifling than all the rest. He wants someone to preserve his family name, and he's dying to become a father. How will he make his dream come true? I can't face having sex with him. We can't take on the responsibility of a child in a country where life is hard and expensive. He's failed to provide for our needs, and having a child would only add more demands. He got lucky when you turned up, otherwise we'd be in a very dire state."

"Darling," he said, "don't worry about the demands of life. If you have a baby, I'll do all I can for you and the child. The decision is yours. I'll do what I have to for Nafie's sake, and not allow you to go without anything. I'll be by your side and take on the whole burden in order to make everything easy for you. I'll help you with everything to do with the baby. Don't let worries about bringing him up or looking after him be a source of anxiety."

"It's easy for you to say that. You live far away from me in your secure house. It's me who has to bear life's many hardships. How can I have a baby when I can't look after it or even feed it? Who says a baby who's going to suffer wants to be born? Our unstable life would be a disaster for it."

"What can we do about this situation? I'm tied down by my wife, my family, and my job."

"What about the pregnancy? My body and soul are wracked with grief. I can't get physically intimate with Nafie. How can I get pregnant, then?" She started crying in despair.

"Go easy on yourself, my darling. Don't despair. I'll find a way out, don't worry."

When she heard the Doctor's words, Maliha looked at him in teary confusion. She did not fully understand what he meant by a "way out". The situation was serious and couldn't be ignored. They had entered a new stage of their affair, and were about to face an issue they hadn't considered before. They had never thought about pregnancy or having a baby. They had thought life was simple, a walkover, without consequences.

They lived in London; they celebrated their rituals at the small flat thousands of miles away from home. They enjoyed the Doctor's money and the things it bought. The two men would continue serving Maliha and making her comfortable. They both acted to avert her fury. They both longed for her kindness and affection. They both loved her madly.

Now Maliha knew the truth of what she had long tried to deny. The Doctor wanted the relationship to continue as it was. His priority wasn't saving her from the frustrations of her life. Perhaps it was the opposite. He wanted to see her split in half: half for him and half for Nafie. Being split in half made her weak; and weakness made her dependent on Nafie, diminishing her chances of freeing herself from his clutches. Maureen also knew what was going on in her husband's life away from home. She knew about his relationship with Maliha – Cynthia the receptionist had told her. She knew the details of the intimate relationship between the Doctor and the Arab lady, who met him at the surgery on her own, and that whatever went on, went on. The Doctor had fallen in love with her. When she learnt of the affair, she became a bit more accommodating. She tried to reassure herself that what he did outside the house didn't matter, and it helped that he stuck to his duties at home. He always came back, however late. He hadn't messed around with the routine of his life. She took the situation he had created in her stride. His family life was tethered to his wife and children, while his selfish ego was tied to Maliha and the time he spent with her. Maliha represented his egotistical side. Maureen stood for real life, even though it was a horribly bitter reality.

Maliha symbolized the romance and seduction of the orient. Maureen symbolized the English reality that the Doctor lived as an alien. He was caught in between the two, wanting to keep them in balance. All his thoughts and feelings revolved around that contradiction.

14

After their stormy confrontation at the surgery Maliha returned home. She intended to release Nafie from his captivity in the flat and suspected that as soon as she opened the front door, he would immediately broach the subject of having a baby. Much to her surprise, however, he ran over, took her in his arms, and begged her forgiveness. She thought his apologies would draw a line under the matter and that there would be no further talk of it seeing as she had made her unwillingness clear on account of her poor health.

But disaster struck, and again, in bed that night, he started going on about conceiving. She became furious. He was still trying it on. Every now and again he would grope her and pressure her to respond to him. He tried desperately to have sex with her, repeating his longing to father a child with her. "Listen to me, darling. We mustn't delay having children any longer. Time is flying and we're getting older. I want you to have a child who calls you Mummy. You'll make a wonderful, kind mother."

"Are you joking?" she replied. "If I was able to have a baby, I would have devoted myself to the task. I've told you my opinion innumerable times. I can't have children and am not up to getting pregnant or giving birth." She was so close to him their faces were almost touching. She pointed to her stomach and shouted: "I can't have children, I'm a failure. Do you hear? I'm chronically sick. Recognize the truth and admit it to yourself."

The scenario between Maliha and Nafie continued in this fashion. Nafie made desperate attempts to have intercourse with Maliha, and her rejection hardened. Day by day their relationship grew more fraught. She went to meet the Doctor at his surgery and asked him to deliver her from the sorry state she was in. In a low, trembling voice she said: "Listen to me, Nadim. I've been patient long enough and I can't wait any longer. My head's going to burst. My body's going to burst. I cried my eyes out last night. Nafie's still insisting. He tries to take me in bed. I'm repelled by him and put up a struggle. I've told him I don't want to get pregnant. Tell me what to do, darling? Show me the right answer. How do I deal with it? Thinking about it is making me ill."

The Doctor shock his head in bewilderment: "What induced Nafie to ask you?" The Doctor's heart was afire with jealousy. His rival wanted to land a killer blow. He visualized Nafie pawing Maliha's soft ripe body, caressing her silky smooth skin. The prospect of that soft body was so tempting for him, but not at this moment. Disaster was about to strike and it had to be stopped. How could he let his rival impregnate Maliha? How could he let him deposit his laughable seed inside his beloved? How could he allow that weak man to force her beautiful body to submit to his desires and caresses? The scene in his head was unbearable. The scenario was making him nauseous. He could imagine any eventuality except his darling lover falling prey to Nafie's plans. His jealousy came to the boil. No other man, and certainly not her husband, could be allowed to touch her.

He could assuage his jealousy, however, he thought, with a life-changing event that he had long hoped for. He would have a child from an Arab mother. A child born to an Arab mother would be different to one born to an English woman. A child to inherit from his person, and that he could make fond of Arabic poetry. He had completely failed to teach Arabic to any of his children from Maureen as she was always against the idea. She would say: "Please, don't put too much pressure on the children. Your language is strange and totally different to English. You write the letters and lines from right to left, which is the wrong way round. Arabic is not the same as English, so don't insist my kids learn it." Despite Maureen's dislike for it, he tried to teach his youngest daughter Nahla a few Arabic words and phrases, and gave her some unstructured lessons. But the girl used to say to him: "Daddy, I won't learn anything unless you give me a present or some money."

If Maliha became pregnant from him, not Nafie, his dream would come true. Maliha having his child would douse the jealousy he was feeling. He gathered his thoughts together and focused on how to go about achieving this end. Maliha had to get pregnant by him, not her husband. How could she become pregnant without Nafie realising the truth? A good solution and a secret way were needed. The subject kept the Doctor awake. He had to find a way, and fast. Nafie couldn't be allowed to impregnate Maliha before him and plant his seed in her womb. Many ideas ran through his mind, among them artificial insemination. He had to suggest it to Maliha and so he asked her to come to the surgery to discuss a very important matter.

Maliha arrived, feeling burdened down with worries. She was frightened that her life was spinning out of control and so she would not be able to direct things the way she wanted. The constant pressure had turned her into a woman whose mind was paralysed and she was barely able to tell right from wrong. Dark clouds of depression clouded her face, masking her violent temper and the fire in her eyes. She looked like a ghost. The Doctor could see the state she was in. Caught up in his own concerns, he said: "Since you mentioned getting pregnant I've been thinking like mad. I want to find a way for you to get pregnant without submitting your body to Nafie and the solution lies in artificial insemination."

"But what does that mean? I don't know," said Maliha feigning submission and compliance. She thought it best to dispense with her usual bad temper. She was as afraid of the Doctor now as he was of her, or more. She was scared he would abandon her at a critical point. "As you wish. I don't have another plan, especially as I can't sleep with him."

"But you will have to suggest the idea to him," said the Doctor. "Hopefully, he'll agree."

"Of course I'll suggest it, and I promise you he won't say no. His only interest now is in having a child with me, however it is achieved."

Maliha went home in a calmer frame of mind. She did not speak to Nafie straight away about the new plan for getting pregnant. She waited a couple of days, then went to speak to him in the living room where he was sitting in his usual place next to the trunk and crooning the words to a song by Nasri Shamseddine. She started speaking, but he did not hear her because of the music. She drew closer and shook his shoulder lightly. He turned and said in amazement: "Is everything okay? Has something happened?"

"No. Do you still want to have a baby? Let's go to the hospital and see if there are any tests that can diagnose my condition. I'm not well. God alone knows the reason but some tests might provide an answer."

Nafie was moved by the note of weakness in his wife's voice and the tone of her words. Her face was creased and pale. He looked at her with pity and felt that he was responsible for her being messed up psychologically. He felt so guilt-stricken he thought of kneeling before her and asking her forgiveness. He wanted to confess he had been wrong to press her to get pregnant and was prepared to give up the idea of having children to spare her health and wellbeing.

Now, though, it seemed things had changed in his favour. No doubt she had thought about having children and was willing to get pregnant. He had to agree to her generous offer. He had to talk to their friend Dr Nadim and ask his opinion. He was bound to have useful suggestions and advice. The Doctor didn't know much about their married life. He hadn't asked why they hadn't had children. He saw it as something private and didn't intrude. Nafie would ask the Doctor how best to go about achieving their noble aim. He and Maliha would want to go to the best hospital or fertility clinic for tests and diagnoses. Nafie answered Maliha: "You're right, and I'm overjoyed."

The Doctor came by in the evening for dinner. Nafie waited till Maliha went to the kitchen to prepare the food before talking to him. "We want your advice on an important matter," he said. The Doctor realised what he was referring to and waited to hear it from him. "Maliha and me are thinking of having a baby. We'd love a boy or a girl. We're both getting older and we'll need someone with us to face life's difficulties. Clearly there's a health issue stopping us so do tell us which hospital or fertility clinic to go to. And it would be great if you could come with us when we go and see the doctors.

The Doctor nodded: "With God's help I'll get involved." Maliha brought in the food, but over dinner the matter was not raised.

The next day, the Doctor called Nafie: "I've found a private clinic run by a well-known and very experienced doctor. He's an old friend by the name of Mr Boardman. I can get you an appointment soon. There's no reason to have to wait ages for the NHS as with them an appointment might take a year or two, maybe more." Nafie thanked the Doctor and felt delighted at the news.

When it was time for the appointment, Maliha and her husband went with Nadim for tests to diagnose their problem. Maliha had completely given in to the wishes of the two men. After all, they wanted her to get pregnant more than she did. The couple took the initial tests, and Nadim Nasra interpreted the results. "You're not well Madame Maliha, but Nafie is fine. Your wife hasn't been able to get pregnant because of a problem with her eggs. Mr Boardman thinks the only way for you to get pregnant is by artificial insemination."

"How much will it cost?" asked Nafie.

"Don't worry about the cost," said the Doctor. "I'll pay for the treatment. All you have to do is allow the medical team to do their job."

Of course, there was nothing really wrong with Maliha. The diagnosis of Nadim was just a pretence. Plus, she had been taking contraceptive pills. Artificially inseminating Maliha would give the Doctor the chance to father her child.

Dr Nadim set about implementing his plan down to the last detail. On the appointed day for the artificial insemination, the plan was put in motion. He asked Nafie to bring as much semen as he could provide for inseminating Maliha with at the clinic. Nafie was embarrassed at this innovative way of making his wife pregnant, but agreed to do what was required. He would not, however, go with his wife to the clinic. He would stay at home to ponder an extremely important question: what name to give the anticipated baby. Many names had occurred to him, such as Nafia for a girl, and Abdel Wahid for a boy. He needed to make as long a list as he could, which would take a great deal of thought and time. "I'll leave Maliha in your hands," he said to the Doctor. "Good luck."

Maliha and the Doctor left the flat early in the morning, as though she were his, and not Nafie's, wife so Nafie's absence was perfectly normal. When they arrived at the clinic, Nadim produced a bottle containing his semen and left Nafie's sample in the car. Nobody else knew about the deception, and Maliha was inseminated with Nadim's sperm. Once he had calmed down, Nadim felt happy about the whole process, while Maliha felt terribly confused.

Maliha had to go back to the clinic to check if she was pregnant. Nadim went with her, and everyone thought he was her dear husband. Nafie stayed at the flat on his own. Bluntly, he confessed to his wife: "I'm ashamed at the mechanical way I got you pregnant, that's why I'm not going to the clinic with you."

She reproached him: "You're my husband, and it's the early stages of the pregnancy."

"Damn you Maliha, how can I show my face there. The pregnancy isn't natural. If people knew, they would laugh at my manhood and think I'm impotent."

But still, Nafie felt indescribably happy. His dreams of becoming a father would soon come true. He would have a child and become a dad. His appetite for life grew. He started eating good food, and flirting with his wife. His desire to listen to macho songs also grew. Maliha would complain the volume was too high, and he would say she had to get used to loud noise, since there would soon be a baby in the house, turning everything upside down.

The medical team confirmed that Maliha was indeed pregnant, and passed on the good news to Maliha and Nadim. As her pregnancy progressed and her bump became visible, her unhappiness and dissatisfaction grew. She became prone to depression and moaned continually. She said hurtful things to both men: "Pregnancy is more difficult than I imagined. My back and my legs ache. It's a nightmare. It's exhausted me and changed me completely. The baby is spreading out inside me like an octopus. It's running through my cells like a cancer. And I'm expected to put up with all this for a whole nine months."

Nafie listened to her hurtful words and replied: "That's the Devil whispering to you. What are you saying?"

"Leave me alone," she snapped. "It's the way I feel. It's me who's pregnant, not you. You forced me to get pregnant, knowing full well how poor my health is. It was your idea for me to seek medical help. We made Dr Nadim pay exorbitant fees for the treatment. Aren't you ashamed we have had to depend on others?" On hearing her words, Nafie said nothing and avoided looking into her eyes, taking refuge in silence against her hurtful comments.

Maliha, however, did not stop. She kept up a stream of complaints around the clock. Pregnancy had brought her a lot of complications and she felt she had been forced into it. Nafie and the Doctor tried to take care of her and give her every comfort. They helped her and gave her everything she needed. Nafie cooked; he washed her feet, cut her hair, and trimmed her nails. He took her to the toilet. He consoled her when her frustration and despair overwhelmed her, but even so she spent hours on the sofa curled up in pain.

She was in a state of turmoil, and this showed in her eyes. Then one evening, when the Doctor was at the flat with them, something strange happened. Maliha got up from the sofa, her stomach bulging out as though she was carrying twins. She gave Nafie and the Doctor an irate look, pointed her finger at them, and said: "Listen, I've got something really important to say, and I hope you're going to take it seriously. I've decided to have an abortion. I don't want to carry on with the pregnancy. The weight of the baby is killing me. I can't bear it any longer. Enough! My back's breaking. I've turned myself into a factory for having children.

"In fact, I'm a surrogate mother, but surrogate mothers offer their wombs to those unable to have children in exchange for money. Where's my share? I'm asking you, where's my reward? I want lots of cash to make up for my health and mental problems. The child I'm carrying is for the sake of your happiness, dear husband. You, lying there by the bed. Yes, you, the one called Nafie. You know nothing about pregnancy, and how hard it is on the woman."

Maliha stopped speaking and the two men gradually emerged from their shock. They stood there with fear in their eyes. Nafie shook his head. "What do you mean, woman? How can you say what you're saying? God has given us a baby. It is our dream that we've waited years for. We've come a long way and you and the Doctor have worked hard on the journey."

The Doctor intervened. "Madame Maliha, what are you saying?"

Maliha tossed her head nonchalantly. "You heard what I said. Don't pretend to be deaf. It won't wash with me." She went over to the window. Since getting pregnant, she hadn't been watching the businesses and shop owners down below. She opened the window, leaving the men in shock. A deathly silence descended. Terror had struck them when they heard she wanted an abortion.

They were afraid that Maliha would do exactly what she said. They knew she paid no attention to what they said, and that if they did speak it might make matters worse and intensify her anger. They kept staring at her standing by the window. Then Nafie got a grip on his nerves and said: "Come here, and have dinner with us. Then we can discuss these hardships of pregnancy." Fortunately, Maliha agreed. She closed the window, and flung herself down on the sofa. She refused to eat, though, and her thoughts continued to come thick and fast. Nafie went over to her, and caressed her leg. A thick gloom descended, that only dissipated when the Doctor announced his intention to go home.

15

That night the Doctor left the flat upset, his heart constricted with fear and sadness at the prospect of Maliha carrying out her insane desire. He knew for certain she had suffered a great deal to get pregnant, but more importantly the baby would actually be his. He would never forget that dark evening and his thoughts dwelled on the looming calamity – Maliha having an abortion. His eyes were wet with tears. "Why does Maliha take such pleasure in hurting me so much? Doesn't she understand how attached I am to her having the baby?"

The Doctor had dreamed for so long about having an Arab child of his own flesh and blood, an Arab on both its father's and mother's side, not like his children with Maureen, who were half foreign. He had massive doubts. Would his dream come true? Would his volatile lover submit to his overwhelming longing? Would she agree to her Arab child living under his wing? A strange vision occurred to him. Maliha, in a boat on a river, carrying a child in her arms. The boat surged onwards with the swift current until it reached a stormy sea. He screamed out at the top of his voice: "Give me the child before you drown." Maliha hesitated, and he felt a shiver run through his body. The boat capsized and all those on board sank to the seabed, while he dived in to try and save them.

When the Doctor travelled into central London the next morning, he did not go straight to the surgery, but made a detour via Argos, as he usually did when Maliha was angry with him. Today, he wanted to buy baby clothes. He intended to fit out a complete room for the baby. The shop was closed, so he waited outside. As soon as the doors opened, he raced inside and started looking through the catalogue before filling out the order slip with the items he had chosen. He paid what was due and asked them to deliver the purchases to Maliha's flat. Only then did he go to the surgery.

All day he waited in trepidation for news about the abortion. He did not call Maliha and Nafie to avoid hearing what he did not want to hear: that Maliha had gone ahead and terminated the pregnancy. His phone rang and he answered, his hand shaking. He had been expecting a call from Nafie to tell him the disaster he was desperate to avert had happened. He remained in that state until the end of the afternoon. In the evening, he found Nafie and Maliha waiting for him at the flat. They were about to have dinner, and the Doctor took some comfort when it seemed Maliha's mood had improved a little. He silently thanked God that the idea of an abortion seemed to have been wiped from her mind.

Maliha spoke to the two men in a serious tone and made it clear she felt no emotional attachment to the baby growing inside her. It was puzzling to her, and she could find no explanation for it. It was a mystery. "Why do I have this strange feeling?" she asked herself. "I'm being encouraged by both Nafie and the Doctor, but I have no real desire to have a baby."

Maliha had heard a lot about how pregnant women grow attached to their unborn babies. How they would stroke their stomachs and talk to the foetus growing inside. But for her, no such desire had welled up. In fact, it had happened instead to Nafie. He often tried to touch her stomach, but she stopped him of course. She was the same with the Doctor when they met in secret; she rejected his tenderness.

Pregnant women wait impatiently for their babies to be born and are eager to buy the things the baby will need months before it is due. They choose names in advance as well as the place where they're going to give birth. Maliha, however, was experiencing none of that. She told the Doctor about her strange feelings and the detachment she felt about the baby and how she lacked all maternal feelings. He refused to accept what she was saying, dismissing it with the words: "Darling, once you give birth, everything will change, believe me. You'll see what your feelings for the baby will be like. You'll try to protect him, you'll spoil him, and you'll be full of love and tenderness for him. I promise you, Maliha. You'll remember what I'm saying. You'll be jealous of my love for him, too," adding to himself, "even though I'm his real father."

However, after all the anguish of being torn between having the baby or aborting it, Maliha finally went along with her desire to have an abortion, and found her way to a clinic.

At the reception she told the nurse, Teresa: "I've come to make an appointment for an abortion. I want to get rid of the baby growing inside me."

Nurse Teresa replied: "Why do you want an abortion? Are there medical reasons? Is your husband forcing you? Is it something private you don't want to talk about? Some women who come to this clinic for an abortion are being forced to do it by their husbands or their husband's family. It's usually to do with the baby's gender, and it happens with women from India, China, and Africa. Such families want boys not girls, and if the woman is carrying a girl, they make her have an abortion to get rid of it."

Maliha responded, stammering: "My situation is different. I was raped and am now pregnant. I don't want to have a baby whose father's identity is unknown to me. In the long term it wouldn't be right for the child. I come from a conservative family who won't accept the idea of a fatherless child being raised among them. I hid the truth about the rape from my family, as they would think it was my fault and that I'd brought it on myself. In our culture, rape is a shameful thing for the woman who's been raped, and it affects the child for the rest of their life."

"How many months pregnant are you?"

"I'm in my sixth month."

With panic in her voice, the nurse said: "I hope what I'm going to say won't dash your hopes, but your pregnancy is rather advanced so it's impossible to have an abortion. Terminating the pregnancy at this stage might damage your health. It's also against the law. You should have come to see us a long time ago, in the second or third month, and no later than the fifth. In any case you'll have to see a specialist. No doubt, he'll persuade you that what I'm saying is right. Come with me to see Dr Young."

Doctor Young repeated the same things as the nurse: "I can't possibly put your life at risk at this late stage of your pregnancy, and at the same time risk legal problems for the clinic. If you're set on not taking care of the child once it's born, you can put it up for adoption. The child will be well looked after and a family will be found for it. That's preferable to having an abortion."

Following her difficult meeting with nurse Teresa and Dr Young, Maliha returned to her flat disappointed, her will sapped, feeling more anxious than ever.

She stayed like that – her nerves on edge, in a bad mood, ready to snap whenever she spoke – until her due date arrived. She spent the night desperately fighting off contractions while Nafie stood by helplessly, unable to make her pain go away.

As dawn approached, her contractions grew stronger and closer together. Nafie called the Doctor, who dressed quickly and ran to his car. He drove through deserted streets to Shepherd's Bush. His thoughts alternated between Maliha and her pain and the boy child about to be born. The child would strengthen Nadim's relationship with Maliha because he was the child of an Arab mother for whom Nadim's heart was filled with love. He drove on through the city streets, his mind consumed with a buzz of thoughts until he reached the flat.

16

The Doctor found the couple waiting in the dark at the entrance to their block. They looked drained, with dark shadows on their faces. Maliha had wrapped her exhausted body in a red blanket. She was holding her distended stomach and moaning in pain. The Doctor's heart clenched because he could do nothing. He hurried to help her into the car and tried to calm her down. Nafie relaxed as soon as Maliha got into the car, as though all his problems were suddenly over.

"I'm very sorry," said Nafie to the Doctor, "but I can't go with Maliha to the hospital. I have to go to my damn job. I'll leave her in your care, after God's. Please look after her until she gives birth."

The Doctor was taken aback by what his odd friend was saying, but did not try to persuade him to come with them. He left him to do as he said, and set off, with Maliha sitting beside him groaning in pain. He thought about the baby about to be born and felt delighted, although he was scared about the likely complications after the birth. Would everything turn out okay? Would he fulfil his dream and have a child by an Arab woman?

Upon arriving at the hospital, the Doctor handed Maliha over to the medical team and anxiously waited outside the room in anticipation of the birth. A nurse came and asked him to go in and help Maliha cope with the pain and to encourage her. He went in, stood beside Maliha and gently took her hand in his. With his other hand he stroked her brow which was wet with sweat. The Doctor watched as the baby began to emerge, and followed intently until finally, after great exertion on Maliha's part, the baby arrived into the world. The baby screamed, as if asking for an explanation as to why he had come to this world. A nurse picked up the baby from his mother's side and placed him in the Doctor's hands.

The baby was a boy. the Doctor burst into tears of joy as soon as held him in his arms. He embraced Maliha and placed the baby on her bosom. He was moved to see at last his Arab child, whom he longed for so much. "Fantastic, darling," he said, "I can't tell you how happy I am today seeing our baby alive and well. Finally, our dream has come true."

Maliha gave him a puzzled look. Was it a look of joy or sadness? She sat up a little and tilted her head back. They remained silent for several minutes until the baby let out a loud cry. He was announcing his arrival and demanding his right to be loved and cared for.

"I've come up with the name Sameh," said the Doctor. "I chose it after intensive research in my old and modern books. I considered many beautiful names, but, praise God, Sameh stuck in my mind. Do you agree?" Maliha said nothing, and he continued: "If you have another name you prefer, there's no problem." She just gave a nod to indicate her agreement to the name. The nurse asked the Doctor to register the baby at the hospital office. Without hesitation, the Doctor went and registered the child as Sameh Nadim Nasra, disregarding any problems this might cause the child in future, and the Doctor too, especially when Nafie found out. But his paternal feelings overcame his rational mind.

The Doctor became obsessed with Sameh. He could not believe his impossible love affair with Maliha had resulted in a child. The dear baby had been born despite Maliha's attempt to have an abortion. Fate had delivered Sameh in order to bring joy to the heart of a father long accustomed to sadness. The Doctor was determined to play a big part in bringing him up. Everything was set up: he would be a loving father, bringing up his son.

That evening, Nafie went with the Doctor to visit Maliha at the hospital. Nafie picked up the baby and said, smiling: "I've decided on the name Abdel Wahid, Maliha." She was deathly quiet, but the Doctor rescued the situation by saying: "My brother Nafie, Maliha has chosen the name Sameh, and he's been registered under that name." Nafie nodded and made no objections: "Let it be Sameh then, God bless him."

Two days after giving birth, Maliha and Sameh left the hospital in the company of the Doctor. Nafie was at home, impatiently waiting for them in line with a plan he had agreed with the Doctor to welcome Maliha and Sameh home. On the way, Maliha's state of confusion was indisputable. The Doctor did not ask her why she seemed so distant, but assumed she was tired after the birth.

The Doctor loved Middle Eastern customs and traditions, and it was his family's tradition to sacrifice an animal to God on joyous occasions. As a result, he had agreed with Nafie to bring a lamb from Zein Market. The plan was for Nafie to cut the lamb's throat the moment Maliha crossed the threshold in celebration of the new-born baby and to ward off the evil eye. Everything was going to plan: Maliha entered the flat, and Nafie emerged with the lamb under one arm and holding a knife in his other hand. The Doctor had bought the correct knife this time to prevent a repeat of their previous mistake.

Maliha had frequently said she could not bear the brutality of ritual slaughter and the spectacle of blood spurting out. Nafie threw the lamb to the floor and gave the knife a quick sharpen. He was about to slaughter it, when their neighbour with a limp, Noel, who had heard the lamb bleating, stuck his head round the open front door. As soon as he took in the scene before him, he shouted: "My God! What are you doing to that poor creature? Are you going to kill it? That's against the law. Haven't you heard of abattoirs? In this country, animals are slaughtered at an abattoir. Why don't you do that? Why are you making your neighbours see this?"

Nafie did not respond, but continued in his effort to slaughter the animal. Noel, however, leapt over, grabbed the knife out of Nafie's hand, and threw it to the floor. In a determined tone he said: "The animal has to go back where it came from. If you don't do that, I'll call the police." There was nothing Nafie could do but comply with the demand of the old man. The Doctor said nothing; he was aware how awkward the situation had become, and remembered what had happened when he had carried the carcass from Zein Market on the train. He couldn't do anything like that again. He felt disappointed, but fortunately, it had been old Noel who had stopped them, and not another elderly neighbour, Frank, who couldn't stand the presence of foreigners in the block. Frank had made numerous complaints to the estate office because of the loud music Nafie played.

Once this scene in the doorway had ended, things calmed down. Nafie manoeuvred the lamb back along the corridor, feeling extremely embarrassed and disappointed. The Doctor started blaming himself for trying to do something against the law. How could he have bought a lamb and dared to try and slaughter it, at home, in public? And in a country whose laws he well knew forbade slaughter except in designated places.

If the sacrifice had gone ahead, the neighbours would have called the police and taken legal steps that might have threatened his status as a doctor. He went back into the flat in a state of great confusion. It had all arisen because of his overwhelming love for Maliha. He thought for a while and then burst into tears. He went quickly to the bathroom to contain himself, and then joined the couple in the living room with the baby.

After all the confusion accompanying Maliha and Sameh's arrival at the flat, things calmed down. The Doctor and Nafie vied with each other to help Maliha. One of them would fetch her water, the other food, and both of them asked her if she needed anything. Between the pair of them, Maliha stopped eating and drinking, and rather than thanking them she scolded them severely, saying: "Please, I'm fed up with you asking me what I need. The Good Lord gave me strong legs and I can use them to go wherever I want. Listen carefully to what I have to say, as I'm not going to repeat it, my dears. I've come home and will try to recover from the exhaustion of pregnancy and labour. I've been suffering for nine months. Now I want some time out so it's best if you just leave me alone. Look after Sameh, if you want to help me. What happened just now was stupid, and could have landed us in prison. It really was irresponsible behaviour on your parts, but luckily it turned out okay. Why did you risk doing it, when you both know the law? You especially, Doctor, know enough not to do something like that."

The Doctor felt ashamed and tried to defend himself: "But, Madame Maliha, our family celebrates like that to ward off envy." He turned to Nafie and continued: "Isn't that right, Nafie?"

In a weak voice, Nafie answered: "Yes, in our country, families celebrate a new arrival like that. After the sacrifice, you have to dip a finger into the blood and smear a drop on the baby's forehead."

"Whatever," said Maliha. "Just let the animal go, do you hear! Or else I'll go to the police myself and tell them you've got a lamb here and are planning to slit its throat. If you want to enjoy your old rites, it'd be better to look for somewhere like Amini the Somali and his wife Janet's place. A house with a big garden, a space stretching as far as you can see. Then and only then can you do what you like, slaughter a whole flock or do whatever other stupid things you have in mind. If you really want to celebrate the birth of Sameh and us coming home safely, why doesn't the Doctor spill the blood at his own large house in his big garden? He could do the sacrifice and bring us the meat to share out with our friends and neighbours?"

The Doctor responded, directing his words at Maliha: "The blood has to be spilled at the threshold of the house where the newborn is, that's what brings blessings, and that's why I didn't do the sacrifice at my own house. I swear, it would be an honour for me to slaughter the animal in my garden, even if my English family objected. But the sacrifice has to be done here."

Maliha was furious: "I've heard enough of your harebrained ideas."

The two men were perturbed by Maliha as she looked daggers at them. They were scared of her rage. That day, the Doctor stayed with the couple and the baby until it was his usual time to leave. He felt extremely sad about Maliha's state of mind. It should have been a joyous day of celebration, but it had turned into something dreadful. They had all been waiting for Sameh's arrival to spread delight around the flat that had been empty and sad.

Maliha was in a bad mood when Nafie and the Doctor had been feeling jubilant. She kept quiet, but her feelings towards Sameh were unchanged. She decided not to allow a smile to cross her lips. She did not smile at the baby or play with him. There was no emotional link between mother and child. She took care of him as though she were his babysitter. She was convinced Nafie and Dr Nadim had forced her to get pregnant for their own selfish pleasure and to brag about the baby in front of people, the Doctor in particular. They were both using the poor child to prove their manhood.

At the end of the evening, the Doctor left Nafie and Maliha on the threshold of a new stage in their lives. He felt they were like two people expecting a violent sandstorm or massive flood. His joy was tinged with sadness, and he wished his son could live in a happy family, far away from the damaging effects of his mother's emotional turmoil.

17

Maliha felt feverish all night. She did not sleep a wink as she was constantly waking up to comfort her baby, who was screaming the house down. She had to feed and change him in a state of extreme agitation and exhaustion. This difficult situation went on until dawn. Feeling miserable, she just could not take it any longer. She left the bedroom with her hair in a mess and her eyes swollen. As sad as if taking him to the grave, she carried the baby with trembling hands.

She found her husband in the living room fast asleep. He opened his eyes and looked at her in astonishment. Poor Nafie did not know how desperate his wife had become and that she rejected her baby. She had woken him roughly and had to vent her anger. She talked about her baby nervously and with disgust: "Take the child otherwise I'll lose my mind. I can't bear his crying anymore. My head's going to burst. I've done everything to make him shut up, but he keeps on screaming. I've fed him, winded him and changed him, but it's useless. I'm not used to sleeping with all this screaming and crying. Take him away from me as I've reached boiling point. Wasn't it you who forced me to have him? Take him, and do with him as you want. You were waiting for his arrival like a cat on a hot tin roof, now here he is in front of you. He's yours to do with as you please. After today I won't help you anymore. Sameh is your responsibility, I'm just not up to it. I've done my duty by bearing you a healthy baby. Now it's your turn to deal with everything."

Nafie had no idea what had caused the storm raging over his head. He answered in a hoarse voice with great difficulty: "But, darling, the baby is yours, and you're his mother. No one else in the world will look after him like you. That's a mother's role. I'm a man, and men don't know how to take care of babies, especially when they're breastfeeding."

"I've got nothing more to say," she said. "He's yours and you have complete freedom. I'm going to live in peace, and avoid the toil of looking after him and the problems of bringing him up."

"What about breastfeeding?" asked Nafie sarcastically. "You want me to breastfeed him, too? Your baby is in desperate need of your milk. It's his only source of nourishment at this stage."

"Unfortunately, I have to tell you I won't be doing that, and I don't care what people think. I won't struggle just for them to think I'm a decent mother. I really don't feel any love towards him, and I won't take care of him whatever you do. I shall do exactly what I feel like. I can't take it anymore. I feel I'm paying the price for someone else's mistake."

Nafie shook his head in sorrow at Maliha's words, and started comforting Sameh who was crying loudly, as though he understood what his mother had said and wanted to punish her, but did not know the words. When the sun came up, Nafie moved Sameh's things from the bedroom into the living room. He did not discuss it with Maliha because he realised there was no point.

That day marked the beginning of a long road in the relationship between Nafie and Sameh. Nafie feed him, cleaned him, and educated him. He changed his clothes and stayed awake with him. Dr Nadim examined the boy and brought everything needed for his health, such as his formula milk, as well as plenty of toys and presents. He loved him from the heart. The living room was alive with activity and chaos as a result of all the toys, while the get-togethers of the three friends changed. Conversation revolved around Sameh, and his every action became the main concern.

Maliha remained outside those conversations and gatherings. She never felt any bond with Sameh, and as he grew up the two of them only grew further apart. The neighbours often criticised Maliha and reproached her for her lack of concern for her own child. Her response was to get upset and scream and fly off the handle.

One night she screamed at Nafie and the Doctor, repeating her words of rejection and defiance. She posed new angry questions: "Why doesn't one of you at least understand me? A mother's love isn't spontaneous, welling up in her heart at the moment of birth. She doesn't just fall in love when the baby kicks inside her. It's more complicated than that, gentlemen. Are you unaware of that, or are you just ignoring it? That kind of love is deep and one of its causes is the mother looking forward to the birth and being mentally and emotionally prepared for a baby. But poor old me, I was forced to have a baby. It's divine wisdom that I will never love Sameh. You both have to admit the truth and realise that God's will was for things to change. You, Doctor, I think you know a great deal, as you claim, and you must know something about psychological complexes. It'd be better for you to admit it than to exhaust me with blame. There are things in life contrary to the norm, and this is one of those things that you think is against nature, but that you both have to live with. If I had just one wish, it would be that the pair of you were in my shoes and felt the way I do. It hurts so much. Just leave me be, please."

The days, months, and years passed by and things remained the same. Sameh grew up and the emotional void between him and his mother grew too. When he turned five, it was time for him to start school. He had endured all the family problems and had been affected by his mother's temper. Despite the distance between them, Maliha intervened in this particular matter. She thought it best for Sameh to go to a private school, and proposed the idea to the Doctor. She was afraid that Sameh's education would suffer at a state school as had happened with her. All she asked from the Doctor was to send Sameh to a private school. The Doctor rejected the idea with unpersuasive justifications, and this caused a serious clash between them, the likes of which had not happened before, even over their most intimate dealings. Perhaps the maternal instinct had kicked in and broken through the emotional barriers. That powerful instinct made Maliha desperate to defend her son's interests. She would never accept the Doctor's point of view, especially as she knew the miserable fate awaiting her son in state schools.

"I know I've had nothing to do with Sameh's upbringing," she said, "and that what I'm going to say will surprise you. I know you'll wonder why I'm suddenly interested in him. You and Nafie have raised him as well as any mother could, but I'm asking you to send him to a private school and give him a chance. If you really love him, you must protect him from the risks of state schools. Then you will have fulfilled your role."

"But Maliha," replied the Doctor, "do you realise what you're saying? Private education isn't an advantage, the cons outweigh the pros, don't you know? Private education will alienate Sameh from his background. Around here, nobody sends their children to private schools, unless the child is exceptionally clever. And in any case, those children get scholarships from the government or a school. Going to a private school will almost completely isolate him from his environment, and I don't believe you want that. I will never allow it, because it's not in his interest. Sameh would never forgive me when he grows up. Sending him to a private school will make him a stranger in his own society and cause him social and psychological problems. I promise you, it's not the right thing to do. Let's trust in God and send him to an ordinary school and see what happens."

Her eyes flashing anger and her voices dripping contempt, Maliha retorted: "You're not being honest. I'm certain you care more for your money than you do for him. Do you want me to believe you're worried about him going to a private school? That doesn't make sense. It's your greed and meanness that are standing in his way, and if you want the truth, it's you being a miser that has affected him. You're always worried about becoming worse off and returning to the poverty you knew before. We both know that. Didn't you refuse to marry me because you were scared that getting divorced would cost you a lot? Isn't that the way you look at things? What has poor Sameh done wrong? Trust me, I won't let your wrong-headed thinking mess him up."

The Doctor answered in annoyance: "God, you're so wrong. Everything you've worked out is a product of your fertile imagination. I won't back down. Think it over, and you'll see it's not in his interest. Putting Sameh in a private school will take him away from you and from his background. I don't intend to do that because it's not sensible and lacks any rationale. I swear that if Sameh knew what was best for him, he'd take my point of view, but unfortunately he's still too young. Sameh fits in here, at Nelson Mandela House, and he'll carry on living in this flat and growing up in this neighbourhood around Goldhawk Road, in Shepherd's Bush. He'll love this place and play with the neighbours' kids, the kids of Hanem Ahmed, Ruqiya Saber, Niemat Abdel Ilah, and Vanessa Ayman. Imagine the pain it would cause him to be separated from them. It would be so wrong of us to deprive him of his friends and his background. Private schools have a different social ethos than what he's used to. An ethos that aims to put children into a high social class. That's what English schools do to people, particularly the kind of school you have in mind for Sameh. Those schools divide people in terms of class and knowledge in exchange for vast sums of money in fees in order to buy an education that I can see no justification for. They drum what they call received pronunciation into the pupils, and say that that lets people know how clever and posh you are. That accent is like a social façade that you confidently take with you everywhere you go just to prove to people how much has been spent on your education. That accent is just snobbery and nothing do with education and culture. You'll cause Sameh to be socially and culturally isolated even after he's grown up. He'll find that he's different to you and Nafie and the neighbours."

Maliha responded in a loud and defiant tone: "You're a hypocrite, Doctor. Let me say it out loud, a great big hypocrite, and you don't deserve to be in the position you're in. I've only just realised the truth about you. You're two-faced, by God, that is spot on. Your children from that English woman, Maureen, didn't you spend money and have them privately educated? You weren't worried about them turning out with split personalities like you are for Sameh. Can you deny it? You told me you loved them and sent them to private schools. Go on, tell me, how did you make up these lame excuses? Sameh really needs a private education. It'll help him learn and have confidence. Who knows, one day he might be a famous scientist. There's no harm in Sameh moving up the social scale. The problem is with society. It's only Sameh's right, Doctor, to be given such a precious opportunity, one he'll be proud of when he grows up and when he remembers his loving father who gave him that chance. We live in a class-ridden society and those who do well at school and develop their personality survive, while those who don't get a slice of the pie fade away and disappear. Do you want Sameh to survive or disappear? Do you want him to end up like me and Nafie because he's poorly educated? Admit it, Dr Nadim, your excuses are flimsy and not based on fact. Distancing Sameh from his background isn't sufficient reason to deprive him of such an opportunity. Money comes and goes, and you prefer money over your son."

Having clarified her view, Maliha went on to deal with other difficult subjects that were making her even angrier. She blamed the Doctor for not having helped her escape the poverty she was living day after day. The Doctor could have done that but had not tried, she claimed. He also had the power to rescue her from her marriage. At that point Maliha remembered what Nafie had said to her about loving her until death, and she wept bitterly as her feelings confronted her and left her not knowing what to do. Did Nafie really love her? Did the Doctor really love her?

Maliha imagined herself alone in a boat on the open sea. There was no captain and she was at the helm. In the vast expanse around her no land could be seen. The sky was dark with rain clouds and waves were pounding the boat, tossing it left and right. A huge wave struck the boat and split it in two. She saw the Doctor in one half and Nafie in the other and a vast and bottomless chasm between them. She tried to cling on to the wreckage, but she was too weak. She shouted but no sound came out of her mouth.

She kept looking around herself, unable to understand the riddles entangling her life.

In a desperate effort to calm her down, the Doctor said in a steady voice: "My God, Maliha, you don't see it the way I do. I know about education, and I'm only doing what's best for Sameh.

I'm not worried about my money. I swear I love you and love Sameh and would never let anything bad happen to either of you. Sameh is the product of our love, he's my son, a piece of me. If I thought it was right to send him to a private school, I would do it even if I had to borrow money from the bank. I promise you it's nothing to do with money. One day, we'll see Sameh a doctor or engineer. Then our happiness will be complete. His place in society will never be low or affected by going to a state school. Their only aim is education. I'm an example myself of someone whose education was at state schools, and my social standing isn't low, and I know a lot."

But Maliha shot back: "No one could out-talk you, that's for sure, but the matter remains as it was, and right is right. Believe me, I've nothing left to add and, please, no more lame excuses. You're just a hypocrite. I got pregnant with Sameh and suffered because you made me. But I won't let you ruin his future. Just be sure there'll be a high price to pay. This time you won't escape my deadly anger."

18

Maliha began behaving in a lamentable way, severely depressed, moody, and with a violent temper. Sometimes she talked to herself like a madwoman, and she became very forgetful. When she suffered such an episode, she could be found in the street looking closely at goods on display in the shop windows, arguing with herself about the prices as if an invisible salesman was standing next to her. She mostly lost interest in her relationship with the Doctor, even though he was still passionate about her. Their relationship started to unravel. The Doctor tried to patch things up while Maliha would be tearing them apart. Ultimately, he gave in and left things to her. He was content to sit in his surgery and wait for her. But she did not come, and her cruel abandonment of him hurt. What hurt him most was not being able to bring her back to what she had been like before, although he tried everything possible.

In the past, patching up their relationship meant expensive presents, which she had always loved, but that no longer worked. In despair the Doctor wrote poetry and in his misery sang songs. He composed verses about abandonment and longing. That was the only consolation for his distress and anguish. When he complained to his friends, he would recite to them tearfully:

"*The spiders of your abandonment breed in the abandoned cave of my heart.*

The flame means nothing in the blind man's eye.
I leave my steps behind
and go into myself,
but how can I walk then?"

Nafie, on the other hand, had become very attached to Sameh and loved him dearly. His love acted as a balm for him and helped him face the marital problems that had always frustrated him.

Time sped by and Sameh was growing up under the care of Nafie and the watchful eyes of the Doctor. However, he was very confused and terribly unsure. He would look at Maliha and not know who she was, since she had scarcely given him any love and attention. He would look at Nafie and the Doctor and not know which of them was his father. As he grew older, his confusion increased because of the strange circumstances he was living in. He was confused by what he heard from his friends about their families and the love that bound them together. He was always making comparisons between them and his own sad family life. This made him feel insecure and unhappy. In that broken home he lost any sense of belonging.

But Sameh did sense the Doctor's love for him and reciprocated that love. His feelings towards Nafie and Maliha, however, were the opposite. He had doubts that they were really his mother and father, and were instead his aunt and uncle or some other relation. He often wondered when he would find his real parents and leave behind the tense atmosphere at home. The Doctor came by every day, and after dinner would read him stories and then leave. Sameh always wanted to go with him and hear more stories.

In fact, Sameh felt more attached to the Doctor than he did to Nafie and Maliha since they did not read him stories and could not help him with his homework. Dr Nadim helped him with his homework and explained historical events to him and taught him about the legacy of ancient civilizations. He told him the reasons for the wars that had broken out between the Arab states that had led to divisions.

He often talked to Sameh about the Palestinian *nakba* that had caused the Palestinian diaspora. When he explained that painful historical event, the Doctor would weep bitterly as though the tragedy was fresh in his memory. "Sameh, do you know that many Palestinian families left the keys of their homes under the doormat in the belief they would be back in a few weeks? But the invader occupied the houses by force of arms and the real owners had to go into exile."

With a child's innocence, Sameh asked: "What happened to the children's toys? Did the enemy take them and give them to other children?"

With a lump in his throat, the Doctor answered: "Yes, Sameh. All their possessions fell into the hands of the occupier, the houses and the toys. They were taken by force and given to those not entitled to them. That's oppression and injustice."

The stories and histories stimulated Sameh and ignited his wild imagination to learn more about events. The child had a sharp mind and loved asking questions as much as he did hearing and discussing the answers.

The Doctor did not neglect the importance of Arabic language for Sameh, and spoke to him in Arabic, and explained its grammar and style. Sameh would wait for the Doctor, who had become both his teacher and his friend, to arrive. He even took to calling him Dad. He would impatiently await his arrival at the flat to be led into the world of the imagination, which in the Doctor's absence was completely lacking. The time Sameh spent at home without the Doctor mostly involved listening to stirring songs and watching television. The television was on night and day with Nafie sitting and watching until the small hours, leaving Sameh feeling very lonely.

Every day, when the time came for the Doctor to leave, Sameh would beg him to stay: "I want to go with you, Dad, so you can tell me stories. Don't leave me on my own."

Hearing Sameh's words was heart-wrenching for the Doctor, and he would hug and kiss him. He would usually tell him another story or two to calm him down, and then sneak home without Sameh being aware. But soon enough Sameh would discover the Doctor had left, and he would start crying again, stamping the ground with his feet and becoming hysterical, trying to hurt himself and break things. If Nafie tried to calm him down, he would shout: "I want my Dad."

Directing his words at Nafie and Maliha, Sameh declared: "You're not my Dad, and she's not my Mum. My Dad is my uncle Nadim Nasra. He buys me toys and sweets, and reads me great stories and does my homework with me. You don't love me like he does. You ignore me and just watch the TV. Can't you leave me alone and let me go with him. He loves me and I love him."

Sameh said this while crying his eyes out. Nafie stood by helplessly, convinced that much of what Sameh was saying was true. He tried to calm him down, taking him to bed and reading him a story, but it was one that was not really for children, with little feeling in it. To try and improve their cool relationship Nafie said to Sameh: "Tomorrow, I'll take you to a fast food place and we'll have a delicious burger and fries and a strawberry shake. Wouldn't that make you happy?"

"Hamburgers are bad for you," replied Sameh. "That's what my Dad says and he recommends I don't eat them. He says they're junk food with no nutritional value."

"But who's going to tell the Doctor we went to the restaurant?" said Nafie. "He'll never know."

Poor Sameh was an innocent child easy to persuade. He nodded in agreement and laughed, forgetting everything he had just said as he flung himself into Nafie's arms and hugged him tenderly. "But, Sameh, where did you learn to come out with such things. Who said I'm not your Dad and Maliha's not your Mum? Who said such nonsense? If you tell us who said this, your Uncle Nadim will be very happy and get you more toys."

"People say it," he replied. "They say you're not my parents. My friends Lamar, Anas, Clare, and Su Ling told me, and said I shouldn't tell anyone."

When Nafie heard this he felt extremely sad and full of regret that he had made Maliha get pregnant. He felt he was the reason behind Sameh's emotional problems and felt very guilty. "That's not true, my boy," he said. "I'm your Dad. How could you believe something like that? Isn't it me who stays up all night with you when you're not well? Don't I feed you and take you to school and bring you back home?"

Unconvinced, Sameh answered: "You don't love me like Dr Nadim. He loves me a lot, and says I'm the apple of his eye."

This serious discussion took place in Maliha's hearing, but she said nothing. She was content just to observe and didn't even try to convince Sameh she was his mother. In fact, she agreed with what he had said, and if it had been up to her she would have sided with him against Nafie. All she did was go to her room, leaving Nafie to negotiate his fate with Sameh.

The feelings Sameh fostered towards his parents resulted in Nafie talking frankly with the Doctor. He went to the surgery and told him what the boy had said. "As you can see, Doctor, Sameh is disturbed and full of doubts. He says his friends at school say I'm not his Dad, that you are. I don't know what to do to keep Sameh emotionally stable."

The Doctor's response was to say: "I'm not sure what's the right thing to do, either. How can I convince a child I'm not his father?"

Appearing to show a great deal of sense for once, Nafie said: "Doctor, I have an idea. You tell me whether it's good or bad. I think we have to go along with what Sameh says, and pretend you're his father. It's important Sameh grows up psychologically healthy."

The Doctor was astonished. He was delighted when he realised that this would allow Sameh to grow up knowing he was his father. But he kept control of himself and hid his feelings from Nafie. "Your idea is a good one," replied the Doctor, "and as you said, let's pretend that this is the case for Sameh's sake. It won't do anyone any harm." He remembered the birth certificate that backed up the pretence and showed Sameh was legally registered with the Doctor as his father. Now there was a golden opportunity to tell everyone Sameh was actually his son and not Nafie's. Now he could live the situation he had striven to bring about for so long. Sneakily, the Doctor said: "Nafie, we can change the birth certificate from Sameh Nafie to Sameh Nadim. It's very easy and no problem. Sameh is what matters, and as you know his mood is having a bad effect on his education. Rest assured, doing that tiny thing will improve his performance at school."

As usual Nafie did not argue with the Doctor. "As you see fit," he said. "It's only a piece of paper which means little when we both know I'm his father. I just want to ask whether having him recognized as your son might not cause you problems in the long run. I know that lots of people who adopt children don't want to have them declared their own children, because of potential problems with inheritance when they die. You're comfortably off and have children and a British family with legal rights."

With a broad smile on his face, the Doctor said: "My brother Nafie, who gets to inherit from me, and who doesn't, won't cause me any harm once I'm dead. I'll be resting in peace in my grave, oblivious to it all. Any legal battle will be down to them. In any case, I've already arranged for each of my children to get their share. That's all settled, then, and I don't think Sameh will encounter any difficulties in that regard. What's important now is his psychological well-being, which has started to affect his marks at school. You know I want him to go to a good university to study medicine. We ought to worry about that rather more than problems of inheritance down the line."

The next day, the two men sat down with Sameh. The Doctor looked Sameh in the eye and said: "My son, we want to talk to you about something important. Now that you're a big boy, we have to tell you this. Sameh, I am your Dad and I have always loved you. We didn't tell you because it's very complicated. Do you understand what I'm saying?"

Sameh heard, but couldn't quite take it in. Conflicting expressions of joy, shock, and amazement were visible on his face, but joy and delight soon shone through. He got up and started spinning around and jumping up and down as he repeated: "I knew it. I knew it. So, Uncle, you're my Dad from now on. So why don't I go home with you every day if you're my Dad? Don't you love me? Why do I have to live here with Uncle Nafie, while you live on your own. I want you to take me with you wherever you go. I want to live with you. Take me with you, and we can come and visit Maliha and Nafie every day."

The Doctor became very nervous and avoided looking Sameh in the eye as he answered: "I live in a special department for doctors, and my circumstances don't permit me to have you live with me. It's a place only for doctors, and children can't stay there. I promise I'll come and see you every day and play with you. And some day you'll come with me, God willing. Your Uncle Nafie will be here instead of me, and if you need anything, just ask him."

The little boy was quiet for a while as he took this in. He looked at his "Uncle" Nafie and then threw himself into the Doctor's arms. As the days passed, Sameh became calmer and his school marks gradually improved because he had found the lost half of himself. His temper tantrums ceased and he stopped slapping himself as he had done when the Doctor was about to leave. He accepted the new arrangement and adjusted to it. In the past he had been afraid when the Doctor left because there was no one else to explain his homework. Now he started to rely on himself.

Sameh started imagining a new and beautiful world that he would explore with his young mind. He imagined the house he was destined to live in with his father once he left the doctors' residence. He saw a faraway place on the edge of a dense forest where he imagined playing with the many tame animals that grazed there.

Sameh was comfortable with the seemingly convincing explanation he had been given that he was living with his adoptive parents, Nafie and Maliha. Over time, a dream that had impinged on his thoughts since early childhood began to fade. In that dream Dr Nadim came in a large car to take Sameh and his clothes and toys to a beautiful place where he played every evening after dinner. He imagined himself sitting in the back of the car while the Doctor drove and they both waved goodbye to Nafie and Maliha. His happiness transported him to the clouds. But soon enough he would wake from his dream and feel downhearted when he looked at Nafie and Maliha. When would his torment end and he find himself somewhere like that beautiful garden surrounded by happiness and full of delight?

19

The three friends, Nafie, Maliha, and the Doctor continued living this bizarre vicious circle of despairing monotony for so long it verged on madness. Over these years, the Doctor's feelings for Maliha did not change, but still burnt as hot as they had at the start. Now, getting to the end of his patience, he would wait impatiently to be in her flat, the only place he ever found the chance to be in tune with his feelings. At the flat he could also see his beloved son although he still hated that Nafie was looking after Sameh or showing love for him.

Maliha, on the other hand, did not leave her bedroom. She no longer knew anything about Sameh and his school or personal life. Nafie and Sameh almost lived in the living room. The Doctor would come and sit with them and plan Sameh's future with Nafie. They would discuss how he was doing and how they envisaged his future and the Doctor said Sameh should choose medicine as he was a brilliant student with a good memory. Nafie just agreed, obediently.

Days and years seemed to pass in a flash. Sameh progressed through the stages of his education, always achieving high marks and prizes for getting distinction. With the Doctor's support, he passed his A-levels with flying colours. He was about to embark on a new step that would define his future life: the new world of university learning and relationships. Following lengthy discussions, the Doctor persuaded him to study medicine, as he had wanted. And so Sameh began his long journey. He left the flat where he had grown up and said goodbye to his family of three. He was going to live in student accommodation in a city about two hours from London by train. Once he had settled in, he wrote to them all the time, sending letters and photos of the campus and of his new friends and fellow students.

* * *

The three friends went back to their old ways. They ate dinner around the tray on the low round table, as they had done before Sameh came into the world. They ate meat from the monthly supply by the same butcher on Moscow Road. Things carried on monotonously for another few years, and then lightning struck.

One night the three friends were having dinner as usual when the Doctor received a phone call. "Are you the husband of Maureen?"

"Yes," said the Doctor. "Who is this?"

"It's the Metropolitan Police, Sir. We have to inform you that your wife has been in a bad accident. She is currently in intensive care."

The Doctor raced to the hospital, but it was too late. Maureen had died. She had been on her way to Heathrow Airport by train to fly off on holiday to the Bahamas, but the train had derailed, colliding head-on with another coming from the opposite direction.

The Doctor was in a state of shock for quite a while following his wife's funeral, and his relationship with his children gradually weakened. They each had their own lives in the city, enjoying themselves, and had only stayed in touch at home because they loved their mother, while they had little affection for their father. Now the Doctor lived on his own in the large house. He had complete freedom with nobody asking him what he was doing or watching his comings and goings. He still spent most of his evenings with Maliha and Nafie at their flat, but now paid no attention to how late it got. Over time, he neglected the upkeep of his house and the place became semi-derelict and full of dust. The Doctor realised he had to stop the situation getting worse, as his neglect might result in the trees and lawn dying off, or becoming overgrown, and detract from the house's value. He started spending most of his time there, so sacrificing the pleasant evenings with the woman he loved. After thinking long and hard about the situation and the challenges facing him, the Doctor had a strange proposal to put to Nafie and Maliha: that they come and live with him at his house. Before revealing the plan to them, he had gone and bought a tent, which he had set up in the garden for Maliha as a separate and private place for her. He had also bought another bed from Argos.

Then he told them his idea, hesitating before blurting out: "I propose you leave the flat." Then he shut up for a moment.

Nafie and Maliha heard what he said, but could not believe their ears. In total confusion they replied as one: "Leave the flat?" Maliha continued, "And go where, Doctor? We belong here in Nelson Mandela House. We don't know anywhere else."

"You will come and live with me," stammered the Doctor. "You've lived too long in this cramped flat. I'm now living on my own, as you know, and my house is big enough for a hundred people. I feel lonely, and I'm getting old. Taking the train here and back every day is too much for me. It's so tiring, and I'm afraid our friendship will end if we stop meeting. We've been friends for more than twenty years, and I don't want our relationship to peter out at the end of my life. Please, you have to move in with me, without hesitation, and soon."

Giving a sidelong glance at Maliha and fearful that his view might not match hers, Nafie replied: "That would be great, Doctor. No, Maliha?"

Maliha said nothing. She was fed up with constant suggestions and strange ideas, but felt she had no choice. She was a woman who had complied with the orders and wishes of others for so long that expressing a different opinion made no difference. Ultimately, it was in the hands of the domineering Doctor and her husband Nafie, who followed him blindly.

The next morning, the Doctor arrived ready to discuss the date and arrangements for the move. "What have you decided?" he asked. "Will you leave the flat?"

"Doctor," said Nafie, "are you sure about this? Won't your children be put out by strangers in the house? It's the house they grew up in with their mother, and I doubt they would want strangers living there."

"My children have left, and aren't coming back," said the Doctor. "I haven't been in touch with them much since their mother died. In any case they don't want to live with me. Do you know how exhausting it's been taking the train? To be honest, I've thought about selling the surgery and giving up work for good. I want to concentrate on my other interests, poetry, literature and other things. A few weeks ago, a medical company asked me if I wanted to sell the surgery to a group of young doctors who are looking to start a practice. I think I'll say yes. They offered quite a sum and it's tempting. With that money I could live a good life with you in my spacious house. I can leave medicine behind, and leave the dirt of London behind, too. Its streets are full of rubbish, hardened criminals and drug pushers. I want to move on with my life and make a fresh start with you. It's something I've wanted to do for decades."

"You know your situation best, Doctor," said Nafie. "In fact, it's a tempting offer for us and we're happy to accept. Maybe we'll also make a fresh start in the most beautiful, quietest and poshest suburb of London."

Nafie and Maliha prepared to move. A week later, the Doctor used his key to the flat for the last time, locking the front door, and thereby bringing to an end a significant period in all their lives and inaugurating a new one. He shed a single nostalgic tear for the home that had reminded him of his country. He kept the key in his pocket as a memento, swearing not to give it back to the housing office. They left the flat that had been the site of momentous events: the Doctor falling in love with Maliha, the dinners together, and Sameh's birth and his childhood years. The three friends left in the Doctor's car which was filled with their few household possessions, some frozen meat and plastic flowers. They did not forget the round copper tray table, of course. They headed for Richmond, a calm and pleasant drive away.

So much about them had changed over the years from when the two men had been running after Maliha. The Doctor, Nafie, and Maliha were now all physically and mentally exhausted – each with their own reasons. Nafie, because of his habit of sitting in front of the cassette player and eating fatty food, which he did to lessen his fear of Maliha and calm himself. His body had become very flabby and rounded out like a woman's. His thighs and chest had filled out, and his belly had swelled like a pregnant woman's. His face had become round like a ball, and he was losing his hair and going bald. His movements and his walk were slow due to his weight. He often had an inane smile on his face that revealed the few real teeth he had left, together with a mass of gold crowns. His real teeth were rotten on account of all the sweets he ate and not brushing them enough. His clothes were worn and he paid little attention to his personal hygiene. He wore a baggy woollen jumper that was frayed and full of holes, and loose trousers held up by a belt. But who cared anyway?

The worst thing was that he took no interest in his health. The Doctor had often explained to him just how risky his lifestyle was and told him how he would die a slow death. Nafie would reply that, God willing, he would change, but in no time he would always resume his old habits.

The Doctor, on the other hand, was afflicted with the pain of exile and consumed by feelings of sadness. His long period away from the Arab world could not be compensated for by the poems he had written over the years expressing his longing and home-sickness. His love for Maliha had symbolized the mystique of the orient and grew only stronger. He tried to get close to her again as she was all that remained of his old world. But she had grown away from him, mentally, emotionally, and even physically, because he did not fulfil her demands. She no longer liked meeting with him. Whenever their hands brushed, a shiver went through her and she pulled away. When he tried to have sex with her, she was like a sheep being led to the slaughter and submitted completely. All that only increased his sadness and made him feel terrible. Despite this he clung to her and vowed never to give up on her. He was like a drowning man fighting off the waves, or a man lost in the desert without food or water. Where was the safety of shore? Where were the lights of the town?

The Doctor decided to adopt a new way of dealing with the pain of exile. He became a collector of Oriental and Arab artefacts as mementos of his dear, far-off homeland. He bought paintings, rare books, Persian carpets, and ceramics at galleries and auctions. These objects enabled him to smell, taste, and feel his country. He followed events in the Arab world in the newspapers and attended Arab circles to keep up to date with Arabic poetry and prose. He went to lectures and talks on Arab politics and culture at conferences in London and participated in analysing the most complex issues facing the Arab world such as water and energy.

Each one in this triangle had their own wants and desires. All Nafie wanted was to eat voraciously and sit beside his cassette player. For him that was total happiness and relaxation. The Doctor wanted to return home. Maliha's desires revolved around escaping the poverty she had endured since childhood. She dreamed of the day when she would be independently well off, that was what would make her happy. Another crucial wish for her was to escape the monotony of her life. Her life was routine, dull and boring. She woke up every morning to the same scene and did the same things day after day. She needed to go out on trips and to the cinema and theatre. She lacked fun and entertainment. But she never told the two men how she felt. She was certain nobody would listen to her. Both men were preoccupied with themselves and had no sense of her real mental state.

At the new house, Nafie relaxed. At long last he was living somewhere with space, a big house with rooms full of beautiful furniture. He loved the garden, which reminded him of the groves of pomegranate and lemon, and the abundant mint in his country, where he had grown up playing or sitting in the shade. His childhood memories came flooding back, and he saw himself picking mint to take to his mother to use in her cooking. Now he would have the opportunity to practise his skills as a gardener, something he had loved to do as a child, but had never had the chance in that damned flat.

Maliha failed to register the enormous difference in size between the new house and the old flat. She never felt happy and was constantly obsessing about her poverty. The moment she entered the house, she had sat down on a sofa that looked out on the garden and had stared at it without showing any reaction. She did not go and sit in the garden for a breath of fresh air or to enjoy it. She felt isolated from everything around her, unaware of anything except the Doctor calling to Nafie for him to come and see the room that would be theirs, as he pointed ahead and said: "I'm giving you the biggest room there is."

Nafie and Maliha's room was on the ground floor. It had a large door and, like the living room, French windows on to the garden. Nafie rushed in, delighted to put his bags down in the new room. He was as happy as a child at his birthday party, a happiness he had not felt for years, not since Sameh was born. Life was beautiful and full of delight for him, while his depressed wife swung between despair and madness.

20

The three companions entered an ambiguous phase in their relationship, one marked by isolation. In this new stage, the points of their triangle moved apart as their interaction diminished day by day. Life was no longer how it had been in the Shepherd's Bush flat. None of them was aware of what the others were doing, and whole days would pass without a single word being exchanged between them – at most a few whispered mutterings might be heard. Each one had retreated into their shell, like hermits devoting themselves to worship and contemplation in their cells. The sheer size of the house and garden contributed to their separation. The various rooms of the house became isolation zones where each would do their own thing without the others knowing or joining them. Silent withdrawal and resentment were the order of the day.

The Doctor withdrew to his room and concentrated on his passions. He devoted himself to learning about cultural life in the Arab world and Middle East. He collected books, studied old maps, and read newspapers and periodicals about Arab affairs. Whenever the opportunity arose, he indulged his passion for acquiring more oriental artefacts – Persian, Moroccan, and Turkish rugs, crystal, marble, oil paintings, photographs, and carvings. The house filled up with his purchases, most of which remained in their packaging as there were so many of them and his time was short. The corridors and passageways became blocked, and Nafie and Maliha began to get annoyed.

At auctions, when the Doctor observed the paintings and sculptures, he became temporarily blind to all else. He became a child who would not calm himself until he had what he wanted. He did not care how much an item cost, and that its price might double over the bidding. His bank balance dwindled and he started borrowing money from the bank and even from the auction houses themselves.

The Doctor prized his antiquities, which shop owners and auctioneers had told him were rare and from various periods and countries – Palestine, Jordan, Egypt, and other Arab lands, as well as from Iran, Pakistan and India. When he bought something he would almost hug it. His heart would fill with sadness and his eyes with tears as nostalgia for his homeland overwhelmed him. He wept over those beautiful and valuable pieces even more thinking they had no doubt been stolen and smuggled into Europe. Nobody knew who had stolen them and there were no witnesses or evidence.

Each in their own worlds, the Doctor did not speak with Nafie and Maliha for quite some time. Maliha was still depressed, and Nafie continued his old habits in the new location. He occupied a corner of the comfortable living room where he placed his cassette player and the tapes of Arab singers. Naturally, he did not forget his bags of nuts and the poetry of Antara ibn Shaddad. He protected his corner and forbade the other two from sitting there or walking through it. He did, however, begin to take an interest in the large house. He cleaned the kitchen, and did the laundry and the cooking and kept the garden tidy.

Nafie had a great deal of time on his hands and he found that the ideal way of making it pass was to serve Maliha and the Doctor. He would leave the house at eleven every morning, headphones on and a Walkman fixed to the belt of his trousers, pulling a large shopping trolley behind him, whose big strong wheels made a loud screech. People stared at him in disgust at the noise, but he did not care, convincing himself he wasn't the only person whose trolley squeaked, and so just ignored them. And in fact many people at the local shops pulled even larger trolleys without caring about the noise they made.

After a short walk, Nafie arrived at the local shops. He walked slowly, his heavy body waddling from side to side as he adjusted his trousers that were on the verge of slipping down. He went from shop to shop, buying the things he needed and comparing the prices in order to get the cheapest. In the supermarket, he went to the refrigerated dairy section and then the fruit and vegetable aisle. Perhaps he was cautious as he did not want to spend what little money the Doctor had left, after so much had gone on antiquities. Nafie also felt he was a guest who had to be kind to his host and his property. He might end up being a guest for life. He often wondered what the reason was for the Doctor's generosity. It had to be proof of the sincerity and depth of the Doctor's friendship. The real reason never crossed his mind.

Once Nafie had finished the shopping, he would head home with an inane grin on his face as he pulled the bulging trolley behind him. On the way back, he would go to one of the coffee shops that housewives and pensioners frequented. He would join the queue to get served. He loved cake, especially dark chocolate cake. He would look at the people around him, giving them meaningless smiles. If he felt someone respond to his glance, he would go over and ask if he could sit with them. Some said yes and chatted with him, others thought he was crazy and left.

When he found someone he liked, they would chat about rising prices or the weather. Somehow he would move from talk about prices and the weather to what he was planting in the beautiful garden of "his house". He always managed to create this tenuous link, so he could take out of his pockets dog-eared photos of the garden, and of the vegetables and English roses he was planting. He enjoyed hearing people's comments and seeing the looks of envy that crossed their faces. They thought he was just a foreigner, but he still made the most of a big garden that they themselves, in their own country, could never get their hands on.

In a tone of amazement, one of the people chatting with Nafie said: "I can hardly believe that someone with such a big, posh house and garden spends his time with the old and retired and the unemployed."

Nafie gave a knowing laugh: "Native English people like nothing more than appearances. You'll never find a single one of them who owns a big house and nice garden mixing with ordinary people. The rich don't mix with the common folk who live in council houses and survive on their pensions or benefits."

Then, it was time for him to go back to the house and cook so he said goodbye to his companion and hurried out of the café, dragging the large trolley behind him. He walked fast, allowing nothing to distract him unless he bumped into one of the local women, like Mrs Bennett or Mrs Edwards. Although he was only superficially acquainted with them, he liked to stop and chat. The chat might extend to cover diverse topics such as the price of hair dye and trips out. As soon as he arrived home, he set to work.

Nafie took a particular interest in the garden. He tended it and cared for it as though it were one of the family. He weeded and pruned, watered and fought off pests. This interest in gardening gave rise to a strong, symbiotic attachment with the garden: he watered and nurtured it, and in turn the garden provided the fruits and vegetables that Nafie cooked. The garden also produced colourful flowers, which he used to decorate the house or would present to neighbourhood women as a token of friendship.

Nafie bought new varieties of seedlings, some of which he knew and some he had never heard of. His friends among his new neighbours told him what they were. He planted them, watered them, and tended them, waiting impatiently for them to grow and for their fruits and shape to become an exciting topic of conversation with the neighbours, who also loved gardening.

Every morning, Nafie was awake before dawn to check on his garden, which he would inspect even in the worst and coldest weather. He made sure nothing had been damaged in his absence overnight. His love for the garden grew and it became the focus of his life. Because of his worries for the garden during the night, he asked the Doctor to buy floodlights so he could look after it at night. The Doctor had no objection, and was even pleased at the idea. He bought the floodlights and mounted them high up around the garden, making it seem like a football pitch. Nafie started gardening at night like a madman, pruning at two in the morning. His joy and dream lasted no more than a week as the powerful lights annoyed the neighbours. Bright lights in a residential area were against the law, and Nafie and the Doctor had no choice but to submit to the complaints. As a result, Nafie felt deprived of some of the happiest moments of his life – it was as though he had had a limb amputated.

Nafie started suffering from severe anxiety at being deprived of his right to check on his garden whenever he wanted. He couldn't sleep and spent the nights desperate for first light. As soon as the first rays of the sun appeared he would rush to inspect the trees, talking to each one of them. Perhaps the reason for his strange behaviour was that a woman had told him trees like being talked to. Conversation made them feel wanted and helped them yield more fruit. He spoke to the apple tree as he stroked its trunk, then moved on to the pear tree, apologizing to it for his absence during the night, leaving it alone in the cold and dark. He did the same with all the trees in the garden.

After thinking long and hard, Nafie decided on a plan to buy domesticated animals and keep them in the garden; some would be free to roam and others kept in pens. The constant activity of the animals, jumping from tree to tree, and their various noises, would surely keep the trees company and stop them feeling lonely.

Visiting the pet shop, he was amazed by all the varieties of vividly coloured birds. He stood entranced as he looked through the window, delighted by the hopping birds, playful monkeys, and rabbits munching carrots. He spent the week's money on a collection of birds and rabbits, along with a small monkey.

A week later, once he had seen how successful his idea had been, he went back to the shop and bought more animals: two cats, a goat, a lamb and a sheep, some hens and a goose. The garden was full of animals plus a few tropical birds; a jungle in the middle of the neighbourhood. They proved a lot of work for Nafie: he had to feed them and clean up their waste. He adopted a new plan for planting, and devoted large areas to growing food for the animals: lettuce, cabbage, carrots, and beetroot.

The creatures made a range of noises, some easy on the ear and others annoying. If it hadn't been for the noise, the Doctor and Maliha would not have noticed the animals' existence – Nafie had done everything without telling them in case they objected. The garden was his domain to conduct whatever experiments he pleased. Being in control of the garden restored Nafie's self-confidence, which had been sorely lacking in Shepherd's Bush. He had begun to feel saner after quarrels between him and Maliha stopped. Now everyone was doing their own thing. He was happy with what he was doing, while she was going crazy, imagining things that were not there, and talking to herself.

Nafie gave the animals and birds names. When he called their names, they looked at him as if saying good morning or hello. Although he was in control of the animals, some of the birds flew off when he was cleaning their cages, and some died despite all his care. Most of the birds that died had had their feathers dyed in vivid, fiery colours that attracted the eye, but the dye poisoned them. Their deaths saddened Nafie a great deal and he buried each one. He grieved for them and stopped listening to music while he mourned.

But Nafie became depressed. His interest in the garden waned and he began to lose control over it. Rubbish started to accumulate, marring the vista, and a bad smell replaced the scent of the flowers. The screeching and squawking of the animals and birds become unbearable. This led to problems with the neighbours, who were already aware of Nafie's antisocial antics and could never forget the floodlights that had kept them awake at night. Now they worried the rubbish would attract flies and rats and make people ill. Nafie did not have a licence to keep so many animals, though in their opinion they were dealing with someone who was already an offender. They gave him no choice and united against him. In the end, Nafie had to get rid of the animals, even though they had been very dear to him.

21

The animals had been brought to the garden, they had lived there for a long time, and then they were gone, but none of that was of any interest to Maliha. She had slipped into a despairing madness, and had become very forgetful and unpredictable. Her forgetfulness and mental imbalance had begun during the last days in Shepherd's Bush, and as soon as she arrived at the Doctor's house, she had started wandering all over it as though looking for something she had mislaid. She looked all over, upstairs and downstairs, and one day suddenly asked Nafie and the Doctor about the living-room window – the one in the old flat, in the belief she was still living there. Then she asked where Lewis' the butcher's was, and the jeweller's, and the draper's.

Confusion was etched on her face as she said: "Where's the old window? I can't see it and I can't see the neighbours or the local shops. I want to see the cuts of meat and the rolls of cloth."

"Here's the window," said Nafie, "but you can't see any shops from it, just the garden."

She went over to the window and then stepped back. She could see only the lawn and trees with their thick trunks, which she took to be lampposts. The hustle and bustle she was used to seeing from her window in Goldhawk Road had gone. She was in a new and unfamiliar neighbourhood.

This transformation before her eyes made her snap. "Where is my neighbour Lewis the butcher, and his meat?" she screamed. "Where is my Sudanese neighbour, Haj Mu'tazz and his fabrics? Where is the Indian jeweller, Ramesh, and his gold, glinting in his hands and in the shop window?"

Nafie laughed out loud. He thought that either Maliha was not right in the head, or that somehow she was suffering from amnesia. He said to her rather disdainfully: "But Maliha, dear, that was all at our old house. We've moved in with our friend the Doctor, we're in his house. Can't you see that? After all, you were the one in such a hurry to pack up your clothes and things when it was time to move. Me and you, we now live in a far better neighbourhood and street than we did in London. Here, the air is clean and we can enjoy looking at trees rather than shops, the drab concrete of Nelson Mandela House, and all the bustle below. From the day we arrived here, we no longer had to inhale exhaust fumes. We're living in a large house with a big garden. The choice is yours, Maliha. You can look at the garden or watch TV in your own room. It's so much better than the confines we lived in before, no?"

Maliha kept quiet for a short while. She looked vacantly at the two men, then asked calmly again: "You don't understand what I mean. Where are the shops? I want an answer. Where have the shops and restaurants around our block gone? This place is empty, there's nothing to hear or see."

Nafie gave the Doctor an imploring look: "Please, Doctor, you answer her. She'll keep on asking if we don't convince her."

"Maliha," said the Doctor calmly, "don't you remember, we took your stuff and put it in my car? That day was your last day in that flat. Now you're both living with me at my house." He hoped his explanation would jog Maliha's failing memory.

The Doctor went silent for a while, in an attempt to read the expression on Maliha's face. Then he continued: "Don't you remember our journey here from Shepherd's Bush? We took my car and stopped at a garage and had lunch. Then we continued. You were really happy, singing for joy. You agreed to move, and were keen to leave the small flat behind, and its neighbourhood. You wanted to live, you said, somewhere bigger, and luck had it that you and I could finally fulfil our dreams. You're going to live like a queen. I'll make you happy and protect you with all my might. As for shops and markets, we've some big, beautiful shops here. I'll take you there one day soon. There are also lots of places for us to go and visit."

Tenderly, he stroked her hair, as though spoiling a small child. All of that was in front of Nafie, and then he said, without thinking: "Ah, Madame Maliha, you always said you were fed up of life in that small flat that looked out over a dusty street and you were fed up with your routine, humdrum life." He took her hand and raised it up and said: "Come on. Get up and take a look around the house. Do whatever you like. In the near future, you'll be able to entertain your old neighbours, Umm Ahmed, Manar Hanem, and Attiya. Have dinner with them here any day that suits you."

After that explanation, Maliha stood up in front of the Doctor. She was crying and rubbing her eyes with her hands like a child. She ran to her room and for two days refused to speak or eat, and of course her health deteriorated.

Maliha spent the two days thinking about how she had reached such a sorry state and how her life had changed so much. The great calm of the new house threw her into crisis; she missed the hustle and bustle of Goldhawk Road and its spectacle. She wasn't very excited about the new location, though in fact nothing could get her excited. She would have been moaning whatever her situation.

Maliha's despair had thoroughly taken root. She felt desperately alone, lost, and very confused. She longed to leave the house and add a touch of vitality to her life, so she started roaming around the neighbourhood. She went out early in the morning and came home late. It was the only way she could think to make herself feel better. She started seeing shops and people again, which was what she had long wished for. The Doctor and Nafie did not know where she had gone to or when she would be back. Whenever they thought of asking her, they dropped the idea, fearing they would only make her mental state worse if they stopped her from going out. Maliha would leave wearing one set of clothes, and arrive back wearing something else, but neither of them asked her how come. Of course, the Doctor and Nafie were both puzzled and wondered what on earth was going on, but they didn't do anything about it. They ignored her behaviour, not because they didn't care about her, but because they were all doing as they pleased – Maliha did not interfere with them, so they had no right to interfere with her.

On one of her walks, Maliha had seen people selling things in the street, and she was taken back to her childhood. She had sold things when she was at school, and now a loud voice in her head was telling her to start selling again. She began to collect together stuff from the house nobody wanted: junk, things nobody used, as well as her own makeup and accessories. The particular place she carried her merchandise to only went to show that she was by then completely mad. She climbed up onto a low roof with them and in a melodious voice started calling out her goods and their prices. She called to people she imagined were there and invited them to come and buy from her, and then haggled with them over the price. Maliha only came down from the roof for two reasons: because of the rain, when it soaked her things, or because it was dark, when she couldn't see anything. She continued doing that for two whole days, but no one came and bought anything from her. After noticing the absence of customers, she climbed down and headed off somewhere else where she thought she could find some. She laid out her wares in the Doctor's garden and started selling in a loud voice. Whenever she saw Nafie or the Doctor approaching, she would continue calling out her merchandise just as she had done at the school gates when she was a girl.

She called on the Doctor and Nafie to come and buy but the two men completely ignored her, just saying: "Please get up so you don't catch cold." She called to them again and they answered: "Please come inside, may God give you peace." But she was not happy about that. After they started ignoring her, she began bargaining with imaginary people, trying to persuade them to buy. She imitated the gestures of her old neighbours, Lewis the butcher and Haj Mu'tazz the draper; she repeated their turns of phrase in the hope that someone would buy from her. But even the people she conjured in her imagination ignored her, so she gave up and looked for another way to spend her time. She started helping Nafie to water and tend the garden, and also continued leaving the house early in the morning and coming back late.

After a few days, Maliha went back to selling. This time she occupied a spot outside the house near the front door. She displayed her wares, which consisted of some old cups and bowls, a few bent knives and forks, some empty perfume bottles, old clothes and shoes, plastic flowers, and used cosmetics. She even included old newspaper cuttings that she had picked up from the Doctor's desk. People walking by gave her mocking and derisive looks. Some looked at her with pity, while others who noticed her beauty were very surprised and wondered: "How come this beautiful woman is selling junk outside a posh house in a rich neighbourhood? The house suggests her family are well off, but she's acting like she's homeless." They also wondered where the police were, and why they weren't upholding the law. Maliha needed a permit to sell things in the street, otherwise she was breaking the law. People whispered and pointed at her and kept their distance. Once again, Maliha's project failed, and she was forced to look for another site.

She started to use the technique of peddlers, roaming the streets with a large bag of junk slung over her shoulder. She kept walking until her legs grew tired and she then went home. She realised she had to find a pitch to set out her stall. In the beginning it was hard to choose. Then she saw old Mr Hayley selling newspapers at the train station, alongside Mandy's flower stall, each plying their trade. What aroused Maliha's interest was the sheer quantity of people – foreign, British, and tourists – buying from Mr Hayley and Mandy. She had finally found what she was looking for, she thought, and started to sell her household junk outside the station. The passers-by looked at her suspiciously as they went in and out. They eyed her up and gave her a wide berth realising she was not quite right in the head. Only a mad woman would be selling junk there. Maliha could not attract customers and she was very disappointed. She thought long and hard and decided to change what she was selling. In place of the junk, she brought different kinds of food from the kitchen at home: olives, tomatoes, lentils, rice, onions, honey, oil, sugar, nuts, biscuits, and meat from the freezer. The freezer at home was full of the monthly supply the Doctor still bought from Zein Market in London, as well as fish and chicken.

The passers-by were amazed at the strange products Maliha was now selling. They looked at them in disgust, particularly the pieces of thawing meat on the pavement, swimming in blood. Obviously, no one bought anything. At the end of the day, Maliha gathered up her wares and put them back in the bag and went home. She was so exhausted she didn't even put the meat back in the fridge or freezer. She just left it in the bag. The next morning after breakfast, she picked up the bag with what was now rotten meat. She made her way to the station with a foul smell accompanying her. Her pitch soon attracted flies, and people were repelled. They started making a fuss, and soon called the police to report a mad lady selling rotten meat without a licence and to complain about the terrible smell and health hazard she was causing. In less than five minutes, the police arrived. They were immediately aghast at the smell of the rotting meat and covered their noses. One policeman asked Maliha to stand up and asked her: "Madam, what are you doing here?" She did not reply and did not move. Another policeman said: "What you're doing is against the law and could land you in jail." Maliha stayed there like a statue, not moving. The policemen realised what they were dealing with, and gently led her off to the police station, where they interviewed her about selling rotten meat in the street without a permit. During the interview, they confirmed she was not mentally competent, and were content to give her a warning. Then they took her home without any further legal action against her.

* * *

After her run-in with the police, Maliha stopped selling food for a few days, then went back to selling junk. Nafie and the Doctor were well aware of what she was doing, and knew it was against the law. They talked to her about it a number of times, but she did not respond. In the end they left her alone, mainly because they were both busy with their own things. The Doctor was still mad about acquiring antiquities. He bought maps that showed the borders of Arab Palestine and proved the right of the Arabs to their ancestral land, and maps showing the rivers and watercourses of Iraq. He bought pieces from archaeological digs and coins discovered in various Arab countries including Egypt, Syria, Lebanon, and Algeria.

As for Nafie, his day was divided between cooking, doing the washing and ironing, and looking after and watering the garden. While he did these jobs, he listened to martial songs. The small Walkman was still there, hanging round his waist, and the earplugs were still in his ears.

In his new surroundings, Nafie had come out of his shell. He had changed into somebody new, a sociable person. The move had opened new doors for him and broadened his horizons, especially after freeing himself from Maliha's control. In the past, she had belittled him and blamed him, never admitting the good things he had done for her. Now he had rid himself of the oppression that had ruled him for so long, he began to make friends. He had his hobbies at home and also went out to meet people and enjoy life.

Nafie began to make new friends with people he met in the neighbourhood during his daily rounds. Once he was done with the housework, he went to the local pubs with his friends to spend time socializing. He would arrive home late or go to the cinema or one of the clubs for retired people, where he played cards or did aerobics or listened to lectures on gardening, health, or cooking. He learnt flower arranging and how to make cakes. Sometimes he went out to one of the many local Indian or Chinese restaurants.

Nafie often invited his friends round to the house. They would sit in the garden, and he would offer them mint tea, sandwiches, and cakes, and then they would all take a tour of the garden.

Sometimes his friends even stayed the night; the Doctor did not interfere, since he paid no attention to what Nafie's guests did.

Among his group of friends was a widow called Connie Bennett, or as she was known to her friends, Mrs Bennett. The relationship between them flourished and they became very close friends indeed. Mrs Bennett was a large, round-faced lady with grey hair who laughed a lot. Her husband, who had been a builder, had died a long time before as a result of lung disease brought on by long-term inhalation of cement dust. She had wanted to sue the construction company for having caused her dear husband's death by not safeguarding its employees against the risks posed by building materials. After medical research and studies undertaken by universities and medical research institutes revealed the health risks of cement dust, Mrs Bennet was able to bring a case against the company. The case went through several appeals, but in the end the company lost and Mrs Bennet was awarded substantial compensation.

Nafie and Mrs Bennett often talked about their gardens and love of gardening, what they were planting, and how to look after what they could harvest. Mrs Bennett told Nafie about the profit she made from the produce of her garden, which she sold at the local farmer's market every Sunday.

Over the course of these long conversations, the friendship between Mrs Bennett and Nafie grew stronger and turned into mutual admiration. After years of emotional drought for both of them, their hearts started to beat with love. Nafie sang to her and recited love poetry to her. He flirted with her and ran after her for no reason. Nafie stole his first kiss from Mrs Bennett in her garden when they were standing under an apple tree. She was talking and he suddenly interrupted her, took her hand, and started saying sweet words to her until he assailed her with a kiss, that was followed by others. After each kiss, they looked at each other with longing and tenderness. Nafie sang her a song by Umm Kalthoum, "Sing to me a little and capture my heart". Mrs Bennett was overwhelmed and enchanted by the words of the song, even though she did not understand a word. Love was knocking on the door of two hearts that had not known love for years.

Mrs Bennett became a regular visitor to the house. They would sit together in the garden, or water and prune the trees. Maliha and the Doctor were oblivious to the love story developing between them. On Sundays they went with the produce from their gardens to the farmers' market or visited their friends. Every detail of Nafie's life changed, with the exception of not giving up his martial songs. He kept on listening in the face of Mrs Bennett's objections. Whenever it was too much for her, she would look at him disapprovingly, but Nafie now had the self-confidence not to change his almost sacred habit.

Mrs Bennet would reproach him saying, "Naf" – that was her nickname for him, given she could not pronounce the Arabic guttural at the end of his name – "it's absolutely clear you think you're a teenager or a black pop star. One of those who stick headphones in their ears and roam the streets of New York. Remember, you're not one of them, Naf. Act your age, and take off the headphones before I take them off for you." She said this as she tried to pull off his headphones. But he pulled away and tried to keep them on. Nafie got annoyed and said: "Get your hands off my headphones. They're mine and they don't do anyone any harm." But she replied that they were harming her, because she had often called him for something important and he hadn't heard her. The only thing that came between her and Nafie were the headphones. If not for them, he would have been hers in body, mind, and soul.

The love between Nafie and Mrs Bennett grew. They passed

beautiful, tranquil days almost free of problems. This calm and peace encouraged Mrs Bennett to ask Nafie to come and live with her. That was naturally what Nafie wished for, but he couldn't, and apologised for still being married to Maliha, as well as being busy with his domestic responsibilities. It would not be fair to abandon Maliha and the Doctor to look after things themselves, given the sorry state they were both in. So, things remained as they had been for Nafie and his new love. They saw each other every day and kissed in secret. They also took trips together to London and neighbouring towns. Neither Nafie nor Mrs Bennett knew what fate had in store for them. They had started a journey whose destination was unknown. Their relationship seemed futile because it was heading for a dead end and was driven only by blind love. Where would it all lead?

22

Another year passed, things changed, relationships formed. The Doctor remained preoccupied, while Maliha took a break from her previous activities. After her brush with the law, she ceased her mad, desperate actions outside the house. She spent her time helping Nafie, imitating him by speaking to the plants and stroking the damp branches. Sometimes she would wander around the house like an aimless and directionless ghost. Nafie spent a lot of time out of the house, visiting Mrs Bennett, providing a golden opportunity for the Doctor to take Maliha once more in his arms.

The Doctor spoke to her in a voice dripping with pain that did not hide his longing and innermost feelings. "Maliha, my sweet darling, how could we have grown so cold with each other, so far apart? Why has our relationship reached such a low point?"

Maliha did not respond to the question, and he repeated it while giving her a gentle and despairing shake on her shoulder. She looked at him in surprise and gave an embarrassed smile like a child. She covered her face with her hands and ignored his question and complaint.

He realised her mind was blank. He looked at her and asked:

"Where have you gone, Maliha? Where have you disappeared to? What happened? Your eyes have lost their magic sparkle. You no longer put eye shadow on your big beautiful Arab eyes. I wish with all my heart that you'd come back. I'm ready to do all I can to bring our love back to life.

"You've neglected your complexion and it needs attention. Please look after yourself like you used to. Come on, darling, come closer and dazzle me with your eyes. I want to dive into their depths and sail their waves. The kohl has overflowed and runs with the course of your tears. Let me wipe it away and with it your pain and sadness." He took a tissue and wiped away the streaks of kohl. He looked right into her eyes and stroked her cheek tenderly.

"Come, darling, sit next to me. Let's awaken our sleeping feelings, our dulled senses. Do you remember the sweet feelings we used to have? Throw yourself into my arms. I'll kiss you tenderly and remind you of the beautiful moments we had when we met at the surgery. That was at the beginning of our beautiful love, let's bring it back. Maliha, I'm asking you how we could have let those days of happiness slip away?"

Maliha did not reply but smiled shyly. The Doctor took her hand and said: "My darling, let's enjoy being alone together. Believe me, I've missed you so much, as much as I long for my home country. I miss your Arab perfume that enchanted me. Your scent that has not changed because it is the elixir of life."

With ardour and longing he embraced her and kissed her passionately. Then, very calmly, he removed her clothes. She did not object or resist as she had in the past when she fled from him like a lamb from slaughter, and hid her desire for him. She did not hurry to undress like she had done when she had been fed up with their sterile relationship. Then she had stripped off in a flash and had sat naked on the coffee table urging him to hurry up himself:

"Come on, this is what you've invited me here for."

Now, Maliha was offering her body to the Doctor to do with as he pleased without a word of love or hate. She submitted in silence as he drew near and pulled her powerfully to him. She gave him her body to do with as he wanted.

* * *

At this point of time, Maliha had been feeling bored with doing housework and thought again about selling things in the street. This time she decided to sell something valuable that would easily fetch a high price. She said goodbye to meat that had gone off and to old junk. She moved on to the Doctor's antiquities. One day she took some valuable pieces out of their boxes and headed off to the train station with them. She set out her stall, with some paintings and ancient tablets, next to the old newspaper seller Mr Hayley and Mandy's flower stall.

Unlike before, she had no difficulty in drawing attention. People bought the valuable pieces from her and asked her where she had got them from. Maliha just ignored them and did not answer. The people were drawn to the beautiful woman selling antiquities; they flocked around her like vultures and not a single item remained. They could not believe that genuine antiquities were being sold so cheaply. But in less than an hour, everything had gone – pieces worth thousands sold for a few quid.

Maliha went home very happy, clutching the money she had made. Finally, she had found a successful occupation. She hid the money in the bathroom, just as she had done as a child when she had hidden it from her brother. The Doctor did not notice the disappearance of his possessions because he had so many. Maliha started going through the antiquities, sorting them out and pricing them for sale the next day.

There were so many pieces that no one would notice a few had gone, she thought and the Doctor never imagined Maliha could come up with such an idea, especially as she had never mentioned it or shown any interest in his antiquities. And so she carried on selling off his things, and she made marked progress in the number of customers she attracted and achieved unrivalled success.

* * *

On one occasion when she was selling her wares a tall, well-built man with a broad face and shoulders came up to her. His nose was bent, and his teeth were yellow from neglect and smoking, and covered by fat, cracked lips. A diamond earring sparkled in the sunshine. The moment he saw the antiquities, he stopped short in amazement. He studied them closely; he picked one up and inspected it while scrabbling in his pocket for some money to buy it.

"My dear," he said, "where did you get these beautiful things? Do you have any more? I'll take everything you have, and I promise I'll pay what you want." He picked up a small tablet inscribed in Babylonian cuneiform. "Are you from the Middle East? From the Arab world?" Maliha gave a nod. He told her about his trips to Lebanon and Baghdad. "I've been to Egypt a few times. I loved it. I bought quite a few rare and fine pieces. I got them from dealers at Hadaba Market. Trust me, if I'd bought them here it would have cost me millions, or even more – if you could find them."

Maliha listened to the strange man's explanation without saying a word. He went on: "I'd like to buy everything in front of you, and I'd like to see all the other items you have. I'm a dealer of antiquities, and I'll give you a good price. You'll be able to buy more and better pieces and sell them at a high price. I promise you won't lose out."

Maliha responded hesitantly at this point with an innocent smile still on her face. "When would be a convenient time for you to come to the house and see my whole collection? I have a large collection which is all for sale."

The man's hands clenched and his heart started beating at the thought of this profitable deal. He felt elated. He looked at her and said: "Fine, at this time tomorrow, I'll come here for you to take me to where you're hiding your treasure."

"But there are two men at home," she said. "A tall fat one with powerful shoulders, and one of medium height. They might not let me in and might stop me opening the boxes."

The man thought one of the men might be her father. "Don't worry, leave it to me. I can persuade your father to let us look at what's yours. The antiquities are yours and no one else's business. I mean if they don't belong to those two men, they shouldn't interfere." He took her hand and shook it gently. "No? Isn't what I'm saying true? You're in a country where people don't play around with ownership. Haven't you heard that before, my dove?" He stretched out a finger and poked her playfully on the nose. "Or have those two men kept the truth from you? Anyway, now you know a fact you seem not to have known before."

The man did not wait for Maliha to answer. He grabbed his bag of valuable purchases and gave a quick wave goodbye and blew her a kiss. She remained seated in front of her empty pitch. She folded up the tablecloth and left, holding on to the money he had given her and headed home.

The next day, the strange man came back as they had agreed, but Maliha did not show up. He thought she must be late for some reason, but as the wait wore on, he became very annoyed. He composed himself and started looking round the station for her. He went into the station, thinking she might have changed her pitch and sat down in one of its dark corners. He came up with many excuses for her; perhaps she was waiting somewhere else outside the station. He asked the people working at the station without getting anywhere. He was fuming at the beautiful woman not turning up, but he had no way to find her and had to suppress his anger. He was unaware the beautiful woman had simply forgotten their appointment.

Maliha was mostly unwitting of what she was doing. She had not grasped the importance of the meeting she had arranged with the man and then missed. It was just another of her bouts of absent detachment.

The strange man grew angry again. He was the kind of man no one would dare defy or fail to keep an appointment with. He could be very hard on such people. He promised himself he would not be lenient with her. He swore to himself that if he did not find her the next day, he would knock on every door in the neighbourhood looking for her. Fortunately, the next day Maliha did show up to meet the man. She had new pieces with her. As usual she attracted the attention of passers-by, and a long queue formed. There was quite a scrummage as people tried desperately to reach the front. At that point the strange man appeared.

"Please move away from this woman," he said to the crowd. "Two days ago, she agreed to sell me everything she has. All these antiquities are mine. Please move away, or I'll have the police do it." Some customers objected, but the man lied to them and said he had already paid for them. Even after that lie, two men continued to object, but they backed down after he flexed his muscles and said to them: "If you don't piss off, I'll wipe the floor with you." Once the crowd had dispersed, the man gave Maliha a hard stare and said nothing. She looked calmly back; two things impressed her: his way of dealing with the customers, and his eagerness to buy her stuff. For her, the pieces were worthless. Although she found his behaviour strange, she did not say a word. She just beamed a smile at him as she stared into an unknown horizon.

After a few moments, the man directed his words at Maliha as he tried to suppress his anger and not lose out on the deal. "Where were you yesterday?" he asked. "I came at the time we fixed, but you weren't here." Maliha avoided looking him in the eye, as she did now whenever she talked to someone. Looking at the crowd, she replied: "Yesterday, my father stopped me going out, and I was forced to stay in. But I used the time to look for new pieces which my father had hidden away from me. He hid some in locked boxes, and looking for the keys took ages. But in the end, I was able to find quite a few of them, all for your sake. I'll show them to you this afternoon, so please don't be angry with me for selling things to customers who got here first."

The man heard what Maliha said and shook his head in regret at the pieces he had missed out on. "The things you show me today had better be valuable," he said: "or the consequences won't be pleasant." He gave a crude and sarcastic laugh, then continued: "By the way, the name's Charlie Monahan. What's your name?"

"I'm Mo," she said. "That's short for a long name there's no need to mention. My real name is long and foreign." She fell silent, awaiting a sign from Charlie.

"Mo," he said, "have you changed your mind about us going to see the antiquities you have at home, or what?"

Before she could reply, Charlie had started picking up the corners of the tablecloth. Once he had finished he said: "Let's go to your house without delay so I can check out your things for myself." Maliha nodded to him and set off with him, holding a few pounds in her hand from the day's business. Charlie walked beside her. Every now and then, Maliha would stop walking to re-count the money she had. Charlie looked on in astonishment at her actions until they reached the bus stop to ride to the beautiful woman's house. The buses went speeding past, and for some reason did not stop for them. Charlie became quite worked up and cursed the management of TFL for failing to provide a transport system to meet the needs of the city's inhabitants.

Charlie was on edge and felt bored as the chill wind slapped his face. He paced to and fro under the bus shelter as he waited. He grew tired and sat down on a seat. Maliha did not utter a word, and remained sitting in silence. Charlie started looking her over. He sidled closer until their thighs were touching. He looked at her and started stroking her back with his fleshy hand, then put his arm round her shoulder. After a while he was stroking her long thick black hair. The place was silent the whole time they were waiting. No buses stopped; they just kept flashing past.

Suddenly and for no reason, Charlie turned toward Maliha. She was looking at the ground so he raised her head with his hand. Looking her straight in the eyes, he said: "You're really beautiful, my little foreigner. You're a real beauty, Mo. Where are you from? Let me look into your beautiful dark eyes. They're so much prettier than the eyes of British girls, which are so full of defiance and arrogance they lose their femininity. Their eyes don't have the touch of childlike innocence in yours. This is the kind of woman a man's looking for."

Charlie continued to explain: "Do you know how they get those eyes filled with defiance? It's all because of the sterile laws passed by parliament and applied by judges. Those laws have encouraged women to be rebellious; it's obvious in their eyes. They challenge men. Unfortunate laws that have turned men into women and women into men."

He was silent for a moment, took a deep breath, and went on: "Since you're not originally from Britain, you're bound to be placid and submissive, not rude and aggressive, and you won't have any qualms about men dominating women." Maliha gave him a look he did not understand. Was it denying or affirming what he had said?

The boring wait continued, and when the boredom had reached its height, he realised no bus was coming. He put his arm around Maliha's waist and said: "You're so beautiful Mo. Genuine foreign beauty. Can I give you a kiss? Just one kiss. Please." Before she could say yes or no, he had swooped hungrily on her lips. Without saying another word, he stood up, took her hand, and led her across the road. He had spotted a small hotel in the distance with its lights on.

They reached the hotel entrance and Charlie stood reading the price list with intense concentration. In a low voice he did some sums, adding and subtracting, before returning to the price list. Finally, he had worked out the price of a room for one night. He pulled Maliha by the hand and hurried inside with her, driven on by desire.

They went into the hotel hand in hand. The hotel had a low ceiling and the lobby was dimly lit by a dust-covered chandelier. There was a smell of rotten food. A frail, stooped, young man was sitting behind a small metal desk with many drawers, going through slips of paper and making notes. Charlie went up to him and asked for a small room for one night. The thin young man handed him a slip of paper, and with indolent indifference asked him to sign what was in effect a bill for the room. Charlie signed the paper and the receptionist took it back. Charlie paid what was due and was given the key to room 5 on the ground floor. Charlie pulled Maliha along and hurried her into the room along a narrow corridor. He opened the door and as soon as they were inside, he turned and grabbed her, almost crushing her in his arms. He looked at Maliha's face. "Your eyes are so beautiful. You'll be my girlfriend forever, especially as we share the same hobby. We both love collecting antiquities. We'll go travelling together, we might even go to your native land. But one moment, I don't know where you're from." As usual Maliha did not answer, content just to look at him. He in turn did not repeat the question.

"Sit down, darling," he whispered. "You've done enough standing up today. All those hours standing waiting for the damned bus has knackered us out. Your legs must be tired out. Take your shoes off. Here let me help you." He bent down and took her shoes off. Breathing heavily, he asked: "Isn't that better than burying your feet in tight high heels? Now stretch out your legs and I'll give them a massage."

Before Maliha could reply, he started kneeling down on the floor, and in the process he heard the sound of his trousers splitting. "Damn," he muttered, "how did that happen. I'll kill the tailor for doing such a bad job. He put the rip out of his mind, stretched out a hand, and gently raised the edge of Maliha's dress up as far as her thighs. He stared at her beautiful feet and shapely legs. He leaned forward like a dog and sniffed her skin. He started kissing her feet and rubbing his hands up and down her legs. He only stopped when he heard her voice. "Please leave my clothes alone. Let them cover my legs, I'm starting to feel cold."

"So sorry, love, that I made you cold."

He removed his hand and the edge of her dress slipped down like a drape. He leaned slightly over on his knees and stared at the top of her thighs. "Darling, your skin is so lovely. I'm scared it should get scratched. No doubt we're going to have a good time, but isn't your heavy coat annoying you? Take it off so you can get comfortable. Let me take it off for you." He placed one hand on the floor and tried to stand up, but failed. He tried again, but his bulk prevented him.

He stretched out his hand to her and gave an embarrassed

laugh. "Help me stand up, darling. My knees are stuck to the floor." She gave him her hand and he hauled his heavy body upright. His trousers ripped some more. He turned round and stood behind her and whisked her coat off her shoulders and threw it on an old suitcase in the corner. "At last! You're rid of that heavy coat. Sit down on the bed and relax a while." Maliha complied. As soon as she sat on the bed, it broke and she tumbled to the floor. One leg of the bed hadn't been properly fixed. She held out her hand, and he helped her to back up. He said angrily: "Damn. What did we expect from a cheap hotel? I'm sorry, darling. I hope you haven't hurt yourself."

He reassured her, and spoke to himself as he walked around the room: "Punitive measures should be taken against negligent hotels. They make loads of money. Who gave this hotel a licence to operate? It's absolutely filthy and no more than a trap for ignorant tourists. Where has this country's greatness gone? My country used to be the envy of the world, now it's in a sorry state. I think the only thing left to do is emigrate."

Charlie stopped talking for a moment and covered his face with his hands. Heavy silence reigned. He glimpsed Maliha standing meekly beside the broken bed, and said: "My love, let me order a drink to calm us down. I'm dying for a few shots to calm me down after what's happened. I promise you I'll sort out the broken bed in a way the owners of this dump of a hotel will never forget. In the end, we'll have some fun together on this wonky pile of wood that's supposed to be a bed."

He picked up the phone on the bedside table and asked room service for a bottle of vodka. He went up to Maliha and embraced her. "Wait a bit, my beauty, until I've finished sorting out the bed that almost caused us so much damage. He rolled up his sleeves, revealing two thick arms heavily tattooed with tall, naked women in green with long hair and crimson lips. He bent down and pulled the second leg off the bed and threw it against the closed window, smashing the glass with a loud crash. He pulled off the third and fourth legs and the bed collapsed on the floor. "We'll be comfortable now lying down with the bed on the floor. It won't collapse again. Come on, my love, let's give it a try and enjoy its new stability."

Maliha went over to the bed. Before she sat down, he pushed her forcefully onto it and started kissing her violently. He heard room service knocking at the door with the vodka. He stood up to go and take the bottle, then quickly shut the door and put the tray on the floor. He poured two glasses and offered one to Maliha. She took a sip and threw the glass on to the floor. Charlie realised she didn't like vodka and did not force her to drink it. He took a few gulps of his and felt a lot more relaxed.

He took a pack of cigarettes out of his pocket and quickly smoked one. Out of his other pocket, he took out a small wrap of paper, which he opened with great care, as though worried that the fine white powder it contained might get spilt. With a fingertip he dabbed a few grains of the powder and inhaled them. He offered the wrap to Maliha and she inadvertently smeared her face with the powder.

Charlie shouted in annoyance at what she had done and snatched the powder back. "Give it here, you idiot. Don't waste this expensive gear. Don't you know how much an ounce costs? Haven't you taken it before, you stupid woman?"

Laughing staccato laughs, she said: "I haven't taken it before. I dust my face with fine white powder from Christian Dior that my father buys from the chemist nearby."

As if talking to himself, he said: "Never mind. You don't need the powder. But in a bit you'll play the game I want to have with you."

He lay down under the covers and quickly took Maliha's

clothes off. He took what he wanted from her, while she submitted to his strange predilections. Her feelings were all over the place and her mind was indifferent to what Charlie was doing. She focused on a corner of the room and the ceiling. Frightening images appeared. The ceiling pressed down on her body and the body of the man she was in bed with. The room was like a sardine tin, and she was like one of the tightly packed fish. She struggled to free herself from Charlie's grip and get out of the tin.

She raised her hand to protect her body from the collapsing ceiling. She looked towards the window and saw a black cat with bright eyes and sharp claws, which it was using to tear at and eat the intestines of three rats while blood dripped from its mouth. One of the rats was still alive and gave sad and chilling squeals.

The small backyard of the hotel emerged behind the cat. It was piled with black bags full of rubbish. Legs of lamb poked out of some, which had been slashed with a sharp knife. Maliha became absorbed in the scene and forgot about Charlie on top of her. She let her imagination roam. She imagined that the rubbish bags were large chunks of coal floating on a placid lake in a mysterious world. She started counting the bags out loud from right to left and from left to right. Her heavenly, imagined world was far removed from Charlie's world.

She promised herself that as soon as she was free of Charlie's grip she would go over to the window to see what the cat was doing to the rats and the coal floating on the surface of the lake. She tried a few times to get up, but Charlie roughly reproached her and said: "What are you doing, stupid? There's no need to spoil things. I won't hurt you." He carried on pleasuring himself alone with her.

Lying on the bed with Charlie, Maliha was visited by images of the past. She remembered the days of her fiery relationship with the Doctor. She had offered up her body in the small waiting room to the strains of Arabic songs. She could see the glow of the red candles and smell the fragrance of incense. Her dates with the Doctor had been full of beauty and had had an aura of romance. The aroma of meals of onion rice, chickpeas, and meat spiced with garlic and olive oil blended with the incense to create a unique perfume.

As soon as Charlie had had his way with her, his trembling body rolled over onto its back, a sated beast. He smoked a cigarette with relish. Totally naked, Maliha slipped away from him and went over to the window to see the fierce cat and the placid lake and large pieces of coal floating on its surface. The cat had gone, and the lake was only the backyard, and the pieces of coal only black rubbish bags. Charlie noticed Maliha had got up and ranted at her: "Are you mad? Standing naked by the window like that. Come back to bed right now." She turned to him and gave an embarrassed smile and went back to the bed. He turned from side to side until he had finished smoking his cigarette down to the filter, which he stubbed out in a small ashtray. He stood and picked up his clothes and urged Maliha to get dressed. He went over to the door, opened it and ordered her to leave. He was swaggering along behind her, and had forgotten the split in his trousers that widened with every step.

Charlie and Maliha slipped out of the back door of the hotel without having paid for the vodka. They went to the bus stop; Charlie thought there was less traffic than before. Once again, they started waiting for a bus, but there was no sign of one, which drove Charlie mad with rage. He said to Maliha: "There's no point waiting. I think the damned drivers must be on strike. I suggest we get a cab so we're not late. I've got an important meeting in a pub near my house with a guy who wants to sell a load of antiquities. I suspect they're smuggled from China and South America. What do you think? Should I hail a cab?"

Maliha nodded and said: "But I don't have any money to pay the fare."

"Don't be mean," he said with some force. "Did I ask you to pay?"

She smiled and said nothing. Charlie tried to hail one of the cabs speeding by. One stopped, and he asked the driver to take them in the direction of Maliha's house.

On the way, Charlie kept hold of Maliha's hand, as though he was afraid she might escape. He started to realise she was living in a world of her own. When they arrived, he paid the fare and walked behind her. He looked left and right, amazed at the quiet streets and the large clean houses.

Dr Nadim and Nafie did not notice them come in. Maliha, followed by Charlie, slipped into a room off the hallway leading to the living room.

When Charlie saw the store of antiquities and antiques, his eyes widened and he took a deep breath. In a low voice as though to himself, he said: "Where did they get all these rare and priceless pieces? How can they leave them lying around like this? Aren't they worried they might get stolen? Where to start and what to choose?" He stood with his head in his hands in confusion for a few seconds, then walked between the bags, boxes, and pieces, picking up one and examining another. He forgot himself and the passing of time.

He glanced at his watch and said: "Come on, my beauty, before it gets too late. I've got a lot to do as soon as I leave here. Get some bags and help me pack up the pieces I've chosen. Maliha nodded and left the room.

The Doctor was in his office reading some manuscripts about the glory of the Arabs in Andalusia and what had been lost there after seven hundred years of Arab rule. He read that the forces against the Arabs gave themselves just twenty-one days to end the Arab presence and erase its traces. In record time they had outlawed the speaking of Arab, and anyone who did so went to prison. The Arab cultural heritage still lived on despite the efforts over centuries by the Spanish state to obliterate it by teaching a rewritten version of history in schools.

As he read, the Doctor became sad over the loss of Andalusia. He remembered the land of Palestine and he started crying. Nafie was in the garden mowing the lawn.

Maliha came back with some bags, and she helped Charlie fill them with pieces. Charlie wished a truck would pull up to take away as much as possible. There would then be no need to come back, such a chance would never be repeated. On the way he had thought there wouldn't be more than a few items, but he could barely count or evaluate artistically or commercially the things he was looking at.

He whispered to Maliha: "My beauty, I'll come tomorrow to buy some more pieces. I promise I'll buy most if not all you have."

Maliha nodded and said: "Okay, Charlie. I'll meet you tomorrow at the usual place and we'll come here together." Charlie smiled, went up to her, and pinched her cheek. "There's no need to wait for me at the station tomorrow," he said. "I'll come straight here. Meet me outside the house, so I don't have to ring the bell and disturb your father." As he was finishing packing up the antiquities, Dr Nadim appeared in the doorway.

The Doctor saw a stranger in his house and was shocked. He switched his gaze from Charlie to Maliha, who was helping him pack away the Doctor's precious possessions. "Maliha, what are you doing? And who's that with you?" Maliha looked away, unperturbed by what he was saying. "This is Charlie. He wanted to buy some of our antiquities, that's why he's here." Charlie stopped packing the pieces and stretched out a hand to shake hands with the Doctor.

"Charlie Watkins," he said. "I'm here to buy some of the antiquities owned by the charming Mo. And by the way, Mo and I have started going out and we plan to get married soon."

In astonishment and anger, the Doctor asked him: "What did you say? You'd better leave the bags where they are and leave right now."

"Hold on, mate. My lovely girlfriend wants to get rid of the old worthless things she has. I'll give my darling a fair price, especially as we're intending to go travelling."

The Doctor was getting angrier. "These things do not belong to the lady," he said. "They're mine and this is my house. Do you hear? Now I recommend you leave right away, or I'll call the police to remove you lawfully."

"Shut up, you idiot. Don't you dare threaten me with the police. You're talking to Inspector Charlie from the CID."

"In my opinion you're an ignorant thief who breaks into people's homes. Clear off right now."

Out of his shirt pocket Charlie pulled a fat wallet stuffed with banknotes and various cards. He pulled out an ID card showing his photo, name, and rank of inspector in the police. He waved it in the Doctor's face in an attempt to prove his identity as a policeman. The Doctor turned his head away and said: "I've heard what you're saying, but I'm not going to say any more."

The Doctor made a move towards the telephone to call the police. Charlie pulled a pistol out of his trouser pocket, pointed it at the Doctor's back, and fired several shots. The Doctor turned and gave a final look at Maliha and fell to the floor screaming in pain. Charlie shot him again.

In the garden, Nafie heard the shots and rushed into the house in a state of terror. What had happened? Had a war started? He saw the horrific scene. Dr Nadim on the floor, a dead body swimming in blood. He looked at Maliha whose eyes bulged wide like a scared cat. Then he turned to Charlie. "What's happened? And who are you?"

"Shut up, you stupid pip-squeak or you're going to get what the old man got."

Nafie tried to save himself. Charlie raised his pistol and fired a shot at Nafie that felled him. Charlie tried to leave the house with the stolen antiquities. In his haste, some pieces fell out of the bags. He nearly tripped over but steadied himself with a hand against the wall. It was enough to rattle him and he dropped the bags and fled the scene of the crime as fast as he could.

* * *

A deathly calm filled the place. Maliha took her hands from her face and with one eye cast a glance at the two bodies covered in blood. She went over to the corpse of the Doctor and stood looking down at him for a long time. She heard the usual voices in her head. "It's time for action, Maliha," said the voices. "Do what you have to before it's too late. Try and wake up the Doctor. He has an appointment with the antique dealer at his shop near the British Museum. There's no place for fear anymore. Your brother Abdel Wahid has gone a long way away and is never coming back."

Maliha obeyed the invisible speaker and drew closer to the Doctor's corpse. She gave him a few gentle shakes, but he did not stir. She rubbed his back and told him to get up. "It's time for your appointment with the antique dealer. Wake up. Get moving."

She left him and went over to Nafie's body, a few feet from the Doctor. She shook him and said tenderly: "Wake up, Nafie. You have to take care of the birds, the goat, the rabbits, and the ducks. Your animals are hungry."

But Nafie was dead, like the Doctor. Maliha stepped back from the bodies and sank down onto a large suitcase contemplating the scene before her in a madness of despair. She grew tired and even more confused. She stood up and went back to the Doctor. She shook him gently. She dipped her fingers in the blood around the bullet hole in his back. Her fingers became smeared with his blood. She smeared her forehead and cheeks with it. Then she went over to Nafie and smeared her other hand with his blood and applied a little of it to her lips. She waited for the blood to dry on her face and mouth.

She left the room feeling very confident. She went into the bathroom and stood in front of the mirror. She looked at her face and tidied her hair. Finished with checking how she looked, she felt ready to go to her wedding with Charlie. She remembered Charlie had asked the Doctor for her hand in marriage before killing him.

There was one final thing missing in preparation for the wedding. She left the bathroom and went to her room in search of her wedding dress. She found an assortment of dresses hanging up in the wardrobe. She chose a baggy white gown embroidered in silver. She put it on together, with its matching shoes, and did the dance of joy she had learned in childhood.

She went back into the room where the Doctor's and Nafie's corpses were lying. She sat down in the middle of the room. She had a vivid hallucination that the Doctor had woken from his sleep to accompany her to her wedding to Charlie. But suddenly she felt all alone, totally alone and afraid, a mixture of despair and madness. She heard the voice in her head say: "Your wedding to Charlie has been postponed. Take advantage of the time to do something profitable. You're in desperate need of money. Try and sell the bodies of your lover Nadim and your husband Nafie. That would make a profit."

In complete obedience to the voice in her head, Maliha dragged the Doctor's corpse to the front door. She left him and went back for Nafie. He was very heavy and she dragged him with great difficulty. She opened the front door and pulled the two bodies outside. Then she sat down like a woman selling at a village market.

She rested the head of each body on her thighs, the Doctor on her left leg and Nafie on her right. In a loud voice, like the voice she had used in her school days, she started to sell her wares: "Two bodies for sale. Who wants to buy two bodies? Come on, people, who wants to buy what I have? Come and see the quality for yourselves."

The street was empty and strangely quiet. Suddenly Sameh appeared out of nowhere looking extremely happy. He saw Maliha from afar and as he approached he discovered the terrible calamity.

"Mum, what's happened? Who killed my Dad and my uncle? Tell me! Why? Oh, these bodies? And the blood?" Maliha did not answer. He shook her by the shoulders, hoping to shake her out of her daze but without success. She did not utter a word, just gave a blank smile. Maliha had reached the pinnacle of her madness of despair.

Sameh called the police and an investigation began. The police concluded that Maliha had not killed the two men. The culprit had come into the house from outside with the intention of stealing the Doctor's antiquities.

* * *

The authorities put Maliha in a psychiatric hospital. She received treatment for a number of years, and thankfully recovered. Her mind returned to a healthy state, and she became aware of the absence of the Doctor and Nafie. She inquired after them and learned the truth about their deaths as though she were a child who had been orphaned.

Would the madness of despair envelop her again? No, for this story there has to be a happy ending. For Maliha, after those years of madness, life became beautiful and she began to thrive. A decent man appeared on the horizon, a milkman, known to his friends as Barry. Maliha had got to know him at the hospital and he often visited her and chatted with her. When God granted her a cure from her madness, Barry was the one kind soul she had been able to embrace. Having lost her husband and her lover, her new friend became a balm that healed her hurt and abandonment. The day Maliha left the hospital, she and Barry married, and so began for her a new life full of hope and promise.

Ghalya F T Al Said

Ghalya F T Al Said is a novelist who studied in Oman and the UK, culminating in her obtaining a PhD in International Relations at the University of Warwick. Her novels, preceded by poems and short stories, focus on immigrants in foreign, usually Western settings, and how they try to cope with and adapt to conflicting concepts of belief and culture. Two of these novels are set in Oman and the rest in the UK. They comprise *The Madness of Despair* (2011), in translation here, plus *Days in Heaven* (2005; 2nd edition 2011) of which a part was excerpted in *Banipal 51* (2014), *Sabira and Asila* (2007), *Scattered Years* (2008), *The Tedium of Time* (in two standalone parts 2015 and 2017) and *District of the Blind* (2019). Additionally, in Oman, she has opened one traditional Museum and plans to open a second one soon on culturally related themes.

Raphael Cohen

Raphael Cohen is a professional translator and lexicographer who studied Arabic and Hebrew at Oxford University and the University of Chicago. He has translated a growing number of novels by contemporary Arab authors including *Guard of the Dead* by George Yarak (2019), *Butterfly Wings: an Egyptian Novel* (2014) by Mohamed Salmawy, *The Art of Forgetting* (2011) and *The Bridges of Constantine* (2014) by Ahlem Mosteghanemi, *Status Emo* by Eslam Mosbah (2013), *So You May See* by Mona Prince (2011), this novel by Ghayla F T Al Said, and has translated and introduced *Poems of Alexandria and New York* by Ahmed Morsi (Banipal Books, 2021). He is a contributing editor of *Banipal* magazine of modern Arab literature.

OTHER TITLES FROM BANIPAL BOOKS

Sarajevo Firewood by Saïd Khatibi – 2021
translated from the Arabic by Paul Starkey. 320pp
ISBN 978-1-913043-23-0 • Paperback & Ebook •
The recent civil conflicts of Algeria and Bosnia and
Herzegovina were a raw turmoil of experiences for
Salim, a journalist, and Ivana, a young Bosnian woman,
who both separately fled the destruction, hatred and
atrocities of their respective countries to try to build
new lives in Slovenia. A fictional memorial to the
thousands of dead and disappeared, and to the survivors.
Shortlisted for the 2020 International Prize for Arabic
Fiction.

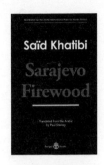

Fadhil Al-Azzawi's Beautiful Creatures – 2021
by Fadhil al-Azzawi, translated from the Arabic by the
author, and edited by Hannah Somerville.
ISBN 978-1-913043-10-0 • Hbk, Pbk, Ebook.
This poetic open work was written in defiance of the
"sanctity of genre" and to raise the question of freedom
of expression in writing. First published in Arabic in
1969 to great acclaim, it has been variously called a
novel or a prose poem, while the author calls it an epic
in prose, divided as it is into cantos.

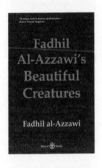

Poems of Alexandria and New York – 2021
by Ahmed Morsi, translated from the Arabic by
Raphael Cohen. ISBN 978-1-913043-16-2 • Paperback
& Ebook.
A renowned painter, art critic, journalist, translator and
consummate poet, Ahmed Morsi's first volume in
English translation captures the modernity at the heart
of all his works, his surrealistic humour, and his visions
of the dramas of ordinary life. It comprises two of his
many collections, *Pictures from the New York Album*
and *Elegies to the Mediterranean*.

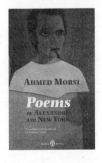

Mansi: A Rare Man in His Own Way by Tayeb Salih
ISBN 978-0-9956369-8-9 • Paperback & Ebook •
184pp • 2020
Translated and introduced by Adil Babikir, this
affectionate memoir of Salih's irrepressible friend Mansi
shows, with humour, wit, and 20th century personalities
centre stage, another side to the author, known for his
classic novel *Season of Migration to the North*.

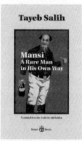

Goat Mountain by Habib Selmi
ISBN: 978-1-913043-04-9 • Paperback & Ebook •
92pp • 2020
Translated from the Arabic by Charis Olszok. The
author's debut novel, from 1988, now in English
translation. The journey to Goat Mountain, a forlorn,
dusty, desert Tunisian village, begins in a dilapidated
old bus. "I enjoyed this book. I liked its gloomy
atmosphere, its strangeness and sense of unfamiliarity.
Eerie, funereal, and outstanding!" – Jabra Ibrahim Jabra

The Mariner by Taleb Alrefai
ISBN: 978-1-913043-08-7 • Paperback & Ebook •
160pp • 2020
Translated from the Arabic by Russell Harris. A
fictional re-telling of the final treacherous journey at sea
of famous Kuwaiti dhow shipmaster Captain Al-Najdi,
with flashbacks to the awesome pull of the sea on Al-
Najdi since childhood, his years pearl fishing and the
industry's demise, and his voyages around the Arabian
Peninsula with Australian sailor Alan Villiers.

A Boat to Lesbos, and other poems
by Nouri Al-Jarrah
ISBN: 978-0-9956369-4-1 • Paperback • 120pp • 2018.
Translated from the Arabic by Camilo Gómez-Rivas
and Allison Blecker and illustrated with paintings by
Reem Yassouf. The first English-language collection
for this major Syrian poet, whose compelling epic
poem bears passionate witness to Syrian families fleeing
to Lesbos through the eye of history, of Sappho and the
travels of Odysseus.

An Iraqi In Paris by Samuel Shimon
ISBN: 978-0-9574424-8-1 • Paperback • 282pp • 2016
Translated from the Arabic by Christina Philips and
Piers Amodia with the author. Long-listed for the 2007
IMPAC Prize. Called a gem of autobiographical
writing, a manifesto of tolerance, a cinematographic
odyssey. "This combination of a realist style with
content more akin to the adventures of Sindbad helps
to make *An Iraqi in Paris* a modern Arab fable,
sustaining the moral such a fable requires: follow your
dreams and you will succeed" – Hanna Ziadeh, *Al-Ahram Weekly*

Heavenly Life: Selected Poems by Ramsey Nasr
ISBN: 978-0-9549666-9-0 • Paperback • 180pp • 2010
First English-language collection for Ramsey Nasr,
Poet Laureate of the Netherlands, 2009 & 2010.
Translated from the Dutch by David Colmer, with an
Introduction by Victor Schiferli and a Foreword by
Ruth Padel. The title poem was written to
commemorate the 150th anniversary of Gustav
Mahler's birth and is based on his Fourth Symphony,
the four sections of the poem echoing the structure,
tone and length of its movements. It is named after
"Das himmlische Leben", the song that forms the
symphony's finale.

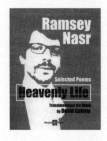

Knife Sharpener: Selected Poems by Sargon Boulus.
ISBN: 978-0-9549666-7-6 • Paperback • 154pp • 2009
The first English-language collection for this influential
and innovative Iraqi poet, who dedicated himself to
reading, writing and translating into Arabic
contemporary poetry. Foreword by Adonis. Translated
from the Arabic by the author with an essay "Poetry
and Memory". Plus tributes by fellow poets and authors
following the author's passing while the book was in
production and Afterword by the publisher.

Shepherd of Solitude: Selected Poems
by Amjad Nasser
ISBN: 978-0-9549666-8-3 • Paperback • 186pp • 2009
The first English-language collection for this major
modern poet, who lived most of his life outside his
home country of Jordan. Translated from the Arabic
and introduced by the foremost translator of
contemporary Arabic poetry into English, Khaled
Mattawa, with the poems selected by poet and
translator from the poet's Arabic volumes from the
years 1979 to 2004.

Mordechai's Moustache and his Wife's Cats,
and other stories by Mahmoud Shukair.
ISBN: 978-0-9549666-3-8 • Paperback • 124pp • 2007
Translations from the Arabic by Issa J Boullata,
Elizabeth Whitehouse, Elizabeth Winslow and Christina
Phillips. This first major publication in an English
translation of one of the most original of Palestinian
storytellers enthralls, surprises and even shocks.
"Shukair's gift for absurdist satire is never more telling
than in the hilarious title story" – Judith Kazantsis

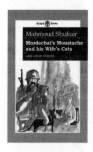

A Retired Gentleman, & other stories
by Issa J Boullata
ISBN: 978-0-9549666-6-9 • Paperback • 120pp • 2007
The Jerusalem-born author, scholar, critic, and
translator creates a rich medley of tales by emigrants to
Canada and the US from Palestine, Lebanon, Egypt
and Syria. George, Kamal, Mayy, Abdullah, Nadia,
William all have to begin their lives again, learn how to
deal with their memories, with their pasts . . .

The Myrtle Tree by Jad El Hage.
ISBN: 978-0-9549666-4-5 • Paperback • 288pp • 2007
"This remarkable novel, set in a Lebanese mountain
village, conveys with razor-sharp accuracy the sights,
sounds, tastes and tragic dilemmas of Lebanon's
fratricidal civil war. A must read" Patrick Seale

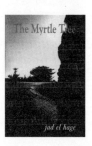

Sardines and Oranges: Short Stories from North Africa
ISBN: 978-0-9549666-1-4 • Paperback • 222pp • 2005
Introduced by Peter Clark. The 26 stories are by 21
authors: Latifa Baqa, Ahmed Bouzfour, Rachida el-
Charni, Mohamed Choukri, Mohammed Dib, Tarek
Eltayeb, Mansoura Ez-Eldin, Gamal el-Ghitani, Said al-
Kafrawi, Idriss el-Kouri, Ahmed el-Madini, Ali
Mosbah, Hassouna Mosbahi, Sabri Moussa, Muhammad
Mustagab, Hassan Nasr, Rabia Raihane, Tayeb Salih,
Habib Selmi, Izz al-Din Tazi and Mohammed Zefzaf.
Translations are from the Arabic except for Mohammed
Dib's story, which was from the French original.